BARBOUZE

Charles Pol Thrillers
Book One

Alan Williams

Also in the Charles Pol Series

The Tale of the Lazy Dog
Gentleman Traitor
Shah-Mak
Dead Secret
Holy of Holies

BARBOUZE

Published by Sapere Books.

20 Windermere Drive, Leeds, England, LS17 7UZ,
United Kingdom

saperebooks.com

ISBN: 978-1-913335-89-2

To my parents

PROLOGUE: ROOM 274

The girl sat on the bed behind closed shutters, waiting. The only light came through a chink in the folding doors leading to the salon. Here two men sat round a polished table playing backgammon.

The apartment was high in a tall street that trapped the salt smells of the port. It was a black night, and a hot wind boomed against the shutters with a sound like the sea. When it dropped the girl could hear the rustle of dice from the salon and the thud of dance-music from a radio behind the apartment wall. The fan above her bed had shorted. She sat dressed only in a pair of pants, and her skin felt dry, and the wind and the dance-music made her head ache.

From somewhere across the city came the braying of an ambulance siren, dying into a distant suburb. She lifted her hands and scooped her black hair up from the nape of her neck; then, without lowering her hands, she stood up and stared at the spear of light between the doors into the salon. She had a bold dark face, and her body was strong and beautifully made.

The two men in the next room sat over their game in silence. Presently one of them nodded towards the bedroom: 'Shouldn't she be getting ready?'

The other glanced at his watch: 'She's got another ten minutes. Better give her a drink.' He was a bony man with a greying crewcut and a cruel sunken face. He spoke almost in a whisper, trembling slightly, staring at the red and white backgammon counters. His companion pushed back his chair and fetched a can of beer from the side-table.

'No, give her some brandy, Serge,' said the bony man, nodding towards the bedroom.

The man called Serge went over to the cocktail cabinet and took out an unopened bottle of cognac fine champagne. He was big and black-haired with a bandit moustache, dressed in a chocolate-brown suit with a white handkerchief sprouting from the breast-pocket. He walked over and rapped on the folding doors: 'Do you want a drink, Anne-Marie?'

The girl put a hand through, took the bottle and closed the doors again. Serge came back to the table where the bony man sat frowning at his hands. From the bedroom a shower hissed like rain in the tropics, making the apartment seem even hotter — cramped and stifling.

'It's your throw,' said the bony man.

Serge took the dice. 'Somebody else should do it,' he said, shaking the wooden cup, 'she's too young.'

'I have decided that Anne-Marie does it. There will be no more discussion on the matter. It is finished!'

'Finished for us,' murmured Serge, 'but not for her.'

The bony man lifted his head and his lips parted as though to yell at Serge; but he controlled himself, drew in his breath and was silent. His fingers lay clasped on the table, the nails working into the palms. Serge threw the dice: a three and a two. He was losing the fourth game that evening.

At the end of the bedroom, behind the shower curtains, Anne-Marie stood smoothing her hands along her wet thighs, seizing the bellies of her breasts and pressing them upwards, throwing her head back and letting the tepid water flow across her eyelids, down her long body.

She walked back into the bedroom, dripping on the linoleum, opened the bottle of fine champagne and poured herself half a tumbler which she drank slowly, letting her skin dry in the close night air. The shutters groaned; her head throbbed with a dull pain. She put the glass down and began to dress.

In the salon the bony man won the fourth game and began rearranging the counters. Anne-Marie came out of the bedroom, her hair scraped back under a blue scarf, wearing a sea-green dress patterned with fishes. A heavy handbag was slung over her shoulder like a satchel.

Serge began to stand up.

The bony man said to her, 'You have everything? It's now a quarter past eleven. You must be out of there by midnight at the latest. The car will be waiting outside.'

Serge grinned at her and said, 'Merde!'

She walked past them to the door.

'Remember,' said the bony man, 'check with the receptionist first, then both bars.'

She nodded and went out, followed by Serge. When they had gone the bony man got up and bolted the outer door.

Down in the street the black Citroën DS crouched on its hydraulic springs like a long toad. Anne-Marie climbed in next to Serge who drove fast and quietly, down towards the sea. There were few sounds in the city. Most of the cafés and restaurants were closed behind wire cages. Occasional cars sped across the intersections, with lights doused, whining into the darkness. It was very hot inside the Citroën, even with the windows down and the dust blowing in their faces. They hardly spoke.

The car turned into a boulevard that ran down to the Front de Mer. Arcaded shops swept past like empty eye-sockets. Most of the street lighting here had been smashed and there were troops at every corner. They passed a cinema still livid with neon, under a pastel-coloured Frank Sinatra with arms outstretched, singing soundlessly into the night.

The car stopped along the Front de Mer twenty yards from the hotel. Anne-Marie got out. There were troops in steel helmets lounging up the street watching. A crushed cigarette carton came bouncing down the pavement towards her. The Citroën drove away. She turned and hurried past a splashing fountain, under palm-fronds that scraped together in the wind like scales.

Inside the hotel the silver-haired receptionist paused over a ledger, his eyes pale as glass. She spoke to him, and he murmured something without expression. Behind him an elderly policeman sat under the key-rack with a machine-pistol over his knees.

She walked across the foyer to the downstairs bar. From the ceilings fans moved sluggishly as though churning water. The bar was almost empty. She stood in the doorway looking round, then turned and walked back across the foyer to the lifts.

A Moslem in a blue uniform bowed and pulled back the gates, grinning at her with gold teeth: '*Quel étage, m'dame?*'

'*Salon de jeu.*'

The lift began to click up the well of the marble staircase, past the first floor — rooms 1 to 100. The casino, with its restaurant and bar, was on the second floor. The Moslem bowed her out, still grinning, murmuring, '*Bin'soir m'dame!*' She strode past him, the heavy bag swinging from her shoulder.

Just beyond the lifts she almost collided with two men coming from the salon de jeu. They were both very drunk. One of them giggled and tried to clutch her arm. He looked like a rabbit, small and white-faced with floppy ears. She pushed past him and he called after her, in a wheedling voice, '*Salut coco!*'

She walked briskly down the passage, across a deserted hall the size of a tennis-court lined with blown-up photographs of French film stars. In the corner an old woman with blue hair sat outside the toilets, knitting behind a saucer of coins. As Anne-Marie reached her she heard the two drunks turn and come up behind her, laughing.

She went into the toilet, put her handbag on the floor and stared into the mirror. Her eyes were huge and black, her face hollow in the bleak lighting above the basin. She realized that her heart was beating hard. She looked at her hands: they were quite still. She ran her fingers down her cheeks and dabbed cold water to her temples. She could hear the two drunks jabbering outside the door. She felt angry and nervous; but whatever happened she must avoid causing a scene. Somehow she would have to get rid of them. She picked up her handbag and turned to the door.

They were outside waiting for her. The rabbit-faced one came squirming up to her, calling her '*Ma p'tite coco!*' She tried to pass, but they stood across the passage leading into the casino. She looked helplessly at the old woman who went on knitting behind her saucer of coins.

The rabbit-faced one plucked at her sleeve; she flinched away and cried, '*Fous le camp!*' The old woman looked up and stared at them. The little drunk simpered at Anne-Marie, shaking his head and saying, '*Pas poli, mademoiselle!*'

She thrust her way between them, shook off the little man's hand and hurried down the passage into the salon de jeu. There was another policeman inside the door near the caisse. He stood with a blunt-muzzled machine-pistol strapped to his hip, looking down the long room where about a dozen

Europeans crowded round one roulette table. The rest of the room was empty, its chandeliers hanging in darkness high above tables shrouded with dust-sheets.

To the left, behind the balcony that looked across the gaming-tables, lay the restaurant and bar. Here was a frenzied gaiety: men in tuxedos and women in cocktail dresses laughing and yelling at the overworked Moslem waiters, and Army officers in biscuit-coloured uniforms talking noisily over champagne. On the far side of the room great uncurtained windows looked out across the darkened bay.

Anne-Marie examined the people round the roulette table. The man she was looking for was not there. She turned towards the restaurant and the two drunks appeared at her side, laughing and winking at each other. The policeman looked at them all without interest. A fat-necked man with a silver-topped cane was being paid out 100 Nouveaux-Franc notes at the caisse. The little drunk was trying to talk to Anne-Marie, to grab her by the arm and pull her back. She thought quickly, with anger turning to alarm: *I mustn't do anything to attract attention. I must keep calm. I must go to the bar, order a drink, ignore them.*

The man she was looking for was not in the restaurant. She went over to the bar. The two drunks stayed behind her, the little one giggling and mewing, '*Ah, elle est bien, elle est jolie, la coco!*'

The barman flashed an enamel smile at her and asked what she wanted. There was a lot of drinking going on at the bar. She hesitated, glancing down the row of faces. Beside her a journalist had his head down, one hand over his ear, bawling into a telephone. The man she was looking for was not here either. She said to the barman, '*Un Scotch!*'

'*Blackanvite, mademoiselle?*'

She nodded.

'*Trois blackanvite!*' a voice called behind her. It was the rabbit-faced drunk. He was smiling up at her with a look of malevolent, cock-eyed cunning. The barman turned to pour the drinks. The second drunk pressed beside her against the bar. He was a large man with curly hair and a flushed, damp face; he grinned at her, showing teeth the colour of dirty wax. She could smell his breath, and tried to draw back, but the rabbit-faced man was behind, wedging her in.

She looked at the barman, who stood with his back to them, measuring out the whiskies. She looked at her watch. It was 11.37. She had barely twenty minutes left. There was a pocket of cold air deep in her stomach near the base of her spine. The rabbit-faced man suddenly leant out and grabbed her by the wrist. She reacted without thought, swinging the handbag off her shoulder and striking him in the face. He gave a squeal and lurched back, both hands over his nose.

The barman spun round holding a glass of whisky. An officer at a nearby table stood up. Somebody laughed. The journalist went on yelling into the telephone. Anne-Marie did not move. The second drunk had gone over to the rabbit-faced man who had begun to straighten up, his eyes filling with tears, screeching, '*Salope! P'tite salope!*'

The barman moved swiftly round, laid a hand across the little man's chest, and said to Annie-Marie, 'What happened?'

'They're drunk. They're annoying me. Get rid of them.'

'*Salope!*' said the little man again, wiping his nose on his sleeve. The barman ignored him; he said to Anne-Marie, 'Do you wish to make a complaint, mademoiselle?'

From across the room she saw the policeman making his way between the tables towards them. 'It doesn't matter,' she said, 'I don't want to cause any trouble.'

The barman turned to the drunks: 'Get out of here!'

The little one began to whimper in protest, but the other took him by the arm and hustled him off, just as the policeman came up. The barman said something to him. The man turned, his machine-pistol swinging round with him, and looked at Anne-Marie: 'We don't want any trouble here, mademoiselle.'

'It's all right,' she said, 'they were just drunks.' She put up her hand to arrange some hair that had fallen loose from under her scarf. The policeman nodded and turned away. The two drunks had reached the end of the restaurant. The barman said, 'Do you still want the Scotch?'

She looked up, and realized she was shaking all over. She put out a hand and gripped the edge of the bar. 'Yes please,' she murmured, and the barman pushed the glass over to her. The time was now 11.41. She swallowed the whisky neat and started to take some money from inside her dress; she did not touch the bag.

The barman waved a hand: *'Ca va, c'est payé!'*

She tried to smile, and said, *'Merci'*, then turned and walked hurriedly across the restaurant, past the woman in the blue hair, back to the lifts. The whisky had steadied her nerves; but her heart still beat hard and her face felt hot and throbbing. None of the lifts were at the floor. She started up the marble stairs. Room 274 was down to the left. There was no one in sight. She began to walk at a controlled pace along the dim carpeted corridor.

She reached the corner and turned. Behind her she heard a door close; a typewriter tapped in one of the rooms. She counted the decimal numbers set in the dark-varnished wood: — 68 — 70 — 72 — 74. She stopped, steadied herself, then lifted the handbag. None of the doors had handles, they locked automatically from the inside. She snapped open the bag and took out the pass-key; inserted it, twisted it to the left, pushed the door open and walked in.

It was dark inside. A passage led past the bathroom and toilet to the bedroom door, which stood ajar. She left the outer door open a couple of inches. There was no sound from the bedroom. She moved quickly, throwing the door wide-open. The shutters were closed across French windows and there was the metallic smell of air-conditioning. Through the darkness she could just make out the shape of a man lying under a sheet on the double bed. The wind roared outside and she could not hear him breathing. Her hand dropped the pass-key back into the bag and came out holding a revolver with the barrel wrapped in a bandage. She held it up level with her right breast and fired.

The bandage reduced the explosion to a loud thump, followed by a cracking sound. An arm moved out from under the sheet. She stepped forward and fired again. The first bullet had torn a white splinter out of the bed-top; the second thudded into the pillow.

The man's head came up and began shouting. His voice was high and cracked, and she tried not to listen to it as she took aim again and fired. The man was half out of bed now, dragging the sheet with him. She stood gripping the gun with both hands, watching him come round the bed towards her, still pulling the sheet and screaming at her.

She fired again, and a bottle of mineral water shattered on a table by the bed. He lunged at her, tripping in the tangled sheet. With the next shot she aimed lower and heard him choke. She fired twice more; he stumbled and half his face disappeared.

He was kneeling on the floor now, and the room was full of his choking screams and the burnt smell of the gun. She watched as the upper half of his body grew dark; and he sank forward on to the carpet and died.

She stepped back and collided with the wardrobe, groped round it and bumped into the open door. She was shuddering, stumbling past the bathroom into the passage. She looked both ways, then started to run. Behind her a door slammed. She turned the corner and almost ran into a pot-bellied man in a dressing gown who stood gaping up and down the corridor. He called to her as she passed, 'What's happened? Is somebody hurt?'

She ran on without answering. Somewhere her mind began to register door-numbers: 307, 305, 303. She reached the stairs and started down three steps at a time. The lift passed her on its way up. From above she heard shouting. She came to the next landing and read quickly the gilt letters on the mirror opposite: '*Troisième étage.*' The floor with rooms 200 to 300. The floor with Room 274. She did not stop: the handbag swung wildly as she leapt on down the marble stairs. The realization was coming to her that she had been on the fourth floor. She had killed the wrong man. As she ran across the foyer towards the hotel entrance she could see him clearly, kneeling in the dark with half his face gone.

Her body felt like water, and when she reached the doors and saw the Citroën parked without lights across the street she was weeping.

PART 1: ON THE HOLY MOUNTAIN

CHAPTER 1

The Dutchman, Pieter Van Loon, stopped under the monastery wall and sat lighting his meerschaum pipe, waiting for Neil Ingleby to reach him. The Englishman was a good fifty yards below, plodding up the slope under the weight of a small rucksack and portable typewriter.

The two of them had been on the move now for more than fourteen hours, leaving the last monastery of Chilandariou at dawn and tramping all day up the spine of the mountain peninsula. They had stopped only for a lunch of bread, olives, and retsina offered by some monks in a vineyard, and to pause for regular gulps from Van Loon's litre-bottle of ouzo.

Neil Ingleby arrived at the head of the path, exhausted.

The Dutchman grinned and breathed black smoke into the still air: 'You are not so tough, Neil old fellow!'

The Englishman unhoisted his rucksack and Olivetti 22, and sank down on the stony ground beside Van Loon, head on his knees. The Dutchman brought out the bottle of flawed green glass with no label, half-full of ouzo mixed with water. They both drank deeply, feeling the milky-white liquid spread through them with a sweet aniseed warmth, as they sat looking down the walls of the valley to the isthmus far below, where the dried-up Xerxes Canal once severed the peninsula from the Greek mainland. Beyond, they could just see the little town of Ierrissou with its jumble of white houses and the stone jetty where the girls went walking arm-in-arm in the evenings.

'That would be a good place to live,' said Van Loon, 'you could take a pretty girl there and live quietly, and when you are fed up with her, you come over the canal to escape.' He laughed and shook his head, enjoying his little fantasy over another gulp of ouzo.

The valley was growing dark with a grey-green twilight that smouldered out of the dense olives and vineyards. Mists began to crawl down the foothills of the mountain, trailing like cobwebs from the tops of the pines and walnut trees; and the heat was rapidly going out of the earth.

Van Loon stuffed the bottle back into his rucksack and said, 'Come, we go before they close the gates.'

Neil followed him wearily round the wall which climbed two hundred feet above them: a stone face pitted with age, its balconies and buttresses honeycombed with the nests of wild birds. The gate was sunk under a gloomy arch; Van Loon tugged at an iron lever and a bell chimed distantly behind the wall.

They had come to the Bulgarian monastery of Zographou, built in the twelfth century. It is one of more than thirty monasteries on the Holy Mountain of Athos, which rises from a finger of land pointing down into the Aegean off the north coast of Greece. For centuries the peninsula has been the refuge of thousands of monks, hermits and holy men belonging to the Orthodox Church; but with the spread of Communism cutting off the flow of novices from the east, and with the growing agnosticism of the West, the population of Athos has now dwindled to a few hundred stooped and senile men whose memories of the outside world ended before the murder at Sarajevo. Today their ancient palaces, lying in the folds of valleys or clinging to precipices over the sea, are falling silent, into decay.

Mount Athos is still governed by the oldest democracy in the world: an elected assembly of monks whose rule is respected by the Greek Government. No female creature, except birds and insects, and no wheeled vehicle is allowed on the peninsula; the mules and donkeys, which are the sole form of transport, have to be bred on the mainland. Only once, when a band of Communist guerrillas, including sixteen girls, attacked the monasteries to loot food in 1946, has a woman ever put foot on Athos. One of the few concessions to modern bureaucracy is a grubby office in Salonika where prospective tourists to the peninsula are issued with visas by a bearded monk in the chimney-pot hat of the Orthodox Church.

Neil, who had first met Van Loon on the bus from Salonika five days ago, had come to see this womanless civilization before it died out altogether; but now, standing in the gathering gloom, limp with tiredness, his head throbbing with the fumes of ouzo, he had to admit to himself that he found it a dead and dispiriting place.

There was a grinding like clockwork behind the wall and the gate creaked inwards, held open by a monk bent over a knotted stick. He raised his hand in welcome, turning to them a face swathed in a cocoon of dirty white hair hanging over his shoulders, revealing one black eye that shone at them with unnatural vigour.

They passed under the stone arch, into a courtyard full of the sweet stench of rotting vegetation. Walls of blind windows rose round them, under a belfry where a clock had stopped at five to one. The monk led them up a spiral staircase, past four floors, out on to a wooden gallery that looked across the sagging roofs into the black valley below. Out of the stillness came the chant of evensong.

By misfortune Neil and Van Loon had arrived on Athos during one of the fasting periods, so — as travellers, enjoying the traditional hospitality of the monasteries — they had to make do with a diet of bread, dried fish and olives. But local wine, and the fierce spirits ouzo and arak, had flowed without stint, and after the gruelling marches uphill, drinking freely on an almost empty stomach, Neil was feeling in poor physical condition.

Back in London, where he was a successful political journalist, he had grown slack on a routine of well-ordered luxury. He had come out here on a three-month leave of absence from his newspaper, ostensibly in order to write a book about Greece. But the book was unimportant: after two weeks all he had to show were a few scrappy notes. He had really come away to prove to himself that he could resist the comforts and creeping sloth of his London life.

On Mount Athos he had been attracted by the legendary virtues of solitude and enforced chastity; but unfortunately, Neil Ingleby did not have the mental resilience of a religious man. While he liked to think of himself as an enlightened liberal, able to reject the vulgarities of materialism, he was also the victim of habit: he depended too much on a fat salary, good restaurants and fashionable friends. On Mount Athos he felt exhausted and depressed, while Van Loon seemed to thrive, dark with the sun and tough as whipcord.

The monk had reached a wooden door down the gallery and stood bowing them inside. The cell was cramped and dark; there were two beds laid with straw under blankets of sackcloth, and a tiny window, shut and caked with dirt. Everywhere was the same sweet smell of decay. The monk shuffled in after them and picked up a rusted oil lamp from under one of the beds. After a lot of grunting and fumbling, he lit it with a box of matches from beneath his habit. The flame gave off a ribbon of black smoke, and Neil saw with distaste that the ceiling was hung with a canopy of cobwebs.

The old man put the lamp down between the beds, then straightened up and swept the hair from his face, giving them a totally toothless grin. The one black eye glinted mischievously, while the other was closed up, weeping down the hairy cheek. He looked like a shrunken miniature of Rasputin. He stood to attention and muttered a blessing in Bulgarian, then went out, closing the door. Neil stretched himself out on the bed, wondering if it wouldn't be better to give in and go back to Salonika or down to Athens.

Van Loon sat down and smoked his meerschaum; and soon the black shag began to overcome the smell of rot and burning oil. For some moments they said nothing. Neil found this one of the most restful things about their relationship. They talked to each other without effort, often in monosyllables, and there was no compulsion to impress or score over the other in intellectual combat.

Van Loon was a simple man: enormously strong, with a pleasant bovine face, blue eyes and a spiky blond beard. His hands were the size of spades and he had a great capacity for alcohol. He was a sailor by profession, but had done many jobs, never sticking to one for more than a few months. When they had met each other on the bus from Salonika he had been on the first leg of his journey round the world; and during the past five days the whole of Van Loon's sad saga had been unfolded to Neil, as they tramped side by side from monastery to monastery.

He was travelling on a bounty of sixty pounds — all the money he had in the world — saved up while tree felling in Finland during the summer. For four years he had been in love with a Norwegian girl who worked as a secretary in Amsterdam. ('A little black-haired girl, not like a Norwegian girl at all,' he had told Neil, 'with cat's eyes and a thin white body.') They were always making plans to get married, when Van Loon would become restless and set off on some trek. The last one had been to the forests of Finland where he had chopped logs for ten hours a day and spent the nights drinking wood spirit, collapsing to sleep it off in the snow. When he returned to Amsterdam three months later he learnt without warning that his girl had married a Dutch civil servant, and that the two of them had already left to live in a trading station in Borneo.

At first he had been stunned, incapable of belief; then had turned to rage and drink. ('She goes with a stupid little government dog!' he had roared at Neil. 'Bald with spectacles! I would have killed them both!') But unable to get his hands on either of them he had instead revenged himself on the bridegroom's father whom he had thrown into one of the canals, followed by a passing policeman. Two more policemen had arrived to restrain him, and they had gone into the canal too, dragging him with them; but he had managed to clamber out and escape through the back of a warehouse where he had tripped and fallen into a vat of sugar. ('I came running out into the square, white like a snowman!' he told Neil, grinning.) Covered in sugar, he had been chased across half Amsterdam; then at the police station he had run amok, putting three men in hospital before they had been able to get him into the cells.

He had gone to prison for four months. As soon as he came out, just three weeks ago, he had left on his journey round the world. Through endurance and a good deal of guile, he had managed to exist on seven pounds since leaving Amsterdam, impelled by a wild hope that one day he would reach Borneo and get his girl back. ('She might come away with me,' he told Neil. 'Perhaps the little husband is already a drunkard and she will divorce him. All the Dutch officials out there become drunkards. Rain and snakes and nothing to do but drink.')

He sat on his bed now in silence, sucking his pipe and listening to the chanting of the monks outside. A bell clanked dismally — a short cracked sound that made Neil shudder. It was growing cold in the cell and he wrapped the sackcloth round him, feeling the straw prick through his drill trousers.

'This is a pretty poor place,' said Van Loon, staring into the flame of the oil lamp. 'These old monks here can't have such good vineyards. Or maybe they drink all their wine. I wonder if we get any food tonight.'

'Let's have some ouzo,' said Neil. 'We might as well enjoy ourselves. It's too dark to read.'

As Van Loon was taking the bottle from his rucksack, there was a slow tread along the gallery and the monk appeared with a tray laid with fish, olives, a jug of wine and two tumblers of arak. He put it on the floor and Van Loon offered him some ouzo. He grinned coyly, taking the bottle and swallowing at least an inch in one draught; then dribbled into his beard and chuckled, his one black eye shining fiercely. Van Loon clapped him on the shoulder. 'That's a good old man, that!' he said to Neil, when the monk had gone.

Neil was tasting the fish. It was so dry that it crumbled in his fingers like biscuit. 'He might have brought us something better than this,' he muttered.

Van Loon was trying the arak. 'The trouble with you, old fellow,' he said, with a sudden insight that rather jarred Neil, 'you have too good a life. Look at that old man. He lives to be perhaps a hundred years old. He says his prayers, he eats this food, he drinks a bloody lot and he is happy!' He took another gulp of arak and added, 'This stuff he gives us is much stronger than my ouzo. After this, you eat anything!'

Neil picked up his glass, frowning, and sipped the transparent spirit. It burned his mouth raw, and his fingertips felt hot and dry. He bit into a lump of fish, chewed a couple of shrivelled olives, and lay back on the bed and thought of London, and of long-legged, small-breasted Miss Caroline Tucker: going to L.C.C. Russian classes and being whisked out of taxis through dim foyers to eat snails and listen to Hutch.

He finished the arak and Van Loon passed him the jug of wine. It was sweet and strong, washing out the salt taste of the fish, and together they drank in peace: Van Loon talking about how he would change his ways when he got back to Amsterdam — he would marry and buy a Vespa and drink only one beer in the evening before going back to his wife.

They finished the wine and returned to the ouzo. The Dutchman rambled on, and Neil lay in thought. Compared with Van Loon's griefs, his own problems were somewhat academic. He worked for one of Britain's most respected middlebrow Sunday newspapers. In twelve years spent in journalism, since graduating from Cambridge with a History First, he had established an enviable reputation. His political column each Sunday was well-informed and occasionally witty. He was a bachelor; made more than £3,000 a year, including television appearances; ran a Mini Cooper; lived in a spacious flat overlooking Battersea Park; and enjoyed the attentions and flattery of famous people: luncheon with Tory MP's on the borders of Westminster, dinner parties with young Labour MP's in the Boltons. He was a success. He had begun to drink too much, grow weary of his work, get up late in the morning and feel stale and morose.

His main affliction was a hopeless, lingering affair with a girl nearly ten years younger than himself. Caroline Tucker, pretty and penniless, was secretary to the editor of a fortnightly fashion magazine. He had met her at a cocktail party given by a junior Cabinet Minister, had invited her to dinner afterwards at Wheeler's and taken her to bed the same night. She was gay and shallow and affectionate in spasms, and he loved her with a passion that was neither dignified nor enjoyable. They had nothing in common; she was grossly unfaithful to him but always came back, smiling and unashamed, curling up beside him with the curtains drawn against the park and a bottle of wine by the bed.

He had asked her to marry him many times, but she always laughed and said she didn't want to marry anyone. He had taken her to Italy in the summer, motoring down the fast straight roads of France, and she had told him then that she loved him and that whatever happened between them she never wanted to lose him.

A few months later she had begun going out with a racing motorist called Tommy Drummond who drove Lotuses and was said to be on the way up. Neil had decided to withdraw nobly; he knew that she would come back to him eventually, as she always did. He had taken £250, packed a rucksack and left for Athos.

He was now feeling drunk enough not to care anymore. Van Loon rolled over and was asleep. Neil turned out the oil lamp, hunched himself under the sackcloth and thought of how, in a few weeks' time, he would go back to London and take Caroline out to an expensive meal, fill her up with wine and begin all over again.

Sometime later in the night the bell clanked twice from the courtyard. He woke suddenly. At first he thought it was the wind: a low whining sound that rose and fell for several seconds, before giving a high-pitched whistle and dying out altogether. There was a pause. He looked at his watch: it was nearly half past two. He could now hear a voice muttering somewhere behind the wall. It went on for a long time and he guessed that one of the monks was praying in a nearby cell.

He dropped back to sleep, but woke again in less than ten minutes. The voice had stopped. There were footsteps moving up and down the gallery outside. They passed the cell twice with a steady creaking, turned and started back, reached his door and halted.

He was wide awake now, sitting up, waiting for the next step. But the only sound was Van Loon's breathing. Then, very gently, he heard a number of clicks, each followed by a ringing sound. He counted eight before they stopped. There was silence: the footsteps did not go away. He lay still, listening; then got up, felt his way across the cell and opened the door.

There was a moon outside and the walls shone stone-white across the courtyard. A man was standing opposite him, his back turned, staring over the balustrade into the yard. He swung round at the sound of the door and for a moment they faced each other in silence. Neil could not see his face against the moonlight: all he could make out was a tall spare figure with arms gripping the balustrade behind him. Neil took a step forward and the man snapped, '*Qui êtes-vous?*'

Neil stopped. He still felt muzzy with wine and arak. He squinted at the man and slurred in his competent French, '*J'suis anglais — j'm'appelle* Ingleby.'

The man seemed to relax; his arms slipped from the balustrade and he murmured, 'Ah, an Englishman!' He stared at Neil, then added, speaking French, 'My name is Martel. Pierre Martel.' He held out a hand that was dry and cold like a doctor's then turned and took a coin from his pocket, which he held over the balustrade and dropped into the yard below. It landed with the clicking sound that Neil had just heard from the cell. Without turning, the man took out another coin. Neil moved closer and saw that it was a ten-drachma piece, worth about half-a-crown. Monsieur Martel leant out again and dropped it carefully over, at exactly the same spot as before. Neil wondered if it was some kind of game. The man was looking down into the yard and said absently: 'I dropped something. I was just taking a walk and I dropped it over the edge.'

For a moment the two of them stood side by side, peering into the darkness.

'What was it?' said Neil.

'A coin. A gold coin.' The man had taken out another ten-drachma piece and dropped it over after the others.

'What are you doing?' said Neil.

Monsieur Martel straightened up suddenly and faced him. It was a gaunt grey face; the hair was the colour of white pepper, cropped over a round scalp, and his eyes were a sunken slate-grey with a curious shallow glare in them. Neil had a feeling that he had seen him somewhere before.

'It's an old trick,' the man said, 'didn't you ever play it as a boy? You lose something, and you send something else after it.' He jerked his head towards the yard: 'There, in the morning, I shall find that all the coins have fallen in a limited area. The gold one will be somewhere among them.'

Neil suddenly wanted to laugh; he said, 'I've got a lamp in my room. We could go down and look for the coin now.'

The Frenchman shook his head: 'Thank you, I'll go myself. Goodnight.' He nodded, unsmiling, and walked away down the gallery.

Neil watched him go, then went back into the cell. Van Loon grunted, half-asleep, 'Who are you talking to?'

'Some old Frenchman,' said Neil. 'He was dropping coins into the yard.' He climbed down under the sackcloth, and Van Loon muttered, 'Must be crazy!'

Neil thought again about that whining sound he had heard earlier; he decided that it hadn't been the wind after all. He wondered where he had seen that gaunt face before.

CHAPTER 2

By the time they were up next morning M. Martel had already left. They washed at a well in the corner of the yard, and Neil noticed that the coins the Frenchman had dropped had now gone.

They set off by eight o'clock, after a breakfast of jam and thimble cups of sweet gritty-black coffee. For the first four hours they trudged up through warm pines, round the shoulder of the mountain. At about noon they were given some grapes by a hermit living in a tree: a decrepit old man with shoes made out of slices of car tyres who sat on a bed of branches built between two pines. Soon after they came out over the sea. From here the path became a ridge winding up the steep pyramid of Mount Athos. Knotted olive trees clung by their roots high above the Aegean, which stretched out below like beaten silver. There was no wind. They walked all day, till the sun sank low and the sea darkened to copper-brown veined with shifting shadows; and in the distance they saw the Russian monastery of St. Panteleimon, its clumps of green cupolas bristling with crosses of dull gold.

An hour later they reached the gates. They were given a whitewashed room with windows over the sea. The beds were laid with coarse clean linen, and there was even a washbowl and a Tilley lamp under a gold-framed photograph of Czar Nicholas II, with an inscription in Russian and French: 'God bless and Protect the Ruler of All the Russias.' Neil smiled at the thought of these ancient men perhaps believing that a Romanov was still enthroned in the Kremlin. Many of them — now shuffling in their high black boots towards evening prayers — would remember sleighfuls of fur-wrapped women sliding down the Nevsky Prospect to the opera. Or perhaps monks did not think about women, unless they were the ones who had fled here from unhappy love affairs. They were more likely to have memories of the crowded darkness of a Midnight Mass in St. Isaac's Cathedral: of snow wastes and forests and wooden seminaries where moths flitted about the bowls of oil lamps on a summer evening.

Van Loon was prodding the beds: 'They are pretty rich, these old Russians, huh?'

Neil nodded and began emptying his rucksack: shaving-case, socks and pants and cigarettes, and paperbacked editions of Conrad, Graves, Raymond Chandler, Roget's *Thesaurus* and a couple of books on Greece.

Van Loon unpacked only his bottle of ouzo, now barely two inches deep, and they shared it till it was empty and a bearded monk appeared to summon them to supper. The refectory was vast and dim, with peeling frescoes round the walls, musky with incense. There were less than fifty monks left in the monastery; they stood now along two wooden tables, heads bowed, as the abbot intoned a sepulchral Russian grace. Neil and Van Loon were led to places reserved at the head of the abbot's table. Opposite them stood M. Martel. He gave Neil a stiff bow; and again Neil found the man's face oddly familiar.

The grace continued for a long time. Many of the monks began to grow restive, like schoolboys, muttering to each other and fidgeting with their pewter knives. As soon as it ended they clattered over the benches and began pouring out wine from earthenware jugs along the tables.

Neil leant across to M. Martel and said, 'Did you find what you were looking for last night?'

'Looking for?' The man's face froze for a moment.

'Yes — the gold coin you lost in the yard.'

'Ah, that!' He gave Neil a faint smile. 'Yes, I found it' He turned and introduced them to the abbot.

Neil and Van Loon were sitting on either side of a bald wrinkled monk who spoke English with an American accent; he explained that he had left his home town of Kharkov in 1912 and spent his whole life on Mount Athos, except for a break of ten years between the wars at a Russian seminary near Wisconsin. His Middle-West accent was coloured with a Damon Runyan vernacular consisting largely of gambling expressions. He kept turning to them both and yelling, 'C'mon, kids, let's anti up with the vino!', refilling their mugs every few minutes. Conversation with him was not easy as he was very deaf. At one point Neil asked him if he had ever been to Chicago. The old man bent his head sideways: 'Come again!'

'Have you ever been to Chicago?' Neil repeated, louder.

The monk thought for a moment, then nodded: 'It is twelve miles from the sea.'

Neil gave up.

The abbot was talking to M. Martel in French, telling him about the illuminated manuscripts in the monastery library. The Frenchman listened intently, asking specific questions about the Sanskrit writings and some ancient texts that were believed to have come from Persia.

'You would do better to go up to Simonpetra for the older works,' the abbot explained. 'Here we have mostly Russian writings from the Middle Ages. We lost many beautiful texts,' he added, 'when the Communists attacked us after the war. Those were bad times. They came here with rifles and there was shooting up in Karyes with the gendarmerie. They even brought women — women who carried guns and laughed at the old monks who could not understand.' He shook his bearded head, and the wrinkled monk shouted at Neil, 'I read a couple o' books of Mr. Arnold Bennett! You ever read him?' Neil said he had. Beside him the abbot was telling M. Martel, 'Before I die I should like to leave the mountain for a few months and see what the world outside is like.'

'When were you last there?' asked M. Martel.

The abbot thought for a moment. 'I left St. Petersburg as a novice fifty-seven years ago.'

The Frenchman smiled grimly: 'You will find things very changed.'

The abbot nodded: 'Yes. But there is nothing wrong with change. Life is a great country that must be advanced across, not retreated over. It is the things that have not changed that I fear most — like the violence and cruelty of Man.'

'Violence is sometimes necessary,' M. Martel murmured.

'It is never necessary,' said the abbot gently. 'Violence is an act of stupidity, of impatience and intolerance. It achieves nothing, it only destroys. God did not create Man in order that he should be violent.'

'Man has to defend himself against his enemies,' said M. Martel. 'Do you think that stupid and wrong?'

The abbot paused. 'That is a hard question. I can only answer by saying that I believe we should always try to reason with our enemies.'

'Reason!' cried the Frenchman. 'Reason with the Communist bandits who came to burn your Sanskrit writings, to pillage your oneels and jeer at your monks?'

'Yes,' said the abbot, 'even with them. We have been attacked and pillaged many times. By the Turks, by pirates, by ignorant godless men who came with no motive but to destroy us. But God understands and he protects us.'

While the abbot had been speaking, Neil had sat watching M. Martel. The man's eyes were a luminous ice-grey, and his hands had tightened round his mug of wine till the knuckles were bone-white. He was listening to the abbot with a small, cruel smile. 'Monsieur l'Abbé!' he said at last. 'You talk of Turks and pirates. But all that was many years ago — before my time or yours. You talk of the Communist guerrillas. They came and burnt your old manuscripts, and the gendarmerie fought them in Karyes. You were lucky then. The Communists were beaten back — defeated by the forces of order. They had no time to destroy you, to wipe you off the face of the earth so that all this' — he waved his long hands round the vaulted refectory — 'all this would be nothing!' He paused, his eyes fixed on the abbot with a fierce glare.

'Yes, you are protected, Monsieur l'Abbé!' he went on, with controlled passion. 'Protected by these walls, by the Greek Government. It was not you who defeated the Communists. When one has to make decisions that will affect history it is not so easy to sit over wine talking about — pacifism!' He almost spat out the word; then sat back and sighed, his fingers loosening round the mug of wine as though a great tension had been released within him.

The abbot inclined his head: 'There is much wisdom in what you say, Monsieur. Many great men have felt as you do, and it is not for any of us here to pronounce you wrong.' He passed the wine round and was silent.

Neil glanced at the Frenchman, who was chewing a lump of bread and staring at his plate. He decided that he did not much like M. Martel.

When supper was over he and Van Loon groped their way up to their room. Neil opened the door and struck a match. He saw at once that there was something wrong. The moon glared in across the sea, on to a large black metal box in the middle of the floor. A pair of steel-backed hairbrushes lay beside the washbowl, under the photograph of the Czar. On the bed, where Neil's rucksack had lain, there was a pigskin suitcase with silver fittings. The match went out. He was just turning, when a powerful light flared into his face. A voice from the door said in French, 'What are you doing here?'

Neil stepped back and blinked. 'I'm sorry —' he put a hand across his eyes — 'we must have the wrong room.'

Monsieur Martel swung the torch on to Van Loon, round the walls, on to the black metal box, then back to Neil. 'What are you doing here?' he said again.

'I told you — we made a mistake. We've got the wrong room. They're all alike.'

'Get out!' said the Frenchman.

Neil stared into the light, began to flush with anger, then shrugged and said, 'Certainly. And thank you for your good manners.' He turned to Van Loon: 'Come on, let's get out of here!'

Martel did not move: 'Wait! I'm sorry. I thought for a moment —'

'It doesn't matter,' said Neil. 'Goodnight.'

'No, wait!' The Frenchman stepped back and closed the door: 'I didn't mean to be discourteous. I thought for a moment that perhaps —' He paused, the torch pointing at the floor.

'You thought perhaps we had come to steal something?' said Neil.

Martel hesitated: 'I have some valuable things in here. There are people who might try —'

'It doesn't matter,' said Neil, 'we both made a mistake. Goodnight, Monsieur Martel.' He started towards the door.

'Stay and have a brandy,' said the Frenchman, 'I have some excellent Armagnac.'

'Armagnac!' cried Van Loon, 'O.K., we accept!'

'*Bien!*' Martel strode across the room and lit the Tilley lamp, pumping up the pressure till the gauze bulb glowed a livid white that made his face look like a skull. Neil stood reluctantly by the door. 'Sit down, sit down!' said Martel, 'I'm afraid we'll have to make do with only two glasses.' He opened the pigskin case on the bed and brought out the brandy.

Neil and Van Loon sat on the other bed. The Frenchman poured out two tumblers, handed one to Neil, took the other and sat down on a chair beside the black box. There was a heavy silence. It was broken by Martel.

'What are you both doing on Athos?' It was not so much a polite opening to conversation as a blunt question that demanded an answer.

Neil gave it: 'I'm writing a book. My friend here's going round the world.' He passed the brandy to Van Loon: 'And you, Monsieur Martel?'

The Frenchman hesitated, his eyes sliding away from Neil's. 'I am here for my health. I was advised to take a holiday.'

'You're French, of course?'

'Yes.'

'From Paris?'

The man's eyes flicked back to Neil and the lids made a fluttering movement like a pair of camera shutters. 'No, not from Paris. I've spent most of my life overseas. I'm a professor — retired now.' He paused, his luminous grey eyes still on Neil: 'What is your book about, if I may ask?'

Neil sipped his brandy, trying to relax. There was something very unnerving about those eyes. 'It's supposed to be about Greece — when I can get down and write it. I'm aiming at an experimental travel book, working some of the ancient myths into background of life in modern Greece.'

Martel had leant forward, his fingertips pressed together: 'That is an idea with interesting possibilities. If I may be immodest, I once published a book myself — on the Islamic countries.'

'Are you a professor of Arabic?'

'Not exactly. I've studied a little classical Arabic.' He poured out more brandy and for the next few minutes he talked to Neil in scholarly detail about the complexities of Arabic semantics, and how the language had degenerated as it spread west from Egypt to the Maghreb.

Van Loon yawned.

'I'm boring you,' said Martel.

'No, no!' said Neil, embarrassed and annoyed with Van Loon.

There was a pause. His eyes strayed round the room and settled on the black metal box in the middle of the floor. 'How do you travel about on Athos, Monsieur Martel?' he asked.

The Frenchman's eyes followed Neil's to the black box. 'I have a mule I hired in Karyes.'

Neil nodded. Van Loon sat with his square hands hanging between his knees. Neil felt it was time to go. He was draining down his brandy, when Martel said, 'Did you have any trouble coming to Athos?'

'Trouble?'

'Yes — trouble with the police. Were you stopped at all?'

'Only by the official who checked our visas. We didn't see any police.'

'Which way did you come?'

'Through Ierrissou — over the Xerxes Canal.'

Martel nodded slowly, as though to himself: 'So you didn't come by boat to Daphne?' He stood up and emptied his glass: 'Well, Messieurs, it's getting late. I have to be up early tomorrow.' His stiff grey face stretched into a smile.

At the door, Neil turned: 'Monsieur Martel, do you mind if I look at that gold coin you lost last night?'

The Frenchman stared at him for a moment: 'Certainly.' He stepped over the other bed, opened the pigskin bag and drew out a slim leather case like a jewel box. Inside, set in a cushion of black velvet, lay about two dozen coins. Most of them were small and misshapen, black or yellowish brown, almost bald with age. Martel lifted one out that was larger than the rest, about the size of a florin, bearing the stamp of a heavy Roman profile.

'*Voilà!*' He placed the coin on Neil's palm. Neil knew by the weight that it was gold; he turned it over and saw a series of almost illegible numerals.

'Those are what makes it valuable,' said Martel, 'special numbering for money in circulation outside Rome. This coin was used to pay off Brutus' troops in Egypt. The date shows that it must have been minted after his murder in Alexandria.'

Neil saw a loving passion in the grey eyes, as the man laid the coin back in its velvet bed. 'It is safe there,' he said, snapping the case shut, 'I carry it about with me as a talisman. When I have problems, I keep it in my hand. It has always brought me luck.'

Neil smiled, wondering what problems M. Martel had had last night as he paced the gallery at Zographou at half past two in the morning. 'Goodnight, Monsieur Martel.'

'Goodnight,' said the Frenchman, 'and please excuse my behaviour earlier this evening. I have been under some strain lately.'

'That's all right,' said Neil, smiling.

He and Van Loon went along the passage to their room. As the door closed, Van Loon said, 'He is a pretty odd fellow that, huh?'

'A mad professor,' said Neil.

'Not so mad. He is frightened.'

Neil laughed: 'What would he be frightened of here? You've been drinking too much.'

'I don't know what he is frightened of,' said Van Loon solemnly, 'but he is frightened of something.'

'You go to bed,' said Neil.

CHAPTER 3

It was not until several days later that they again heard of M. Martel. They had come down off the mountain and arrived in Karyes, the administrative centre of the peninsula. It is no more than a couple of wooden streets, a church, a police station manned by a posse of men lent from the mainland, and a café where the monks come to play dominoes and read the newspapers.

They reached the town in mid-morning after six hours' march from the last monastery, walking down the Street of the Holy Ghost, where travellers are forbidden to smoke, wear a hat or ride a donkey: and entered the café, sweating and in need of a drink. The only person inside was a young gendarme in a grubby uniform who sat alone over an empty glass of ouzo. He came over and joined them, leaning across the table and whispering in English, 'You have cigarettes please?'

Neil offered him a packet of Patras filter-tips. The boy helped himself to five, lit one and stowed the rest away inside his tunic, then sat down and ordered three ouzos. 'Here no cigarettes,' he said, 'I come from Salonika. I come here first with cigarettes, guitar, radio, everything. But the monks take them away. It is like prison here.'

The ouzos came and the boy swallowed his in one gulp.

'There can't be much work for you,' said Neil. 'Why do they have police here?'

'I don't know. Perhaps there is sometimes trouble.'

'Has there ever been trouble?'

'No.' The boy looked into his glass and thought for a moment; 'Not trouble. But sometimes perhaps funny things happen. Yesterday a big boat come in the night — it come to Daphne and a man get on it. We hear this from the monks.'

'Is that bad?' said Neil.

'Not good. Everybody who come to Athos must be controlled. This man come down from the mountain with much luggage — big boxes and things, and get on the boat and goes. The police know nothing.'

'Did anyone see this man?'

The boy looked at his empty glass and called the waiter. 'He had white hair — that is all I know.' He ordered three more ouzos.

Neil glanced at Van Loon, who grinned 'The old Frenchman, huh?'

'You know this man?' the boy asked.

'I think so,' said Neil, 'we met him in the monasteries. Is it a serious matter?'

'The police make a report. They tell Salonika.' The boy shrugged: 'Perhaps it is serious. I don't care. I hate this place.'

They finished their ouzos and got up to leave. The boy wanted to go on talking, offering to pay for all the drinks, but they told him they had to be down in Daphne to take the afternoon boat to Athens. He waved goodbye, looking small and miserable, sitting there in the morning sun in his hot uniform, starting on his fourth glass of ouzo.

They left the town, tramping down the mule tracks towards the sea. After an hour they came to an opening in the trees where they could see the steamer approaching, its wash spreading out in a silver fan towards the horizon. They reached Daphne just as the ship was tying up. There were only two passengers — Greek officials with briefcases who had come to check the wine quotas. There was no sign of any police in the town. They had their visas stamped by a little man in a peaked cap with a black moustache who looked like Stalin; then bought deck-class tickets for the night trip to Athens. Neil would have liked a cabin, but did not want to offend Van Loon who couldn't afford one.

They had to wait an hour before the steamer left. They bought some bread and cheese and a wicker-bound jar with four litres of retsina which they lugged between them up the gangway past a brass plate engraved with the name of John MacIntyre & Sons, Glasgow, 1907.

'This should last us the night,' said Neil, as they set down the monster jar on the deck and settled against the bulkheads, using their rucksacks as cushions.

'I think perhaps if we stay on Athos a few months we become drunkards,' said Van Loon, drawing the cork which was the size of his fist.

'And live to be a hundred years old,' said Neil, smiling.

'It is because they have no women,' said Van Loon; 'if I had no women I would go crazy.' He heaved up the jar with both hands and took a long drink. 'I think after Athens I go to Beirut,' he added. 'The girls there are pretty good, huh?'

'That'll cost you money,' said Neil.

The Dutchman shook his head: 'Ah, I wish I had some bloody money!'

They sat watching the mules jog down to the jetty laden with wine casks which were exchanged for coffee, sugar and paraffin. Just after five o'clock the two Greek officials came up the gangway. A moment later the rusted smokestack gave a boom that bounced off the mountain, and the engines started up.

'You know that old white-haired Frenchman?' said Van Loon, as they pulled away from the shore. 'I think he is a smuggler.'

'Oh yes?' said Neil, lifting the jar which was growing lighter.

'He has a black box and gold coins and a boat that comes in the night to take him away,' said Van Loon; 'that is like a smuggler.'

'And what was he smuggling?'

'Gold coins.'

Neil laughed: 'Those were all collectors' pieces. Besides, most of them weren't even gold.'

Van Loon stared at the receding mountain. 'Well, perhaps he smuggles diamonds. Whatever it is, he is a bloody odd fellow!'

Neil thought that M. Martel was indeed an odd fellow; but he didn't think he was a smuggler.

PART 2: THE FAT MAN

CHAPTER 1

They woke as the edge of the sky began to whiten over the hills of Attica; and they sat on the deck, drinking Turkish coffee and watched Athens grow out of the dry dawn.

The sky-line straggled, the colour of dust and sand, from the jumbled port of the Piraeus, where Van Loon's mind was already planning some low debauch, to the gaunt square rock on which the Acropolis stands — looking, Neil thought, like a piece of broken balustrade.

They drew closer, to the groan of ships' horns, smells of tar and tobacco, with gulls gliding over the oily water. There were two men waiting on the quayside as the boat tied up. One was thin, in a brown suit with dark glasses. The other wore the blue-grey uniform of the Greek police.

As Neil and Van Loon came ashore, the plainclothes man stepped in front of them. '*Les papiers!*' He stood with his hand thrust out, while the uniformed man watched with a dark closed face. Neil and Van Loon took out their passports; the plainclothes man flipped through them, snapped them shut and put them away in his pocket. He looked up, his glasses glinting in the sun. '*Suivez-nous!*' he said, jabbing his thumb towards the customs shed. The uniformed man fell in behind, and the little squad began to march briskly across the quay.

After a few yards Neil said to Van Loon, 'Peter, we're under arrest.'

The Dutchman shrugged: 'Oh, some bureaucratic idiocy. It is nothing.'

Neil, who had never been detained by the police before, did not feel the same composure. He turned to the plainclothes man and tried — in French, then in English — to ask what was happening.

The Greek replied brusquely, '*Affaire de police!*' and nodded again towards the customs shed.

But they were not taken into the customs shed. Instead they were led round into a yard where a black Ford sedan stood parked behind locked gates leading into the street. A second policeman, who had been waiting by the car door, came forward to meet them. He was a stout man with a severe puffy grey face. He stepped up to Van Loon and frisked him under the arms and down his hips and thighs. Van Loon laughed. The policeman straightened up and snarled something, then turned and repeated the operation on Neil, who stood very still and did not laugh. The man's breath had a rancid smell and his fingers felt hard and prepared for violence. The first policeman was searching both rucksacks.

Finally the stout man stepped back; they were both handed their luggage and pushed into the rear seats of the Ford. The plainclothes Greek climbed into the front next to the stout man who was driving; the other policeman unlocked the gates, and they purred into a white street where shutters were being rattled up and waiters were sprinkling the pavements and setting tables out in the early sun.

Neil was beginning to feel very uneasy. He whispered to Van Loon, who was relaxing in the deep seats, 'I don't like it, Peter! What the hell's happening?'

'Some idiot formality. We find out.' He grinned: 'Nice taxi, huh!'

They turned into a square, past a brown Byzantine church with a humped brick dome where an old man was selling lemons under the wall. The two Greeks rode in silence.

'This isn't any formality,' said Neil, 'the Greek police don't arrest tourists unless it's something serious.'

'O.K., they think we are dangerous gangsters. It is a joke for us.'

Neil sat back and said nothing. It was too early for him to have a sense of humour. He needed a shave, and his mouth felt black and dried up after the retsina of the night before. The car drummed over cobbles, past trams sparking along the waterfront into Athens. In the seat in front, the driver's neck bulged over his collar like a swollen lead pipe.

'Perhaps they find something wrong with our papers,' Van Loon added, lighting up his meerschaum.

'There's nothing wrong with our papers,' said Neil. He was becoming irritated now with the Dutchman's complacency.

They drove past banks and shipping offices and down dusty treeless avenues into Constitution Square, lined with concrete pillars and the blue shields and white cross of the Hellenic Kingdom. The Ford pulled up in front of the King George Hotel. The policeman who had been driving stayed behind the wheel, while a doorman bowed the other three through the revolving doors. Van Loon, rucksack on his back and pipe between his teeth, grinned ecstatically at the marble and chandeliers, his roughshod feet sinking half an inch into the carpets over to the lifts.

'Perhaps they send us up champagne and dancing girls!' he cried, as the lift doors hissed shut and they rose, as gently as mercury in a barometer, to the top floor. A door at the end of the passage was opened by a small neat man with a nut-brown head. The plainclothes Greek handed him the two passports, and Neil and Van Loon were shown into a suite with bars of sunlight across a wine-red carpet.

In front of the French windows sat an enormously fat man. His head was the shape of an egg, with a sharp little beard and a lick of hair pasted across his brow in a kiss curl. He looked to Neil like a French professor out of some nineteenth-century farce.

The nut-brown man waved a hand at two armchairs in the centre of the floor. '*Asseyez-vous!*' he said, strutting over to a table near the wall. The plainclothes man had taken up his place beside the door.

The nut-brown man stood looking down at Neil and Van Loon, thumping his thick fingers on the two passports: 'Messieurs, I am Captain Spyros of the Athens police.' He spoke French with a strong accent.

Neil interrupted, in English: 'Just a minute. We're not French. I'm English and my friend here is Dutch. And we'd like to know what all this is about.'

Captain Spyros held up his hand and continued, in French: 'Please, my colleague here, Monsieur Charles Pol' — he nodded towards the fat man — 'speaks only French. You are both familiar with the French language? Exactly! So we will proceed.' He opened the two passports.

All this time the fat man, M. Pol, had been watching them with an amused expression which rather unsettled Neil. His moist red lips were parted like two cherries, showing a pair of glistening front teeth.

Captain Spyros looked at the passports. 'You have both been on Athos, I see? You applied for permission in Salonika three weeks ago?'

Neil nodded.

'Which of the monasteries did you visit, please?'

Neil told him the names of the ones he could remember, then added, 'I think we're still entitled to know what all this is about.'

The Greek raised his hand again: 'Please, first we must determine certain facts. Why did you visit Athos?'

Neil shrugged. 'To see the monasteries. Tourism.'

'Tourism?' said Captain Spyros, fixing Neil with small black eyes. 'You did not perhaps have business to do on Athos?'

'Business? What sort of business would I have there?' Neil glanced round at M. Pol, who sat passively watching him with his cherry-lipped smile.

Captain Spyros was looking again at Neil's passport. 'It says here that you are a journalist. Perhaps you visited Athos in order to interview someone?'

'No, I told you, I went as a tourist.'

At that moment M. Pol leant out and whispered something to Captain Spyros, who handed him Neil's passport. The Greek now turned to Van Loon: 'It says here you are a sailor by profession?'

'Oh, I am many things in my life,' said Van Loon, shaking his head slowly like some mystic.

'What were you doing on Athos?'

'Escaping from a girl.'

Monsieur Pol looked up and gave a small peal of laughter, shrill, almost a woman's laugh.

Captain Spyros frowned and adjusted his cuffs. 'You have known each other how long?' he said, with stiff dignity.

'We met on the bus to Ierrissou three weeks ago,' said Van Loon.

The Greek nodded with a look of disappointment, laid the passport back on the desk, and turned again to Neil: 'Did you meet any other tourists while you were on Athos?'

Neil hesitated. Monsieur Pol had leant forward, his chair giving a little crack under his weight. 'Yes, there was a Frenchman we met,' said Neil, 'a Monsieur Martel. He said he was a retired professor.'

'What did this man look like?' It was Pol who spoke, in a rich melodious voice like a tenor.

'Tall — white-haired — about fifty.'

The fat man leant out and picked a folder off the table in front of Captain Spyros. He opened it and handed it to Neil. Inside lay two photographs. They were both of M. Martel; one showed him in a dark suit with the ribbon of the Legion of Honour, standing at attention in a parade in a Paris street. In the other he was behind a desk in the uniform of a French Army officer. Neil knew now where he had seen the face before. It had appeared on the front pages of the world's Press some eight months earlier.

Pol said softly, 'Was it this man?'

Neil nodded and handed the folder back.

CHAPTER 2

The man was Colonel Pierre Broussard, commander of a crack paratroop regiment which had been involved in an abortive coup the year before in one of France's less happy North African Protectorates.

It had been the climax of several years' guerrilla warfare between the French and the Moslem Nationalists, who called themselves the Arab Front. An exhausted French nation had finally agreed to open tentative peace talks as a prelude to granting the Protectorate independence. The European population, a strong minority of nearly a million, had reacted at first with hopeless anger — rioting, burning official buildings, calling strikes.

Then, eight months ago, a clique of Army officers, headed by General Paul Guérin, a former Commander-in-Chief in the Protectorate, had defied the Government and for four days had threatened to drop paratroopers over Paris and seize the city. The revolt had collapsed when the rest of the Army, undecided to the last, had finally failed to give the rebels their support.

Paul Guérin and a number of high-ranking officers, including his second-in-command, Colonel Broussard, had gone underground and been sentenced to death in absentia. Out of the rump of eighteen-hundred disbanded paratroopers and Foreign Legionnaires, and the leaders of extremist civilian groups, Guérin had founded a clandestine organization calling itself the Secret Army.

France now found herself trapped in a three-cornered fight. Burdened with mutinous officers, she was trying to extricate herself with the remnants of dignity, from between two fanatical terrorist organizations. While her struggle against the Arab Front still continued, the power of the Secret Army had been growing to frightening proportions, steadily eroding the foundations of law and order within the Protectorate until now even the stability of Metropolitan France was threatened.

Monsieur Pol now explained that during the last two weeks, while Neil had been on Athos, innocent of world affairs, the Secret Army had begun an indiscriminate terrorist campaign against Moslems in the capital of the Protectorate. Their aim was to disrupt any future peace talks between Paris and the Arab Nationalists. French security forces — the CRS (the Campagnie Républicaine de Sécurité) and the shock troops of the Gardes Mobiles — had tried, with the dubious backing of the Army, to break the organization, but with no great success. Many arrests had been made, but the main conspirators, including Colonel Broussard, had slipped out of the Protectorate to Spain, Sicily and Greece, where they were now believed to be planning a new coup to overthrow the French Government.

Pol confessed to Neil that the Deuxième Bureau had known for a while that Broussard was operating from somewhere in Greece; then, the night before, an agent in Salonika had reported that he might be hiding on Mount Athos. Instructions had been given for the Greek police to detain all travellers leaving the peninsula.

Pol spread his fat fingers across his knees: 'So you see, gentlemen, it was necessary to bring you here this morning in the interests, let us say, of security… Many of Broussard's men were in the Foreign Legion — Germans and Spaniards, Dutchmen, even Englishmen. We couldn't take any chances — these people are very well organized.' He clapped his hands against his enormous thighs: 'However, now you are here, perhaps you could tell us something about this Monsieur Martel. Was he alone?'

'Yes,' said Neil.

'What did he talk about?'

Neil paused: 'The only things he talked to me about were Arabic semantics and old coins.'

Pol chuckled, wagging his head: 'Ah, our friend Broussard is an intellectual! An intellectual killer. One must not underestimate him. He was one of the great heroes of the French Army — a survivor of Dien Bien Phu, decorated with the Legion of Honour, the Médaille Militaire — an expert on psychological warfare and a leading French authority on classical Arabic. He wrote an excellent book on the history of Persian poetry. Formidable man. Unfortunately, in Saigon he began relying too much on opium. After Dien Bien Phu he had a nervous collapse and spent a lot of time in a psychiatric clinic near Grenoble. He's a little insane.'

Neil told Pol about the night at St. Panteleimon and the black box that the colonel had lugged about the mountain.

'That would have been radio transmitting equipment,' said Pol, 'he was keeping in touch with the Secret Army agents here in Greece.'

Neil remembered now the whining sound and the voice behind the wall that he had heard at Zographou on that first night he had met M. Martel. Finally he told Pol of the conversation he had had with the gendarme at Karyes, and about the boat that had arrived during the night.

Pol listened solemnly to this. When Neil finished, he nodded and said glumly, 'So it looks as though our friend Broussard has flown. You say two nights ago?' He turned to Captain Spyros, who had been staring at his manicured nails. 'Captain, we must still check all the boats and roads from Athos. Keep the Salonika police alerted — warn the coastguards, the ports, the airfields. It is just possible that the man is still in Greece.'

Captain Spyros bowed, smiled obsequiously round him, and hurried from the room, followed by the plainclothes man. The door closed. Neil and Van Loon rose to leave, but Pol jumped up with amazing agility and clutched them both by the elbow with his pink fleshy fingers.

'One moment!' he cried. 'I have a debt to pay! I have had you both seized in error as common criminals in a land which is neither mine nor yours. I owe you at least a drink' — he glanced at his watch, it was not yet nine o'clock — 'and a good breakfast.' He pushed them back into their chairs and waddled over to a side table where there were three white telephones and several bottles of Scotch and Perrier water.

Standing up, he reminded Neil of the man in the Michelin tyre advertisement: his great body bulged out of a shiny blue suit and balanced on a pair of delicate feet in soft slippers like ballet shoes. He was sweating heavily and the hair on the back of his head grew in damp rings like a whirlpool.

He stood slopping whisky into three cut-glass tumblers, adding ice from a thermos bucket. 'Now we can behave like free men!' he cried, trotting back with three huge golden drinks. 'These policemen are bores! They are also stupid. They wanted to arrest you formally and take you to headquarters for questioning. It was my idea you came here!' He beamed at them both and took a deep drink.

'You are not a policeman?' said Van Loon suspiciously.

'*Merde, non!* I'm a businessman. I run a supermarket behind the Gare St. Lazare.'

Neil smiled. 'Would it be indiscreet,' he said, 'to ask what you're doing here in Athens?'

The fat sweating face became suddenly sly. 'Monsieur Ingleby, for a man with a secret there are never indiscreet questions, only indiscreet answers.' He chuckled and finished half his drink: 'Now, breakfast! They do a very good Greek dish here — or you can have bacon and eggs.' He clapped Neil on the shoulder. '*Le bon breakfast anglais avec du* Johnny Walter!' he cried, with his peal of girlish laughter.

'I'll settle for the Greek dish,' said Neil. Van Loon chose the same, winking at Neil over his drink, as Pol waddled back to the table and spoke into one of the white telephones. Neil wondered who was paying for the suite: was it the Deuxième Bureau or the Paris housewives who shopped at the supermarket at St. Lazare?

'Monsieur Ingleby, how long are you staying in Greece?' Pol asked, coming back from the table after refilling his drink.

'A month perhaps. And you?'

'Ah, that rather depends on our friend Colonel Broussard, alias Monsieur Martel.' He squinted quizzically at Neil across his glass: 'In any case, we shall be seeing something of each other, I hope?'

There was a knock at the door. A waiter wheeled the breakfast in on a trolley: jug of sweet, burnt-black coffee, bowls of yoghourt covered with a yellow crust and fat green figs wrapped in vine leaves.

The three of them ate with silent concentration: it was the first civilized food that Neil and Van Loon had tasted for more than two weeks. Pol shovelled it in at a ferocious rate, yoghourt dribbling into his beard, washed it all down with another tumbler of Johnny Walker and returned to his row of telephones. 'If you want a bath and shave,' he called, 'it's straight through.' He dialled a number and began a long conversation in French. From what Neil could hear from the bathroom he was giving a series of urgent instructions. His voice held a note of authority that had nothing to do with a cheerful businessman gorging himself on an expense account.

Neil sank into the bath, finished his second whisky, scrubbed himself with the scented soap until the water turned grey, and decided there were worse ways to spend one's first morning in a strange city. He shaved with Pol's razor and dabbed on one of Pol's aftershave lotions, noticing that the bathroom shelves were crowded with bottles of Eau de Cologne, creams, talcum powders, deodorants and vitamin pills. It amused Neil to realize that the man was vain.

Back in the sitting-room Pol was listening excitedly on the phone, another full whisky in his hand. He motioned Neil into a chair, while Van Loon went through to the bathroom.

'*Oui! … Oui! Entendu!* That's all we can do for the moment, except wait.' He hung up, came back streaming with sweat, and collapsed into his chair by the window. For a moment the two of them sat in silence, sipping their drinks and feeling the warm breeze stir through the blinds from the Aegean. It was Pol who spoke first: 'Would you be interested in this affair professionally, Monsieur Ingleby?'

'Of course. I'm going to write a piece about Broussard on Athos, if that's what you mean.'

'That is a good little story, I agree. But I was thinking of something that might be even more interesting.' He paused.

Neil sensed a sudden electric tension spring up between them. He said warily, 'What sort of thing?'

Pol made an ambiguous gesture with his pink hands: 'I'm afraid I can't be very precise at this stage. But I think, if my guess is right, that things will shortly be happening over in North Africa.' He clinked the ice cubes in his glass. There was another pause, full of irrelevant sounds: a horn from the Piraeus, Van Loon in his bath.

Pol wiped his brow, careful not to disarrange the kiss curl: 'When I saw the name in your passport, Monsieur Ingleby, I recognized it at once. I have read several of your articles — they were reprinted in *Le Canard Enchaîné.*'

Neil inclined his head, flattered.

'There was one I particularly liked — about the crisis in the Protectorate last year.'

Neil remembered the article. It had been a facetious piece written while General Guérin was threatening to drop paratroopers over Paris. Neil had suggested that one way to avert the danger, as well as effectively to humiliate the rebels themselves, would be for loyal French pilots to fly the paras across the Mediterranean, but instead of Paris, to drop them over Wigan and Blackpool and let them find their own way back.

Pol chuckled and took a long drink: 'I should like to have thought up that one myself! In moments of crisis the best solutions are often the most unorthodox.'

'It wasn't meant as a serious solution,' said Neil.

'No, not. Not serious perhaps. But as a plan it might have worked.'

Neil looked at him with a superior smile: 'It still wouldn't have prevented those paras from killing a few hundred people — even in Wigan.'

'Ah, *les paras!*' said Pol, shaking his head sadly. 'I'm afraid that France is obsessed with phantoms of military glory. We are becoming almost as morbid as the Germans.' He took another deep drink: 'You see, I have always been radical in my views. I think if the circumstances were right I might even be a revolutionary. I am hampered by the fact that I am also a capitalist. But don't misunderstand me! When Fascism raises its head — when men like Guérin and Broussard try to ride the tide of history — then I draw my sword, Monsieur Ingleby! — I become a warrior!' He sat back and mopped his face: 'I think, from what I have read of your articles, that you are also something of a radical — a man of the Left?'

Neil, with the instincts of breeding, disliked having his politics discussed by a stranger. He said evasively, 'Well, more or less.'

'And you hate Fascism?'

'Of course.'

'Exactly!' Pol smiled. 'I think, Monsieur Ingleby, that you and I may be able to work a little together.'

'Work together?' Neil frowned: 'I don't quite follow you. Are you suggesting that I work for the French Secret Service?'

'Ah, you are very suspicious!' Pol sounded almost unhappy.

'Certainly I'm suspicious — and with some reason, I think. Since putting foot in this city two hours ago I've been arrested, searched for arms, then brought to an hotel suite and questioned about a terrorist leader by a man who tells me he runs a supermarket for French ladies' underwear. Doesn't that sound suspicious to you?'

'You exaggerate,' said Pol. 'I specialize in tinned foods and kitchen utensils. It is a perfectly respectable business.'

'But you work for the Deuxième Bureau?'

'I have told you that I am not a policeman. Please! I find policemen the most tedious brutes. They are even worse than soldiers — they drink less for one thing — and they are quite as corrupt as politicians, except they don't do so well out of it.' He paused and grinned.

'Then who do you work for?' Neil persisted.

'I work,' said Pol reluctantly, wiping his brow again, 'for the French Government — not because I love them, but because France deserves to be ruled by better men than Guérin and Broussard. Besides, I enjoy the adventure of the work — it's the only thing that keeps my fat down.'

'You mean you're a secret agent?' said Neil, smiling suddenly at this preposterous man, with his kiss curl and white telephones and whiskies for breakfast.

'I am an amateur agent,' said Pol, heaving himself up to refill his drink, 'I am not employed by any of the security departments. What in France we rudely call a barbouze — a "false beard".' He tugged at his own little goatee and grinned hugely: 'Only mine is real!'

Neil followed him to the table, his head growing light. 'Monsieur Pol, you mentioned just now that we might be able to work together. You obviously didn't mean in your tinned food department.'

Pol turned and rocked on his slippered feet. An impish smile illuminated his enormous face; he put a hand on Neil's shoulder and pulled him closer till Neil could smell the whisky on his breath. 'Monsieur Ingleby,' he crooned, still smiling, but with eyes that had become peculiarly hard, 'you are a journalist, you are interested in what goes on in the world — in what goes on behind the scenes. Now I like to help journalists whenever I can. I think in English you have an expression, the scoop? Well, I may be able to give you a scoop. In a week, two weeks, perhaps a few days. I cannot tell you about it now, but when it comes it will be worth writing about, believe me!'

Neil felt exhilarated and amused and rather drunk. At the back of his mind a tiny instinct warned him that this burst of speculative generosity might not be as innocent as it sounded. But the whisky bottle was three-quarters empty, and Van Loon had come back into the room, and Pol, with his short little arms outstretched, was seeing them to the door, inviting them to lunch with him at the hotel at one o'clock.

'We'll meet in the bar,' he cried, 'for a good American cocktail!' He laughed, and Van Loon laughed, and they all shook hands.

'He is a terrific fellow, that!' Van Loon said, as they rode down in the lift. 'I think a sort of spy, huh?'

'Something like that,' Neil said; and they went out into the hot sun.

CHAPTER 3

They found a cheap hotel that looked down Kolokrotni Street towards the Acropolis. Their room had a stone floor and no hot water and smelt of charcoal and mutton. But there was a solid table in front of the window where Neil hoped he might work.

The whisky had made them both drowsy, and they stretched out on the lumpy beds to rest before their lunch with Pol. Neil stared at the ceiling and dozed and thought; and the more he thought about Pol, the more intrigued he became. His own enthusiasm had been dissipated by the soft life; what he needed now was a crude dash of adventure. Pol was an adventurer, and Neil envied him for it.

At exactly one o'clock, he and Van Loon were back at the King George Hotel. Neil went to the reception desk and changed a £10 travellers' cheque from his remaining stock of £200. Beside him stood two corn-haired Americans in seersucker suits with cameras the size of binocular cases. 'Can we do Delphi and Marathon in a day?' one of them was asking.

The foyer was empty, except for a slim man with dark glasses and steel-grey hair who was sitting opposite the lifts behind a copy of *L'Aurore*. The second American was saying, 'What about that place Byron was at — Cap Sunion or something?'

Neil stopped at the hotel bookstall on their way to the bar and bought yesterday's Paris edition of the *Herald Tribune*. The bar was crowded, full of the subdued roar of lunchtime drinking, breaking about them like surf on a beach. They pressed past the crush of shantung and mohair, and found a place in the corner under a fan.

Pol had not yet arrived. Neil ordered two Bloody Marys and glanced at the *Herald Tribune*. Guérin's Secret Army was on the front page: during the past twenty-four hours thirty-nine Moslems had died in acts of street terrorism in the French Protectorate in North Africa. Six of them, including a woman and a fourteen-year-old boy, had been dragged from a tram in a European working-class suburb and beaten to death in front of a crowd of several hundred. Neil folded the paper up and felt sick and angry.

Twenty minutes later, Pol had still not arrived. They were beginning to feel hungry. 'I'll go and see if he's been delayed in his room,' said Neil.

The receptionist lifted the telephone and listened for a moment, then shook his head: 'Sir, there is no reply from Monsieur Pol's suite.'

Neil detected a faint stir behind him; the slim steel-grey man had shifted his copy of *L'Aurore*. The receptionist added, 'I have not seen Monsieur Pol go out this morning, sir. His key is gone — he should be somewhere in the hotel.'

'There may be a message,' said Neil, 'the name's Ingleby.' He turned his head slightly and thought he caught the edge of the slim man's eyes shining at him from behind their dark glasses. It gave him a queer, uneasy feeling, as though he had been surprised in some compromising act.

The receptionist turned back: 'I'm sorry, sir, there are no messages. Shall I have Monsieur Pol paged?'

'Please,' said Neil, 'say he's wanted in the bar.'

He went through and bought Van Loon another drink and watched the bar empty for lunch: waiters whisking up glasses and flicking napkins and collecting ashtrays. And still Monsieur Pol did not come.

'Perhaps he is drunk,' Van Loon suggested.

'Perhaps,' said Neil, thinking that more likely Pol had just forgotten, or had had another engagement and hadn't bothered to leave a message. He put down some money on the bar and was just leaving, when a bellboy touched his arm: 'Mister Ingilbee?'

'Yes?'

'Telephone please!'

In the foyer Neil noticed that the slim grey man with *L'Aurore* had gone. He went into one of the airless cells and lifted the receiver. The line crackled as though it were long-distance.

'Monsieur Ingleby? This is Charles — Charles Pol!'

'Where are you?'

'Monsieur Ingleby, can you hear me? I'm sorry I couldn't meet you for lunch. Something has happened.' The voice faded into static and Neil shouted again: 'Where are you?'

'I'm in a café near the Acropolis — in Kalidon Street. It's called the Olympic. Have you got that? Take a taxi. And don't tell anyone in the hotel. Hello!'

'Hello!' Neil shouted. 'What's happened?'

'I will explain when you get here. And bring your Dutch friend. You understand?' The line was so indistinct that it was hard to recognize Pol's tone. 'It is very important,' the voice went on, 'very important that you come, Monsieur Ingleby!'

'Are you in any trouble?' said Neil.

'I shall wait for you, please hurry!' The line went dead.

Neil hung up and joined Van Loon outside. 'Something's happened to Pol,' he explained, 'he wants us to meet him in a café in Kalidon Street, wherever that is.'

Van Loon stroked his blond beard and grinned: 'A bit of horseplay, huh?'

'I don't know. Let's go and see.'

Outside, while the bellboy went for the taxi, Neil paced up and down in the hot sun and puzzled over what sort of scrape Pol could be in. He had the Greek police eating out of his hand, so why was he so urgently summoning him and Van Loon?

It took just over a quarter of an hour to reach Kalidon Street, bouncing over alleys through the meat-markets, the cobbles wet with melting ice blocks. The Olympic Café was in a small street in the shadow of the Acropolis Rock. It was a barn-like building, full of sad-eyed men with black moustaches sitting in front of empty coffee cups and glasses of water, playing backgammon and dominoes.

They saw him at once, his balloon-like back facing them from the far end of the room. He sat down at a marble-topped table over a glass of dubious brown liquid, sweating heavily.

'Monsieur Pol!'

He swung round: '*Ah voilà, mes amis!*' he crowed with delight, grabbing up chairs and waving for the waiters.

Neil said, 'What's happened, Monsieur Pol?'

'I've had a bit of trouble at the hotel. A small complication. What will you drink?'

A radio behind the bar began to blare out a deafening Greek lament. 'What sort of trouble?' said Neil.

'There are two men at the hotel looking for me. That's why I couldn't meet you for lunch. I'd have left a message, but I didn't want to risk them picking it up.'

'Who are they?'

'They belong to Broussard — Secret Army men. There was one at the front and one at the back. I had to slip out through the kitchens.'

The waiter arrived; Neil and Van Loon ordered a list of Greek dishes at random and glasses of Fix beer. 'Why didn't you call up Captain Spyros and have them arrested?' said Neil.

Pol shook his head: 'I don't want them to know I suspect them. It's better they think I'm still at the hotel — at least until tonight.'

'But why are they after you?'

'They want to make sure I don't leave Athens.'

'Why?'

Pol looked at them both: 'You haven't heard the news?'

'No.'

'There's been another military revolt in the Protectorate.'

Neil sat back and said, 'My God! When?'

'Early this morning. The reports are still coming in. It's all very confused, but it looks as though the Secret Army has taken over the whole centre of the capital and dug themselves in behind barricades. The airport's been closed and all the frontiers are sealed off. Nobody really knows what's happening yet. Broussard arrived sometime yesterday and is behind the barricades with General Guérin.'

The waiter returned with dishes of shellfish in an oily grey sauce, shish-kebab on wooden skewers, a lot of dry white cheese and glasses of pale beer with a head like seafoam.

'From what I can gather,' Pol went on, 'two regiments of paratroopers were supposed to move into the capital at dawn this morning to reinforce the security troops. Then at the last moment they went over and joined Guérin. They've seized all the administrative buildings and the university. Most of the paras and the Foreign Legion units are now with them behind the barricades. And the Army, of course, sits on its arse and does nothing — each half waiting to see what the other will do.'

'And what are you going to do?' said Neil.

'Go over there.'

'But how?'

'By sea.' Pol took a gulp of his muddy-brown drink and grinned: 'And you and Monsieur Van Loon are coming with me — tonight.'

'Huh!' cried Van Loon.

'I've only a small boat and I need a sailor. The crossing will take two days and two nights.' He turned to Van Loon, whose eyes burned with a fierce blue light. 'Can you get us across?'

The Dutchman smacked the table with his huge hand: 'Bloody hell, I get you five times round the world if you want!'

Pol leant over and patted him affectionately under the ear, then turned to Neil: 'The boat belongs to an old friend of mine, Monsieur Biaggi, who lives in the King George most of the summer. He knows all about it, I've been prepared for this to happen for some time. You'll go to the French Consulate first and collect your visas and military permits. Ask for a man called Molyneux, he's very discreet. I've already warned him by phone that you're coming.'

'You think of everything,' said Neil, with a grain of sarcasm. Perhaps it was the man's appearance, but he still found it difficult to take Pol quite seriously.

'Then go back to the King George,' Pol went on, 'and get the boat's logbook and harbour permits from Monsieur Biaggi. Suite 24. I've phoned him too and he's expecting you. He's very rich,' he added. 'No problems. I've told him we're going down to Crete with some female company for a long weekend — doing a bit of archaeological research!' He let out his peal of laughter, and Van Loon laughed with him.

Neil said earnestly: 'So he doesn't know we're going to Africa?'

Pol gave a grand gesture: 'Ah, Monsieur Biaggi is very broadminded. He comes from Marseilles — we've known each other since the old Vichy days.' He looked at his watch. 'It's now ten past three. I want to be out of Athens by sunset. I shall wait here, and expect you both back not later than six.'

'What about your luggage?' said Neil.

Pol produced from inside his jacket the proverbial toothbrush, plus a tin of Max Factor talcum powder. 'I travel light,' he said, holding up the tin, 'a necessary luxury. One sweats so much in this climate. I could borrow your razor, perhaps?' he added.

Neil nodded, then just as he was leaving, he pointed down at Pol's glass: 'By the way, what is that stuff you're drinking?'

'This, my dear Ingleby,' said Pol, lifting the muddy glass to the sunlight, 'is Hellenic Excelsior Scotch!'

They left him shaking with quiet laughter.

CHAPTER 4

The door was unlocked. A voice called from the darkened bedroom: 'Who are you? Sit down.' Heavy curtains were drawn against the afternoon sun. Monsieur Biaggi lay on the bed in his underpants, propped up on a heap of pillows. Neil could just make out a brown body running to fat, its chest and legs fledged with black hairs like seaweed.

He stepped in and said, 'I've come from Charles Pol. I'm Monsieur Ingleby.'

'Ah, you're the Englishman!' A hand groped out and switched on the bedside light: 'So Charles is off to Crete at last, is he? The old dog!' Monsieur Biaggi gave Neil a tired grin and poured himself a glass of Vichy water from the side table. He had a ruined face, creased like an old glove. 'Is she pretty?' he added.

'Who?'

'Charles' girl. He told me he'd found a girl to take to Crete.'

'Oh yes. Not bad.'

'Ah! He's been looking round for that girl for weeks. I hope she treats him well.' He took a sip of water and closed his eyes. 'I'm sick,' he added, 'are you a sailor, Monsieur Ingleby?'

'No,' said Neil, 'but we've got a sailor with us.'

'Ah!' Monsieur Biaggi nodded, eyes still closed. 'You want the ship's papers? They're on the desk.' He flapped a hand in the direction of the window. The documents and the ignition key were in a greaseproof envelope marked 'Serafina'. Neil checked through them to make sure they were in order.

'I want her back after the weekend,' Monsieur Biaggi murmured, 'I've got a couple of girls I'm taking over to Naxos on Monday.' He opened his bloodshot eyes and smiled with a row of gunmetal teeth: 'What's today?'

'Wednesday.'

'Ah!' He lay back and patted his hairy stomach. 'I'm sick,' he said again, 'haven't eaten since February.'

Neil looked at him lying there with eyes closed, his head sunk back in the pillows: 'Thank you, Monsieur Biaggi.'

'Salut!' the man called, lifting one hand up a few inches above the bed. 'Take care of her — the "Serafina", I mean.'

Neil paused by the door, feeling guilty and sorry for M. Biaggi. He disapproved heartily of rich idle men who spent their lives whisking girls off in pleasure-boats. But M. Biaggi was not going to whisk his girl down to Naxos on Monday. His pleasure-boat had been commandeered for a revolution in North Africa and would probably never be seen again. Still, it was Neil's job to get across to the Protectorate by the quickest means available. The responsibility of the boat was Pol's; and Neil held his tongue and left M. Biaggi, closing the door gently behind him.

Van Loon was waiting in the foyer with the luggage which they had collected from their hotel on the way from the French Embassy. Monsieur Molyneux had turned out to be a quiet-mannered little man who had spoken about a dozen words and given them their visas and permits in ten minutes.

Neil went over to reception to cable his office that he was on his way to North Africa. There were two men at the desk. One was the slim grey man who had been reading *L'Aurore* in the armchair before lunch. The other was heavily-built, with a rubbery face and cropped black hair like a wire brush. As Neil reached them the receptionist nodded towards him. Both men turned. The slim one took a step forward and addressed Neil in

French: 'I understand you have been asking for a Monsieur Pol?'

Neil hesitated. The man's face was smooth and steel-grey like his hair, his expression dead behind the dark glasses.

Neil nodded.

'We are also looking for Monsieur Pol,' said the man, 'would you happen to know where he is?'

'I'm sorry' — Neil saw the man turn his head a fraction and glance at Van Loon — 'I haven't seen Monsieur Pol since this morning. I don't think he'll be back until later tonight.'

The two men looked hard at him, then nodded together and left the hotel without another word. Neil filled in the cable-form and called for a taxi, then explained to Van Loon: 'I think those two men may be the ones who are after Pol.'

The Dutchman shook his head and grinned: 'It's all crazy! That old fellow Pol is completely crazy!'

The taxi was a Chrysler with a radio and a gramophone shaped like a toaster under the dashboard. As he was getting in, Neil noticed a dark-blue Renault Gordini parked about fifty yards down the street behind them. The taxi driver pushed a button above his knee and they rode off listening to 'Never on Sunday', with English lyrics.

Neil sat back and glanced out of the rear window: the little blue Renault was behind them, winding between the traffic about thirty yards away. He frowned. The Chrysler drifted across Omonious Square; a dock chimed half past five. The Renault accelerated, cutting across a lane of traffic, and Neil could see now that it had a Paris TT registration number. There were two men inside: the driver wore dark glasses.

They had turned into Democracy Avenue. The Renault was still behind, keeping its distance of about thirty yards. Neil felt a prickle of fear and his pulse quickened. He turned to the driver: 'Can you go faster!'

The driver spoke English: 'O.K.! I go real fast!' The Chrysler hummed and swerved out in front of a dusty bus; a policeman waved a baton; lights above the street turned red; the Chrysler slowed down with a moan and stood ticking over. The Renault was directly behind.

'Damn them!' said Neil. The lights changed.

'What do they want?' said Van Loon, watching the Renault pulling away after them from the lights.

'They want Pol.'

'Why him?'

'Presumably because he's dangerous to them. These boys have just started a revolution. They don't want him getting over there and cocking the whole thing up!'

The driver had his hand down on the horn, and all the cars round them were blowing their horns too and nobody was moving. 'This is a bad time for traffic,' said the driver, 'no good for going fast.'

Van Loon sat stroking his beard. 'But that fat fellow cannot be so dangerous,' he said.

'Well, those boys in the car behind obviously think he is!' Neil looked anxiously round again. The Renault was still there. Ahead the traffic was strung across the avenue in a wedge of bicycles, buses, American limousines and old dog-carts. The driver told Neil he was going to cut down into one of the side-streets leading to the vegetable market. They honked and jerked their way through the ambling crowds, braking every few yards, the Chrysler rocking on its springs like a motorboat in a heavy swell. They seemed to have lost the Renault. They turned into a quiet street that curved away under a wall enclosing a garden of cypress trees.

'Now fast!' Neil yelled, and the car roared gently and slid away with a wake of dust.

They had gone perhaps two hundred yards when Neil saw the Renault again. It was coming after them through the dust like a torpedo, slowing and dropping back when it came in sight of them.

'That was a mistake,' Neil muttered. 'Now they know we're trying to lose them.'

'Oh to hell with them!' said Van Loon. 'Let's just stop here and see what the idiots will do.'

Neil hesitated. Ahead there was another main street and a stream of traffic. He told the driver to pull up and wait just before the intersection. The Chrysler bumped softly on to the edge of the road and stopped. The driver slipped a new record into the machine under the dashboard and they listened to the opening bars of 'Venus in Blue Jeans', as the Renault came up alongside and passed them. They watched it reach the intersection, stop for a moment, turn left and disappear.

Neil sat up and sighed. 'Go on to Kalidon Street,' he told the driver, who was beginning to look puzzled. They crossed the intersection and headed down towards the meat-markets huddled under the Acropolis. It was 5.50. Neil calculated that if all went well they could be out at sea by half past seven.

Van Loon gave a shout and grabbed Neil's arm. The driver turned his head in surprise and they missed a cyclist by less than an inch, the rider wobbling away, shaking his fist. The Renault was coming up behind them again, its little Gordini engine whining like an angry insect.

Neil rammed his fist into his palm and swore. They were back now in narrow crowded streets where speed was impossible. Neil was trying to think hard, feeling the wet ridge of sweat round his collar. Whatever happened they must not lead the Renault to the Olympic Café. He told the driver to stop again. They could get out and try to slip away on foot; or telephone Pol and arrange to meet him later at the Piraeus.

They were outside a pastry shop in a crooked, sloping street. A moment later the Renault drove past. They watched it go on down the street for about fifty yards, then stop. Nobody got out. An old man with white stubble was hobbling towards them, following his shadow along the wall. The gramophone in the Chrysler switched itself off; and the two cars stood in the narrow street and nothing happened.

'You wanna stop or go on?' said the driver, shifting uneasily, as though he expected to be hit over the head.

Neil looked at his watch: it was three minutes to six.

'You wanna go on to Kalidon Street?' asked the driver.

'Wait a minute,' said Neil. Still nobody had moved inside the French car. The old man with the white stubble shuffled past them. Suddenly Van Loon seized the door handle and jumped out. 'I'm going to see what they bloody want!' he cried, and before Neil could stop him he was striding down the street towards the Renault. Neil was about to follow, when the driver caught him by the sleeve: 'You wanna go on?'

'You wait here,' said Neil, 'you've got our luggage. Just wait!' The driver sucked at a knuckle and nodded. Neil got out and hurried after Van Loon, who had reached the Renault.

The steel-grey man had the window rolled down and was listening with a tight nasty look on his face, while Van Loon shouted in his ugly French: 'You come from the hotel! You follow us here! What are you doing here? Huh?'

The man muttered something to his companion with the black crewcut, who shrugged and went on staring ahead.

Neil came up. He looked awkwardly at the Frenchman and said, 'Good afternoon!'

The man said nothing.

'We met back at the King George,' said Neil.

Van Loon yelled, 'You follow us here, don't you!'

The man did not look at Van Loon. He said to Neil, in a measured voice, 'You are quite sure, Monsieur, that you do not know where the man Pol is?'

Neil edged Van Loon aside and bent down till his face was a few inches from the Frenchman's.

'I've already told you I don't know where he is. Nor do I know why you have been following us here. But if you're not on your way within thirty seconds I'll call the police.'

The man stared at him, quite expressionless. Neil straightened up and said to Van Loon. 'Come on, let's get out of here!' As they were walking away, the Dutchman turned and shouted into the car, '*Vive Guérin!*' and blew a raspberry through the window.

The Frenchman reacted as though he had been struck. He leapt out and slammed the door, standing in front of Van Loon with a little nerve tugging at the edge of his mouth: 'Monsieur, be careful. Be very careful. We don't like those sort of jokes.'

Neil took Van Loon's arm and muttered, 'Come on, let's get out of here!'

Van Loon grinned: 'Oh, to hell with these people! Stupid white kaffirs!'

The Frenchman stood rigid for a moment, then turned and got back into the Renault. The car shot away down the street.

'You're a damned fool!' said Neil, as they walked back to the taxi.

'To hell with them! They were following us, weren't they?'

'That's not the point. You've now told them we know they're members of the Secret Army. For Christ's sake, these people aren't fooling around!'

Van Loon shrugged and got into the Chrysler: 'O.K., they have gone now.'

'They may be back,' said Neil. He told the driver to go on to the end of the street, then return to Omonious Square. But there was no sign now of the Renault. They headed back towards Kalidon Street. Neil paid the taxi off at the corner and they walked the last hundred yards to the Olympic Café.

Pol was sitting just as they had left him, smoking a cheroot and drawing wet rings on the marble table with another glass of Excelsior Scotch. When he saw them he raised both arms with a roar of welcome, splashing whisky on to the floor. 'You're six minutes late!' he cried.

Neil sat down and told him about the Renault. Pol chuckled: 'Ah, that's old Jadot! Former paratroop captain who served under Broussard in Indo-China. He disappeared after the coup last year. I thought he'd turn up sooner or later.'

'Is he dangerous?'

Pol chuckled again, his eyes beginning to look a little glazed: 'Captain Jadot, my dear Ingleby, has the reputation of being able to hit a man in the head with a pistol from forty metres.' He thumped the table: 'We'll get him one day!'

'You still don't want to call Captain Spyros?'

Pol shook his head: 'Too much trouble. We couldn't hold Jadot for long — there's no proper warrant out for him, In France we might get him under the emergency regulations, but not here.' He belched. 'No, the only real way to deal with men like that is shoot them down like dogs when they're not looking. But unfortunately one can't do that sort of thing in a nice city like Athens.

'We're all right, though,' he added, 'as long as you're sure you got rid of him.'

'I think we got rid of him,' said Neil.

'And the papers?'

Neil patted the greaseproof envelope: 'All here.'

'How was old Biaggi?'

'In bed. He's not well.'

'Ah, yes. His stomach's bad. He thinks too much about women.' Pol stood up and snapped his fingers for the bill, then swayed and lurched heavily backwards into the table. Neil saw with some misgiving that he was very drunk.

The waiter arrived with a fistful of chits which Pol paid for out of a wallet stuffed with five hundred and thousand drachma notes.

Outside, special editions of the Athens evening papers were carrying photographs of ex-General Paul Guérin. Neil could make out a distinguished, middle-aged face with a square jaw under a five-starred képi.

There was no sign of the Renault Gordini. They walked down the street and caught a taxi to the Piraeus.

CHAPTER 5

Monsieur Biaggi's boat, the 'Serafina', was moored under a jetty at the end of the yacht-basin where the tramlines finished. There were a number of other smart private craft tied up beside her, shielded from the rest of the port by a seawall. Behind this lay a row of noisy bars and open-air cafés strung with naked lights where there was dancing and handclapping to the strumming of bazoukis. Two harbour police stood at the end of the jetty, smoking; they wore revolvers.

The 'Serafina' was a thirty-foot converted rescue launch, painted blue and white with plenty of deck room for sunbathing and a good deal of fancy brass fittings. There was a covered wheelhouse with a curved windshield leading into a chromium-plated galley and a carpeted wardroom with leather couches round the walls. Below was a second wardroom with twin bunks under velvet curtains, a radiogram and a cocktail cabinet. The shower cubicle and toilet lay under the steps up to the deck.

Van Loon inspected the boat with awe. She was driven by two Perkins diesels, capable of more than twenty knots. The levers and control knobs were ivory, and the wheel was of dark polished wood. There was a panel of luminous green dials, a navigation table covered with charts of the Aegean and Mediterranean, a giro-compass the size of an atlas globe, shortwave radio, cigar lighter and a sliding shelf fitted with slots to hold M. Biaggi's drinks as he steered himself from one pleasure-dome to the next.

'Bloody fantastic!' said Van Loon, smoothing his hand along the varnished wood.

Pol had waddled into the upper wardroom and now sank down on one of the leather couches, breathing hard. The customs man came on board; Neil showed him the papers, and the man looked quickly through the boat, opening cupboards and peering under the hatch. In one locker he found a crate with a dozen bottles of vintage Epernay '55. Neil lifted one out and fired the cork, hosing champagne into four glasses, with one for the customs man before he went ashore. They finished the bottle and Van Loon put his head under the engine-cover, checking the valves and pumps and oil valves.

'Is she all right?' said Neil.

'Terrific! Beautiful! The tanks are almost full, too. We need perhaps another three hundred litres of oil.' He switched on the ignition. The diesels spluttered and grunted and he eased down the ivory levers, allowing the engines to turn freely. The noise purred along the darkening jetty.

The customs man had told them where the fuel bunker was, a couple of hundred yards along the dock past the sea-wall. Neil said, 'You take her round and get her filled up, and I'll buy some food for the trip.'

'Don't worry about drink,' cried Van Loon, 'we have champagne for dinner and champagne for breakfast and champagne for lunch!'

Neil went into the wardroom and found Pol on his back along one of the leather couches. His eyes were closed and his face had gone an unhealthy mauve colour. 'Hey, Charles!' He shook him. Pol opened his eyes and groaned. 'Aren't you feeling well?' said Neil.

Pol sat up slowly, trying to get his breath: '*Ça va? Ça va!* Just a touch of acid.'

'I should lay off the drink for a bit,' said Neil, 'now listen. Van Loon's taking the boat round to refuel. Have you got some money to pay?'

Pol handed him his wallet. 'There's enough there,' he muttered, rolling back on to the couch.

Neil took the wallet into the wheelhouse; judging by its thickness it must have held at least £150 in Greek currency. He gave it gingerly to Van Loon: 'There's a lot of money there — don't spend it all on ouzo. I'll meet you at the bunker.'

He went ashore, along the jetty past the harbour police; and it was then that he began to have his first premonition of impending calamity. After all, he had only Van Loon's word that the man could navigate a ship across several hundred miles of sea, at night, to a strange shore; and although they had maps and good engines, Neil knew that treacherous weather could blow up off the Peloponnese in a matter of minutes and smash even sixty-foot ships on to the rocks. And now there was Pol, architect of the whole trip, lying drunk and groaning with acid in his belly.

Neil walked through the gates, past the immigration and customs buildings. Ahead there was a lot of shouting and blaring of jukeboxes from bars with names like Spitfire Club and The Captain's Table. He came to a restaurant where he bought food for the two days' crossing: a length of salami, ham, cured beef, olives and oranges and toadstool loaves of bread, a hunk of cheese and three dozen eggs.

Outside, a grey-haired sailor sat in the street muttering to himself. The dusk was falling fast now, the city lights winking on across the bay. Neil was about fifty yards from the port gates when he saw the Renault Gordini. It stood in the shadow of the immigration offices. There was no-one inside it.

He hurried past the gates, showing his passport as he began to run, clutching the bag of food, turning and sprinting down the quay towards the fuel bunkers. There had been lights inside the offices and he had heard several voices talking together.

The 'Serafina' was tied up with a fat pipe screwed into her side like an umbilical cord. The two harbour police stood by watching. Neil leapt on board, almost dropping the food over the side, and yelled at Van Loon, 'Get us out of here! Those two Frenchmen are down by the gates!'

Van Loon nodded gravely. 'Two minutes,' he said.

'Not two minutes — now!'

The Dutchman went over and shouted something at the Greek mechanic tending the pipe. Neil glanced fearfully towards the immigration offices. He didn't think anyone had seen him. Jadot was probably making a routine check of the port. Van Loon had counted out the money to the mechanic and the pipe was being unscrewed. 'Come on, start her up!' Neil yelled.

'O.K., O.K.,' said Van Loon calmly.

Neil, watched him begin to untie the ropes. To spare himself the suspense he ducked into the galley with the parcel of food. There was a mild explosion and something hit him hard in the face just below the eye. He stepped backwards and heard a peal of laughter. A cork bounced against the galley wall. Pol came swaying through with the second bottle of champagne; his colour had improved and his eyes glittered. 'Where's your glass, Monsieur Ingleby?'

'You damn fool!' said Neil, rubbing his cheek. 'That Captain Jadot — he's down at the gates!' Behind him the engines started up with a loud whine, as Van Loon let the throttles full out. Neil ran back to the wheelhouse.

They were coming down the quay, about a hundred yards away. Jadot was in front with the thick-set man at his heels. 'Let her go!' Neil cried.

The deck tilted and shuddered; there was a churning and splashing through blue smoke; and the jetty suddenly swung away, the bows heading into the open sea.

Jadot had broken into a run. Neil remembered about him being able to hit a man in the head with a pistol from forty metres. The needle on the rev-counter jerked round the luminous dial. The boat would be out of range in a few moments now. Jadot reached the harbour police and stopped. He would hardly try to shoot it out with them around, Neil thought.

Pol came into the wheelhouse with the bottle of champagne. 'My old friend Jadot, eh?' he said with a grin, handing Neil a glass. 'Did they see you?'

'I don't think so. But they've certainly got our descriptions from the immigration people.' Neil emptied the champagne in one gulp; he was pale and his hands shook.

'They don't know who we are,' said Van Loon, 'they think we are just tourists.'

'Jadot and his friend will know who we are,' said Neil grimly, 'and they'll know we're not just going over to Crete for a dirty weekend.'

Pol shrugged. 'They're left behind — they can't do anything now. We'll have other things to worry about after tomorrow,' he added ominously, returning to the wardroom.

Van Loon was marking one of the navigation charts, plotting a course due-south across the Saronic Gulf past Aegina and Hydra, down the Peloponnese coast between the isles of Milos and Cythera, then south-west of Crete into the Mediterranean.

Neil stood beside him and watched the dipping lights of Athens drift away to the east.

The sea was growing darker, the sky a luminous velvet with a large round moon corning up over the horizon. The swell began to smack against the sides of the boat; but there was no wind. Neil switched on the radio and tuned in to Europe Number One. There had been nineteen deaths during the day in clashes between the Secret Army and French security forces in the capital of the Protectorate. An hour ago nearly a quarter of a million people had gathered in the Place de la Nation in Paris to demand Government action to crush the revolt. The demonstrators were chanting: '*Le Fascisme ne passera pas!*' It sounded to Neil as remote and nostalgic as a snatch of Christopher Isherwood read again after many years.

Back in the wardroom Pol was peeling the foil off a third bottle of champagne. Neil sank down and drank with him, to the steady beat of the engines. Later they made a meal of the salami, bread and cheese, drank more champagne, and Pol talked about his wife. 'The Germans killed her,' he said, chewing quietly, 'they shot her in Nancy in 1942. They caught her trying to contact some Canadian prisoners.'

'You were both in the Resistance?'

'Yes, we worked together.' He paused: 'I'm too old for women now. Too old, too ugly.' His face had collapsed suddenly, utterly sad, staring at nothing. 'She was something of a bitch,' he went on, pouring more champagne, 'before the war she went off and lived with a man in Hungary. She came back to me after the attack on Poland, and we worked together against the Nazis, but we never slept with each other again.'

There was another pause. Neil said, 'What exactly are you going to do when you get to the Protectorate?'

'Catch General Guérin.' He said it as though he were talking about landing a fish.

Neil nodded: 'And how are you going to do that?'

Pol leant back and looked at the ceiling. Ignoring the question he said, 'When Guérin is gone, the Secret Army is gone! Snuff out Guérin — the movement is finished, it dies like a snake without a head!'

'Snakes go on living when you cut their heads off,' said Neil.

'They go on moving, not living. Without Guérin, the Secret Army will move for a little, it will pretend to live, but it will be doomed and dead! And Fascism in France will be doomed and dead with it!' He laughed and came stumbling over with the bottle, refilling Neil's glass; and Neil lay back, suddenly very tired, drinking Epernay '55 and thinking of the quarter of a million people now swelling across Paris in protest against Fascism.

When the bottle was finished he went into the wardroom below and flopped out fully dressed on one of the canopied bunks.

CHAPTER 6

Neil woke suddenly. The cabin was dark and airless, throbbing to the rhythm of the diesels. He looked at his watch: he had been asleep for just under an hour. There was a shaft of light outside; a door opened and he heard a groan and a gush of water. He sat up, kicked on his shoes and went through to the passage. Pol was squeezed into the toilet, his huge frame crumpled over the lavatory, gasping, '*Ah merde!*' between heaves and retches.

Neil got some Alka-Seltzer out of his rucksack: 'Come on, drink this!'

Pol's mighty head rose slowly, the skin a purplish-white streaked with sweat; the kiss curl had come unstuck and lay across his brow like a wet spider. His eyes tried to light up with a smile which the mouth resisted. 'Too much to drink,' he croaked, gulping the Alka-Seltzer.

'Champagne on Greek whisky,' said Neil, 'you deserve to be ill!' Pol turned miserably back to the lavatory. Neil left him there and went up on deck.

Van Loon was at the wheel, solid as a statue, his eyes on the horizon. He turned as Neil came up: 'The fat fellow is pretty sick with drink, huh?' He laughed quietly and looked back to sea. 'That is the island of Aegina out there,' he added, pointing to a few pricks of light far off to starboard.

The swell was rising and the bows beginning to dip giddily. Neil had always been a good sailor but he was worried about Pol: if the man were now to combine sea-sickness with the effects of whisky and champagne, he was going to be in poor shape to represent the French Republic in its showdown against Fascism.

Van Loon took Neil's arm: 'Look there, a good fast ship!'

Neil saw a sharp light moving swiftly behind them, about half a mile away. He guessed that it must be doing nearly thirty knots. He stood watching it grow closer, feeling the cool salt breeze on his face, and wondered what Caroline Tucker was doing at this moment. The thought was not a restful one. He tried to forget her at once, and went down to have another look at Pol. He was lying on one of the bunks, his breath hissing behind the velvet curtains. Neil was turning away when Van Loon shouted, 'Hey, come quick!'

Neil clattered up to the wheelhouse. The Dutchman was staring out to starboard, just as a light swept round and dazzled them both. The motor-launch was heading directly towards them. When it was no more than twenty yards away, still coming at full speed, he cut the diesels and pulled the 'Serafina' over so that she was riding alongside the launch.

Neil hoped to see a Greek flag or police sign on the launch, but there was none. A man stood shadowed beside the spotlight, which was still trained on the wheelhouse. Van Loon waved, and the man waved back. The launch engines had died down and the two boats drifted towards each other.

It was a two-seater, high-speed motorboat with a covered cabin. It bumped gently against the 'Serafina', then sprang away, rising dangerously on the swell. When it touched again, two men stepped into the blaze of the spotlight.

Neil gripped the rail in front of him and a chill rippled over his skin. The man in front was Captain Jadot. He jumped nimbly across on to the 'Serafina's' heaving deck, followed by the thick-set man with the black crewcut, who tied a rope from the launch to the deck rail.

Jadot looked round the wheelhouse, then said to Neil, almost casually: 'Where is he?'

Neil stared at him, his mouth drying up.

'Where is he?' said Jadot again.

The thick-set man had stepped round in front of the wheel-house door. From inside his short belted raincoat he pulled out a machine-pistol. Neil gaped at it: it had an air-cooled barrel, perforated like a flute.

Van Loon had not moved.

'Have you both lost your tongues?' said Jadot. 'You know who we want. Where is he? The fat man.' He had taken off his dark glasses and his naked eyes were holes of black ice. He stood poised forward, fingers curled at his side like a professional fighter.

Neil said feebly, 'I've told you, he's not here. He's in Athens — he's gone away.'

Jadot pushed past him, through the wheelhouse into the galley. Neil whispered to Van Loon, 'We've got to do something!' The Dutchman nodded and said nothing.

Jadot went into the wardroom, glanced round at the empty champagne bottles, then turned towards the steps below. 'The fat bastard's down here!' he shouted, with sudden ferocity, and started below.

Neil watched, feeling cold and weak; the muzzle of the machine-pistol was barely two feet away, covering them both. He looked again at Van Loon, who was staring at Jadot as though he did not fully grasp what was happening. Neil closed his eyes for a moment, and had an image of Pol waddling over to a white telephone with a triple whisky in his hand: now lying in the dark, sick as a dog under a velvet canopy, while Jadot went down to kill him, from less than one metre.

The Frenchman's head disappeared below. And then Van Loon moved. He moved faster than any human being Neil had ever seen. His long legs snapped apart like a pair of scissors, caught the thick-set man in the groin and lifted him a full inch off the deck. At the same moment he chopped down at the man's neck with the ridges of his great square hands. The machine-pistol clattered on to the deck and he kicked it gently into the sea.

The man sagged backwards over the rail, his rubbery face quite green. Van Loon hit him again, without effort, the man's head jerked backwards with a crack and he went over the side. Part of the body hit the edge of the drifting motor-launch, then plopped into the water and vanished.

The Dutchman whipped round, his big feet as fast as a dancer's. He was halfway across the wheel-house when the shot came: a single blasting roar, then silence, and they could hear the sea lapping against the boat.

Van Loon started down the steps; Neil followed, dazed. The light was on in the lower wardroom. Pol sat in his stockinged feet on the bunk. Captain Jadot was sitting on the floor; his head was sinking slowly and he was making a soft sucking noise. He had been shot through the throat.

Pol had a small black gun in his hand, which he put away inside his coat when he saw Neil and Van Loon. 'What happened to the other one?' he asked.

'I killed him,' said Van Loon.

Pol nodded: 'Jadot was getting careless. He shouldn't have shouted like that. He woke me up. Besides, he had to switch on the light first.'

'Is he dead?' said Neil.

'Almost.' Pol stood up and tottered across the floor: 'We must get him out of here. I don't want Biaggi's carpets messed up.'

Jadot's head was resting on his knees now.

'Give me a hand,' said Pol. Van Loop took the man under the armpits and pulled him towards the steps. Thick dark blood was pumping out over his shirt and trousers. Neil felt sick. The man looked very small, as Van Loon began to haul him up the steps. His legs dangled like a puppet's legs, the trousers rumpled up round the knees. Neil noticed he was wearing blue and white chequered socks.

Van Loon dragged him out on to the deck, propped him against the rail and tipped him over. There was a splash, then the sea was empty, dimpled silver and shiny-black under the moon. 'What about the bloody boat?' he asked.

'Sink her,' said Pol, 'if anyone finds her drifting out here we'll have every patrol in the Mediterranean hunting for us.'

'She will take perhaps one hour to go down,' said Van Loon, jumping aboard the motor-launch.

'We'll have to take a chance on that.'

Van Loon turned off the spotlight and began opening the seacocks: 'Hey, what about the bodies?'

'They won't float up for at least three days,' Pol chuckled, 'then the current could carry them anywhere. They might even turn up on the beach at Cannes!' He took Neil by the arm and began to lead him into the wardroom.

'You know,' said Neil, 'I've never heard a shot fired in anger before.'

'Ah, my dear Ingleby, you'll hear plenty in the next few days!' He shouted over his shoulder to Van Loon, 'When you've finished, better start washing some of the blood off before it dries!'

Neil said, 'I think I could do with some more champagne.'

PART 3: REVOLT

CHAPTER 1

The city came out of the sea-fog, tall and salt-white, rising in a great curve along the margin of the water, with the small square houses of the Casbah climbing on one another's shoulders into the hills beyond.

It was four o'clock in the afternoon of the second day. Van Loon cut the throttle until they were almost drifting. There was no sound now except for the chugging of the diesels. 'It is like a ghost city,' he said, gazing at the sea-front less than a quarter of a mile away.

'There's a general strike,' said Neil.

During the trip they had followed the developing crisis on radio news bulletins from all over Europe. The night before, Guérin had ordered a general strike from dawn till midnight to commemorate the Secret Army's dead in clashes with the security forces during the last forty-eight hours. The French High Command, under a General Metz, had responded by extending the night curfew throughout the day. The city was now in a state of total paralysis.

'Even the seagulls are on strike,' said Van Loon, as they watched the empty wharves grow closer, with the ocean liners and cargo ships lying like coffins among the cranes.

They could now see the white flecks of the CRS police sashes, standing at intervals along the Front de Mer. The 'Serafina' chugged across the dark water under the sea-wall and was less than thirty yards away before they were challenged.

Three CRS men, in blue uniforms with machine-pistols strapped to the hip, came down the steps and stood waiting for them to tie up. There was an officer in front: a small straight man with a tanned face creased with tiny furrows that showed white against his brown skin when he spoke. The metal of his machine-pistol was sweating in the fog: 'Where are you coming from? You know the port's closed?'

Pol took out a plastic disc with a red and blue stripe. The officer saw it and saluted at once: 'I'm sorry, I didn't realize.' He turned and signalled to his men. 'You've chosen a nice time to visit us!' he added, leading the way up the steps.

'It is very bad?' said Pol.

The officer pulled a wry face: 'There's been a lot of effervescence — fighting all last night. They've been killing the Arabs off like flies. And it's going to get worse! How far are you going?' he added, when they reached the Front de Mer.

'The Hotel Miramar,' said Pol, 'is it clear?'

'It's all right till the Place Lyautey, but after that there are Gardes Mobiles. Some of them are shooting on sight — they lost a lot of men yesterday. Are you walking?'

Pol grinned: 'How else?'

'I'm sorry I can't offer you any transport,' said the officer, 'all our vehicles are commandeered.' He saluted and moved away.

The three of them began to walk down the Front de Mer, under the tiers of rococo balconies on one side, the palm trees hanging limp and wet on the other; and all round there was a hush as though they were walking in snow. Somewhere ahead a jeep squealed round a corner and drove away into the fog. The streets that climbed from the Front de Mer were choked with garbage, and the only things that moved were furtive, springing cats.

Suddenly a shot rang out, its echo cracking off the walls like a whip. Neil jumped sideways and Pol laughed. The silence folded back, and they came to the last of the CRS troops and started out across a square with the blackened carcasses of two cars lying beside a statue of General Lyautey. The air was thick and clammy with the smell of salt and orange-blossom. Neil was beginning to sweat. 'How much further?' he asked.

'Five hundred metres,' said Pol.

A car passed in one of the back streets, crashing gears. The walls round the square were scrawled with huge slogans where the paint had trickled to the pavement. Neil read, '*Vive Guérin!*' '*Aux Armes Citoyens!*' '*The True France is Divided Only by the Mediterranean!*'

From here on, the Front de Mer became an uneasy stretch of No-Man's-Land where the Secret Army commandos played a deadly game of hide-and-seek with the Gardes Mobiles. Pol was leading the way down the centre of the boulevard when they heard the armoured car. It came grinding out of a side-street about fifty yards away, swerved round and stopped. They could just make out the white pineapple, emblem of the Gardes Mobiles, painted on the armoured plating above the wheels. There was a heavy machinegun at the rear: a Douze-Sept, known locally as La Doucette ('the Sweet One'). Every twelfth round was an explosive shell, and its bullets could pierce eight inches of masonry and still kill a man.

Pol cried, 'Get back!'

They ducked under the arcades facing the sea. Neil crouched against a shop window, keeping his face turned from the boulevard, listening to the chugging of the armoured car engine. He pressed his face to the steel grating across the window. It was a women's clothes shop. He stared at a slim wax effigy of a girl's torso in nylon brassiere and briefs. Beside him Pol puffed hard, getting his breath back. Van Loon was calm, motionless. On the floor of the shop window lay a pair of scarlet pants with a triangle of lacework over the crotch. Neil glanced back up the boulevard: the armoured car had not moved. He closed his eyes, imagined the noise and pain and death.

They waited under the arcades for ten minutes, before the motor roared and the armoured car began to move off into the fog. Pol grinned: 'If they'd decided to come this way, we might have had some fun!' They kept under the arcades for the rest of the way to the hotel.

The Miramar stood behind a grove of palm trees. Candles were burning in the gloomy foyer, with its mirrors and mock-Moorish arches of brown marble. It was five o'clock and already growing dark. All electricity had been cut off. An Army officer sat alone among the armchairs, staring across the empty floor.

The receptionists, those suave custodians of the international high life, performed their duties now with resigned boredom. There were no more fat tips from the money-men weekending from Paris by Caravelle with their girls and golf clubs. Now there was just a scattering of journalists and military personnel.

Pol made no attempt to avoid these hotel officials, who eyed him suspiciously as he stood with Neil and Van Loon at the desk.

'You are not taking a room?' inquired the head receptionist, a silver-haired man with cool mandarin eyes.

'I'm just seeing my friends in,' said Pol smiling, and walked up with Neil and Van Loon to the two rooms they had taken on the third floor, each with a green-tiled bathroom and a balcony over the sea. Pol had agreed to settle Van Loon's bill as payment for his services on the 'Serafina'. To Neil's mind it was cheap at the price.

'So you're not staying here?' Neil said, as Pol followed him into his room and closed the door.

'Here? My dear Ingleby, I wouldn't last the night. The hotel's full of Secret Army informers.' He stood sweating, loosening his collar: 'Do you mind if I have a shower?'

'Go ahead. I'll ring for something to drink.'

'The phones aren't working,' said Pol.

'I'll see if I can find a floor waiter,' said Neil. At the door he paused: 'You didn't make much effort to keep out of sight downstairs. Do the hotel people know who you are?'

Pol chuckled, unbuttoning his shirt: 'Ah, I'm a very notorious fellow!'

'Aren't you taking a bit of a risk coming up here?'

Pol stepped out of his trousers and laughed: 'I take worse risks driving round Paris when I'm stewed at five in the morning!' He stood naked now in his ankle socks like a monstrously inflated baby.

'It's all very well for you to take risks,' said Neil, 'but I'm staying here. I've been seen coming in with you.'

'You'll be all right,' said Pol, taking out his tin of talcum powder and wobbling into the bathroom, 'they won't hurt an English journalist.'

'I hope you're right!' said Neil, going into the corridor where he found a Moslem in an apron, rooting about in a cupboard near the stairs. He ordered a bottle of cognac and two glasses to be brought to Room 274. The man bowed and scuttled away.

Back in the room Pol shouted above the shower, 'Tomorrow or the day after, Monsieur Ingleby, I will have something very interesting for your newspaper!' He came out rubbing down his rolls of flesh: 'As I said in Athens, I may have a scoop for you.' He dropped the towel and began patting talcum powder under his arms.

Neil stared out towards the balcony. A nasty suspicion was beginning to nag at the back of his mind; it was like that first instinct he had had at the King George yesterday when he had been too light-headed with whisky to care. There was some very good reason why Pol wanted him in the Protectorate: and it wasn't just to do him a good turn as a journalist.

The fog was closing in, dark over the dead sweep of the port. From far away he heard a faint burst of gun-fire. There was a sound in the room behind. The Moslem came in with a bottle of Hine, grinning nervously, and bowed himself out before either of them could give him a tip.

'Poor little devil!' said Pol buttoning up his trousers. 'Probably comes down to work from the Casbah every day. Somebody'll put a bullet in his head before long —'

Neil poured them both a brandy and they went out on the balcony. Pol was wearing vest and braces, his fat arms chalk-white with talcum powder liked salted hams. He looked ridiculous; but there was a hard look in his eyes which was very far from the jovial Pol swilling whisky and champagne, all in the merry course of duty for the French Secret Service. Neil realized suddenly that he knew very little about the man: that behind the fatuous exterior there must lie a core of professional ruthlessness. One did not reach the position Pol held — whatever that position exactly was — without it.

'I shall be staying at the High Command Headquarters,' he was saying, sipping his brandy, 'I can't move around as freely as you, I'm afraid, and it won't be easy for us to meet. What I want you to do is phone me tomorrow afternoon at two o'clock at this number. Have you a pencil?' Neil wrote the number down. 'And don't call me from the hotel — somebody might listen in. Use a callbox.'

The warning light was there again, and with it the whisper of danger. Neil said, 'What sort of thing will you have to tell me?'

'I'm not sure. I shall know more tomorrow.' Pol's eyes were fixed on some point in the indefinite distance across the sea: 'Perhaps a meeting with somebody — somebody interesting. It depends what I can arrange.'

He paused; they heard another distant burst of gun-fire. 'I must warn you,' Pol went on, 'that the Secret Army will know you are in the hotel. During the next twenty-four hours they will contact you. There's nothing to worry about — they contact all journalists. Just be tactful and receptive, and avoid discussing politics with them. They're very sensitive at the moment. And above all, don't mention that you were on Athos. We just happened to meet in the King George Hotel.'

Neil stared out across the dim grey city. Pol had been in the hotel for nearly half an hour, and Neil was feeling strained and nervous. He had slept badly the night before, and the fog and silence now thrust him into a deep depression. He did not yet know what was at stake here but suddenly, desperately, he wanted to be rid of Pol. He could not analyse the feeling; perhaps it was mean and disloyal after the comradeship of the last two days, but his instinct warned him, with something visceral and emphatic, that he was becoming involved in a situation over which he had no control. He turned to Pol: 'You'd better be going now. If they know downstairs who you are —'

Pol finished his drink, went back into the room and put on his shirt, tie and jacket. 'Don't forget,' he called from the door, 'two o'clock tomorrow afternoon.'

Neil nodded; 'Careful how you go — don't get a bullet in your head.'

Pol grinned, tapping his round pate: 'Don't worry, I've got a hard head, Monsieur Ingleby!'

CHAPTER 2

Only a few journalists had so far managed to penetrate the Protectorate since the revolt began. That afternoon a Paris-Match photographer had chartered a plane from Catania and parachuted just south of the capital, but had broken his leg on landing and was now in a military hospital. The airports of Paris and Tunis, Rome and Rabat were besieged by frantic hosts of reporters waiting for flights into the capital.

The doyen of the resident correspondents was a well-preserved Englishman, Mr. Winston St. Leger, now in his sixties. He had made a name for himself reporting the Munich putsch in 1923; but was now best renowned for his habit of sucking toothpaste from a tube which he kept permanently in his breast pocket. An American colleague had once challenged him on this: 'Why d'yer suck that stuff, Winston?' 'Because I like it,' St. Leger had replied, silencing further comment. The habit had originated while he was a correspondent in Moscow after the war and had been unable to obtain indigestion pills. One day someone had suggested that certain brands of toothpaste had the desired effect, and Winston St. Leger had become a toothpaste addict. He admitted that he got through two tubes a week.

He, Neil and Van Loon, and a jumpy little American called Hudson from one of the agencies, were sitting up at the bar on the second floor of the hotel, looking over the empty gaming tables in the salon de jeu. St. Leger wore a waistcoat and pinstriped trousers; only at the height of the summer did he leave them off in favour of ducks and a blazer. He was saying, 'I met Paul Guérin three years ago in Paris. Charming fellow.

Very formal, of course — very much the St. Cyr officer class. Not much gaiety there.'

They watched the candles flickering in the tall mirrors across the room. 'What's going to happen now?' asked Neil.

'Death and bloodshed,' said St. Leger evenly, 'they've got Guérin behind those barricades, while the whole Army's on the fence waiting to see what he'll do. But of course there's nothing he can do until the Army does something. Then, when the Government's moved up enough reliable security troops, they'll go in and smash the barricades.'

'Then you'll see the shit start to fly,' said Hudson.

'It won't be the end of it, though,' said St. Leger, 'the killing will go on. The combinations of terrorism in this place are almost infinite. The Secret Army commandos will go back underground. Then you've got the Arab Front — their terrorists are commanded by a dear little chap called Ali La Joconde. His men have been killing about a dozen Europeans a day right in the centre of the city. We've even had to watch our step going outside the hotel. And on top of that you've got the barbouzes.'

'Barbouzes?' said Neil. He remembered that Pol had said he was a barbouze.

'Yes, "false beards",' said St. Leger, 'special gunmen the Government's been sending in to fight the Secret Army on its own terms. They've become almost a legend out here — none of the Ministries will officially admit their existence. They're licensed to kill without any questions being asked. Some of them are reputed to be Indo-Chinese — agents recruited during the war there to infiltrate the Viet-Minh lines. But most of them are just hired thugs — police informers, ex-convicts, gendarmes who've been kicked out of the force for misconduct. Delightful types.'

'How many of them are here now?' said Neil.

St. Leger took a lick of toothpaste, rolled it round his tongue as though it were a vintage wine, and said, 'Not easy to say — the Secret Army's killed so many of them off. But a few days ago it was thought there were about two hundred of them operating in the city. Their favourite method of working is to get in with some Secret Army commandos and go out and shoot a few Moslems — just to show they're in the spirit of the thing, you know — and then, when they've got the names of the commandos, they either move in and kill them on the spot, or take them off and question them for the names of other commandos.'

'They use torture,' said Hudson, his worried face bobbing about like a tennis ball.

Neil was listening gravely; he tried to form a mental picture of Pol, gun in hand in the wardroom of the 'Serafina'; but somehow the image became distorted with Pol the Michelin Man, rubbing down his rolls of fat with a bath towel. It didn't seem to fit.

'Of course, one might say that any methods of fighting the Secret Army are justified,' St. Leger was saying, 'and using the barbouzes is just one of them.'

'How's it all going to end?' said Neil.

'Personally,' said St. Leger, stroking his long dry neck, 'I see no end to it. Except, perhaps, send in the Brigade of Guards and impose fifty years of paternal British rule.' He spoke without a trace of humour, and Neil did not know whether he should laugh or not.

Outside, the night had closed in and there was a black silence over the city, interrupted by the tapping of machinegun fire. Up in his room Neil began to write a long letter to Caroline by candle light; but he was distracted by thoughts of Pol and Jadot and the barbouzes, and he knew she wouldn't be interested in them. He thought of telling her that he had a colleague here who ate toothpaste, but she probably wouldn't believe him. He went to bed.

CHAPTER 3

Neil woke with the telephone purring by his ear. He lifted the receiver from its cradle and a man's voice said in French, 'Monsieur Ingleby, you are wanted downstairs.'

'Who by?'

The voice repeated, 'You are wanted downstairs. This is reception.' The line clicked dead.

Neil sat up and looked at his watch; it was a quarter to seven. Too early for any of the journalists to be up asking for him, and he didn't think Pol would risk coming to the hotel again. Whoever was downstairs was from the Secret Army.

He felt a tightening in his stomach as he showered, dressed and went through to Van Loon. The Dutchman lay naked on his back, snoring. Neil shook him awake: 'Peter! There's someone downstairs to see me — from the Secret Army. You join me in the foyer in five minutes — not later!'

Van Loon opened one eye and said, 'O.K., five minutes. Don't get killed!'

Neil went out and along to the lifts. The hotel was very quiet. In the foyer the two receptionists stood like sentinels against the sunlight from the door. A dark handsome girl sat alone in one of the armchairs, and a Moslem fluttered about with a duster at the end of the room. Neil went up to the desk. The silver-haired receptionist had been replaced by a thin man with a yellow moustache. Neil tried to keep his voice calm: 'I understand someone is here to see me — Monsieur Ingleby.'

The man gave him a flat stare and nodded past him towards the girl in the armchair. Neil turned, frowning, and walked over to her; he stopped with a slight bow and said, 'I'm Monsieur Ingleby. Were you asking for me?'

She looked impassively up at him: 'You are the English journalist who came by boat yesterday from Greece.' It was not a question, but a statement of fact. Neil nodded, swallowing hard.

'Sit down, Monsieur Ingleby.' She took out a packet of Gitanes, lit one, tossed the match on the floor and sat watching him through the curling smoke. She had fine black eyes that sloped upwards in a wide face, and her nose was straight, in a bold line with her forehead, giving her a dramatic Grecian profile. She wore a crimson sheath of shot-silk cut low over her sunburnt breasts. Her arms were bare and her hands slender and brown; she wore no make-up and no ring. On her left wrist was a loose, heavy bracelet of Berber silver.

'You represent a famous English newspaper,' she began, speaking with the deliberation of a set speech, 'it is important that while you are here you write the truth. Many of the foreigners here tell lies about us. They accuse us of being murderers and Fascists and traitors. That is not true. This is our country. We built it out of the sand. Before the French came there was nothing! The Arabs were nomads — tribesmen who came from outside and profited from what we had built, and now they say the country is theirs. It is not theirs, Monsieur Ingleby! This country is French, and we shall keep it French!' Her eyes were fierce and beautiful, and they confused him: he was not used to political passion so early in the morning. He nodded again and said nothing. There was something both absurd and rather frightening about this lovely girl mouthing political abstractions, while outside she and her friends wielded the weapons of violence and death.

'You must write in your newspaper that we are not Fascists and murderers,' she went on, 'we are patriots!' She paused, inhaling deeply, and Neil mumbled something about trying to be objective and seeing all sides of the problem; then added, 'What is your name?'

'Anne-Marie. You don't have to know my family name.' She looked up sharply. Van Loon was coming towards them across the foyer. He stopped in front of her and gave a jerky bow. Neil said, 'This is my Dutch friend who came with me from Greece.'

She said, 'I know. You're Monsieur Van Loon. Sit down please.'

Van Loon fumbled for an armchair, ogling her with his huge blue eyes. She flicked some ash on the carpet and said to Neil, 'There was a third man with you on the boat from Greece.'

He stiffened and felt that tightening again in his stomach as he thought of Jadot and wondered, how much do these people know? His neck and forehead grew damp. She was watching him carefully now, and smiling a small teasing smile. 'A fat man with a beard,' she added, and her sloping black eyes flashed, almost with amusement, 'he is called Charles Pol.'

Neil licked his lips. 'How do you know all this?'

'We know everything, Monsieur Ingleby. And we want to ask you some questions about this fat man.' She squashed out her cigarette on the arm of the chair and brushed the ash to the floor. 'The car is outside,' she said, standing up.

'Where are we going?'

'You'll find out.' She led the way across the foyer, She was a tall girl, large-boned but graceful, and she walked like a dancer, with beautiful legs, long and suntanned, and without too much muscle; her buttocks were high and firm and slightly pointed under the tight red silk. After three iron weeks on Mount Athos Neil began to feel an uneasy stirring in his loins.

Outside, the sea-fog had cleared and the sun burned down out of a hard blue sky. A big man in dark glasses with an open-necked denim shirt stood in front of the hotel leaning against a black Peugeot 403 saloon. He straightened up and opened the doors. Anne-Marie waved them both into the back seats. Neil's foot stubbed against something on the floor as he sat down. It was a sporting rifle with telescopic sights.

The car accelerated with a skid of gravel and drove fast along the Front de Mer. Now that the strike was over, people were beginning to come out again into the streets. Shops and cafés were opening, and the Gardes Mobiles were at every corner with machine-guns and walkie-talkies; and in the squares and down the main boulevards armoured cars stood with the long barrels of the Douze-Septs trained on the balconies above.

The morning smelt fresh and clean, as they climbed from the Front de Mer, above the white dazzle of the city, into a series of poorer, working-class streets full of slogans and grubby little men idling in the mouths of bars and bistros. They turned another corner, still climbing, and two men in khaki uniforms with no insignia stepped out and waved them to a halt. One of them began talking to the driver and Neil caught the word barbouze several times; then the man handed in a sheet of notepaper scrawled with what looked to Neil like a list of serial numbers. Anne-Marie took the paper and began studying it, as the car drove on. She turned to Neil. 'Car numbers belonging to the barbouzes,' she said, pointing to the paper, 'filthy Government agents!' She laughed: 'We'll find them all before this evening.'

'What'll happen to them?'

She smiled, showing very even white teeth, and drew a finger across her throat: 'Kill them. The Government pays these barbouze vermin ten times what ordinary gendarmes get. They're just hired murderers.'

'They never get paid,' said the driver; 'we kill the bastards first.'

'Do you know,' said Anne-Marie, 'that when they first sent in the barbouzes, the Government agreed to pay them every three months. That way they could wait till most of them got killed, and save themselves the money!'

They turned into a tall street strung across with lines of washing between the tenement blocks. The walls shut out the sun and there was a warm stench of garbage. Anne-Marie smiled at Neil again, her head tilted sideways, and said, 'You know, your fat friend Charles Pol is a barbouze.'

Neil said nothing. It was hot inside the car and he began to sweat. A group of young men in leather jackets were lounging against the corner of one of the tenement blocks. The Peugeot stopped. Anne-Marie got out and led Neil and Van Loon into a side entrance, along a cement passage. The driver stayed with the car.

They heard voices and radio music coming from behind closed doors. At the end of the passage a soldier stood against the sunlight, wearing the mottled battle-dress and white kepi of the Foreign Legion. He stepped out and prodded his machine-pistol into Anne-Marie's stomach. She pushed the gun aside and said something to him, and he grinned at her. He had a thin face with very blue eyes, his neck rough with dead acne. He looked at Neil and Van Loon and spat on the floor: 'Journalists, eh? You be careful what you write here or we put a bullet in your necks!' He spoke with a middle-European accent:

'Go on, get moving!' He grinned again as they went past him, out into the sun.

The street was full of armed men, most of them in baggy leopard camouflage strapped across with grenades and belts of machinegun rounds that gleamed like gold teeth. A hundred yards up the street was the first barricade: a double wall of paving stones, topped with barbed wire skewered down with iron staples. A couple of paratroopers sat behind machineguns inside a nest of sand bags. Loudspeakers, hung from streetlamps, were blaring out martial music: rather gay, facetious music, Neil thought, full of fanfares of bugles and images of men in blue cloaks on prancing horses.

The troops squatted on the pavements, smoking and playing cards, or strolled in groups and sprawled in bars drinking beer and Fastis. There was an atmosphere of idleness and tension.

Anne-Marie led the way down the street away from the barricade. A large group of Foreign Legionnaires, in the flat-visored khaki caps of paratroopers, stared at her, grinning and hooting and shouting after her; and as she walked between them with a provocative swing of the hips, Neil thought sadly of the legend that had grown up round the Legion — of the romantic buccaneers and soldiers of fortune who stole heirlooms to save the family honour, or fled to Africa from an unhappy love affair. But there was nothing romantic about these men, they were just blunt, brutal soldiers. They square-bashed and polished equipment and dug latrines and got drunk and went out on savage raids into the Bled, taking no prisoners and leaving behind them a population stunned and full of hatred for the French. Neil wondered what Colonel Broussard, with his love of Persian poetry and old coins, really thought of them. Perhaps to him they were just the crude instruments of force to ensure him his place of power in the Elysée Palace.

As though reflecting his thoughts, Anne-Marie turned to him: 'These paras are not very polite — but they're good soldiers. They make the Arabs run!'

Van Loon whispered to Neil, 'A tremendous girl, huh?'

Neil nodded, thinking that she was also a dangerous girl.

She led them into a slender apartment-house at the end of the street. In the foyer two paras with heavy machineguns checked their papers, then showed them to the lifts. They hummed up to the tenth floor. A solemn man in a grey flannel suit let them into a wide cool room with a wall of French windows opening on to a balcony that looked down over chequered terraces to the sea. A girl in leopard skin trousers, with a heavy Jewish face, lay on a sofa under a reproduction of Matisse, turning the pages of Marie Claire. She scarcely looked up as they entered. The room was full of the tinkle of the Modern Jazz Quartet from an invisible hi-fi system.

Against the glare of the balcony a large man rose from a chair and came towards them. He wore a hound's-tooth jacket, yellow silk scarf and cavalry-twill trousers, and held a silver-topped riding crop against his knee. He gave Anne-Marie a light kiss on the cheek, then turned to Neil and Van Loon and said pleasantly, 'Make yourselves comfortable, messieurs!' — pointing his riding crop at a semicircle of shallow wicker chairs near the window. He sat down in front of them and smiled. He had big square teeth and the weathered face of a sportsman. A welted scar ran from the corner of his mouth to just below his left ear, and his hair, which was normally black, had been dyed bright orange.

'My name is Colonel Le Hir,' he began, addressing Neil, 'you have probably heard of me?'

Neil gave a stiff nod; he was excited and scared. Le Hir was head of a murder squad known as the 'Gamma Commandos'.

They specialized in killing Europeans who were unsympathetic to the Secret Army; it was they who had scored most of the successes against the barbouzes.

'I'd have called you at a more civilized hour,' the colonel continued easily, 'but unfortunately I have a very full programme today.' He turned to the Jewish girl in the leopard skin trousers: 'Nadia, make some coffee!'

The girl unfolded her legs and slunk sulkily out of the room. Le Hir said to Neil, 'We try to be as helpful as we can to the foreign Press during these difficult times. After all, if it was not for you' — he gave a condescending nod — 'the world would be obliged to believe the Paris propaganda machine.' He paused. Anne-Marie shifted in her chair with a crackle of wicker, exposing an inch of shadowed thigh. Le Hir had begun tapping the riding crop against his ankle.

'However, Monsieur Ingleby' — and his voice now became sharp as a razor — 'in your case there is one small matter which rather disturbs me. It concerns the man you arrived with yesterday from Greece. A man named Pol.'

The only sound in the room now was the tapping of the riding crop. Le Hir's eyes, which were pale brown with a bright yellow light in them, watched Neil without blinking: 'Do you know this man well, Monsieur Ingleby?'

Neil felt his pulse begin to race, and in the silence there was a singing in his ears. He knew that if Le Hir had heard of what happened to Jadot, neither he nor Van Loon would leave this building alive.

He said to Le Hir, 'I hardly know him at all. We met in a hotel in Athens and he offered to take me over here in his boat.' He turned to Van Loon, who was busy igniting his meerschaum as though it were some complicated machine: 'He wanted Monsieur Van Loon here to navigate. That's the only way we got to know him.'

Anne-Marie sat with her legs carefully crossed, staring at a point somewhere just above Neil's head. Le Hir did not move his eyes from Neil's face. The girl Nadia slipped in with a tray of filter coffees. Nobody spoke as the cups were passed round. Le Hir removed the filter bowl, placed it in a metal stand beside him, helped himself to two spoonsful of sugar, and sat stirring his cup slowly, still not moving his eyes from Neil. When he spoke his voice was very soft: 'Do you know who this man is?'

Neil shrugged: 'He told me he was a Paris businessman.'

Le Hir shook his head: 'No, Monsieur Ingleby. He is what we call here a barbouze. Do you know what a barbouze is?'

Neil nodded.

Le Hir smacked the riding crop against his shin and sprang up, looming huge above Neil, legs apart, arms akimbo, his big teeth bared in a grin: 'Listen to me carefully, Monsieur Ingleby. I am a reasonable man. I don't believe in interfering with journalists who come here to do their job. But when you and your Dutch friend arrive in this city with a leading French secret agent I begin to have doubts. I begin to wonder whether you are here merely as a journalist, or for some other motive. You had better explain. As I said, my programme today is very full.' He glanced at his watch.

'I can assure you,' said Neil, in a small hoarse voice, 'that my meeting with Monsieur Pol was entirely accidental. I had no idea what sort of work he was doing here. We didn't discuss it.'

'But he went with you to your hotel last night. Why?'

'He came up to have a shower in my room. He sweats a lot.'

Anne-Marie smiled. Le Hir stood above Neil sipping his coffee: 'Monsieur Ingleby, in normal circumstances I would order you out of this country within twelve hours, under pain of death if you stayed. However, I am satisfied that your explanation is an honest one. I am prepared to let you stay — on one condition. I want to know if this man Pol has made any arrangement to see you again while you are here.'

At that moment Neil panicked. He was still not sure just how much Le Hir knew: whether the news of Jadot's death had reached the Secret Army. Perhaps this was a trap to test the truth of his story. Rashly, he began telling Le Hir about the telephone call Pol had asked him to make at two o'clock that afternoon. Even as he spoke he realized that Le Hir almost certainly did not know about Jadot. But the damage had been done.

'Why does he want you to make this call?'

'He said he might have something important to tell me for my newspaper.'

'What number did he ask you to ring?'

Neil showed him the number Pol had given him. Le Hir nodded. 'That's one of the coded lines to the High Command headquarters,' he said, handing Neil's pocketbook back. 'Very well! Now this is what you are going to do. You will ring this man Pol at two o'clock this afternoon. I want to know exactly what he says to you. Anne-Marie will call at your hotel, and whatever information you have you will give to her.' He finished his coffee and handed the cup to Nadia. 'Messieurs,' he said, 'it has been my pleasure to meet you!'

Neil and Van Loon stood up. Around them the hi-fi released the mewing tones of Johnny Mathis. Le Hir took their hands in a grip like iron. 'Remember,' he said, with his square-toothed smile, 'that when you see this man Pol you say nothing about your visit here. You have never met me — you have never met Anne-Marie.' He paused, and a nasty glare showed at the edges of his eyes. 'But if you do say anything, or if you try to conceal from me anything that Pol says to you, then I shall know about it. I promise you.'

It seemed to Neil that he spoke with the studied melodrama of someone who has seen a great many bad films. Neil was reminded suddenly of a games master he had had at his prep school: a big healthy man who expended charm and flattery on the parents, and used to beat boys with a billiard cue if they failed to get ten runs in a cricket match. There was something grotesque about the man which should have been amusing, but wasn't. And as Anne-Marie led the way with secretarial efficiency down the ten floors to the street, Neil had an urge to run, to escape from this white city where the preposterous Pol on one side and this orange-haired colonel on the other were fighting out the last ferocious act in French colonial history, with N. Ingleby trapped somewhere in the middle.

CHAPTER 4

It was going to be a hot day. The streets already shimmered with a white glare and the sun burned into the bay with diamond brilliance. Outside the barricades a restive unnatural holiday atmosphere was spreading through the city. The squares and boulevards were filling with great crowds. The pavement cafés were packed with almond-eyed girls and dark young men in beach hats and sunglasses, breakfasting under striped awnings, watched by the Gardes Mobiles who stood at the door of every shop and bank and bar, eyes like stone, guns at the ready. And along the Front de Mer sports cars, bright with scarves and sunburned arms, were setting out for the beaches, dodging between the jeeps and half-tracks.

The Peugeot turned down towards the Hotel Miramar. Anne-Marie smiled at Neil: 'It's a good day for swimming!'

'And for fishing,' said the driver morosely, glaring out at the helmeted troops. He braked suddenly. In front of them a large crowd had collected on the corner. Cars stood bumper to bumper, hooting in angry chorus. A group of ragged European children came running down the pavement, laughing and waving their arms.

Neil glanced at Anne-Marie: 'What's happened?'

She shrugged, looking indifferently out of the window: 'A ratonnade, I think — some Moslem. Or perhaps a barbouze.'

A Garde Mobile came down the street, blowing a whistle and signalling the cars forward. He reached the Peugeot and the driver leant out and said, 'What's up?'

'*Attentat*,' said the man, 'don't stay around to watch. Get moving!' He had a huge face, of the same metal-grey as his helmet. The Peugeot crept forward to the corner where a cordon of CRS troops had linked arms and were trying to push the crowds back against the edge of the café.

The first Moslem lay on his face in the middle of the street. He wore a pair of dirty plimsols and faded blue trousers. The blood flowed from his head over the camber of the street and forked into two dark serpents, their blunt noses moving swiftly down the gutter collecting a film of dust. Neil remembered afterwards wondering how so much blood could come from the head of one human being.

The second man sat on the pavement, his face in his hands. He was also a Moslem. A bicycle lay overturned beside him, its front wheel still turning. A bucket had rolled into the gutter. Blood was running out of his trouser legs and trickling towards the café tables. Neil saw a party of bronzed men with several pretty girls shift their chairs to avoid dirtying their espadrilles. One of the girls looked at the wounded man and laughed.

He was trying to stand up. His head was still in his hands; he pulled in his legs and strained forward till he toppled into the gutter, his buttocks in the air. The Peugeot stopped, caught in another jam. The man was directly outside the window now. They sat and watched him perform his slow and terrible ritual, struggling to his feet with a bullet in his neck. Neil cried out, in English, 'For God's sake, we must do something!'

'You do something, you get killed,' said Van Loon.

Neil turned to Anne-Marie: her head was resting on the back of the seat. She did not look at the Moslem. 'We must do something!' he said in French. 'The man's dying!'

'Shut up,' she said without moving. He noticed that her eyelids were lightly freckled like eggshell.

The Moslem outside had begun to plod wearily up the street. His hands were still clutched across his face and the back of his head was dark and glistening. The crowds pressed round and watched. He made no sound. The street was full of the blare of hooters. The CRS were busy waving the traffic on again.

'Why don't those damned troops do something?' said Neil, in English.

'Don't talk,' said Van Loon.

The Peugeot moved forward, past the Moslem as he dragged himself upwards, leaving a sprinkled trail of blood. A man came running down the street towards them. He passed the car and yelled, 'Two Europeans just killed!' He waved back up the street and went on, shouting at the crowd round the café.

What happened next was very confused. The crowd closed in in a rush. People began to run; there was shouting, screaming, a glimpse of raised batons, uniforms struggling, children leaping past the windows of the car; the shriek of whistles, the dismal panting of sirens.

The Moslem had disappeared. The crowds rolled back, and Neil saw two people lying in the café among the wreckage of overturned tables and smashed glass. The CRS were frog-marching two men up the street. The Moslem was lying several yards away, his arms flopped behind his back. He did not move. There was a broad smear along the pavement where he had been dragged face downwards.

The traffic cleared and the Peugeot drove on, into a quiet street shaded by high white buildings. Neil looked dumbly at Anne-Marie; he was not even shocked or sickened, just puzzled. 'Why?' he said again. 'Why did they do it?' He remembered that the girl in the café who had laughed at the Moslem had been wearing magenta tights and open sandals. It made no sense.

Anne-Marie stretched her arms along the back of the seat. 'They were Moslems,' she said, 'we kill them if they come into the French quarters. We have to protect ourselves. Ali La Joconde sends his Arab Front terrorists down from the Casbah and they shoot Europeans all round here, and leave bombs in cafés and do horrible things.' She yawned. 'You must be careful round the Hotel Miramar,' she added, 'it's one of the worst places. They killed a man there this morning, just before I came to collect you.'

'So you kill Moslems in return?' said Neil.

'Certainly. We can't lie down and sleep while these terrorists walk around in our city. They mutilate women and children, you know! You haven't seen anything yet.'

'But those two men back there,' said Neil, 'were they terrorists?'

'I don't know,' she said, 'perhaps, I don't know. But they shouldn't have been down in this quarter — they should have kept to the Casbah. That's where they belong.'

'The second man was lynched,' said Neil, 'kicked to death!'

She nodded: 'Yes, I know. That wasn't good. Our commandos have orders only to shoot people. But sometimes the crowd gets excited — especially when they hear that Europeans have just been killed. They get angry, they lose their heads. It's understandable.'

Neil looked at the tiny hairs glinting along her sunburnt arms. She was a beautiful girl; and in the heat of the closed car he caught her warm, musky smell, healthy and alive, evidence that she lived well and slept well and took plenty of exercise and didn't worry about men she saw lynched in the street.

At the corner of the Miramar she took him and Van Loon by the hand. 'Don't forget,' she said, 'you telephone the fat man at two o'clock. I'll come and collect you at half past and we'll go to the beach. I want to introduce you to some of my friends, to show you that we are not all murderers and Fascists.' She smiled at them both with her wide mouth, and her face was bright and innocent — a young girl planning to go to the beach and frisk about in a bikini, sitting now in a chauffeur-driven car with a telescopic rifle on the floor.

They shook hands with her, and Van Loon stood and watched the Peugeot drive away, muttering, 'What a fantastic girl, Neil! Completely sadistic, I think?'

'I don't know,' said Neil, 'I just don't understand any of them. Let's have a drink.'

They went past the fountain into the air-conditioned darkness of the hotel: smells of oranges and old leather, with a crowd of journalists refreshing themselves at the bar. Winston St. Leger and Hudson were there, together with Tom Mallory, transplanted from El Vino in Fleet Street by way of a three-hundred-mile drive in a hired Hillman Minx across the desert. The chances against his getting through had seemed colossal, but he had made it: now holding up an empty glass and shouting 'Nurse!' at the sleek-haired barman.

He was a journalist of erratic brilliance who had been sacked and rehired during his career by two large London papers, had been under sentence of death three times and expelled from altogether five countries. His face now had a gnarled furious look, purple with good living, framed by a halo of copper-red hair that dropped over his soup-stained jacket. Although a comparatively young man, most of his teeth had fallen out and his voice had sung to a croak which was the only impediment to his legendary rudeness. Neil had met him several times and thought him slightly mad. He murmured a greeting but Mallory took no notice. He was leaning across the bar waving his glass about his head: 'Nurse!' he cried again, in his terrible croak.

St. Leger caught Neil's eye: 'You look a bit green about the gills, my dear fellow!'

‘I’ve just seen a man lynched,’ said Neil, sitting down with Van Loon. He explained in detail what they had seen and St. Leger nodded over his pink gin: ‘Yes, you’ll get used to that sort of thing — what is laughingly called here effervescence. What will you drink?’

They ordered brandies. From down the bar came a hoarse cackle of laughter. St. Leger murmured, ‘As you can hear, Mr. Mallory is with us. A good reporter but in my view rather a hooligan. I hope he doesn’t make any trouble for us all.’

‘Trouble?’ said Neil.

‘Yes, trouble with the powers that be — the Secret Army. We have to be rather careful here, you know.’ He paused meaningfully and nibbled at an olive. Hudson had joined them. He glanced at Neil and Van Loon with a raised eyebrow, and St. Leger cleared his throat. When he spoke again it was with measured gravity, ‘Mister Ingleby, far be it from me to attempt to tell another journalist, especially one of your reputation, what he should and should not do. But in this case’ — and he sipped his pink gin — ‘I feel I ought to warn you.’

‘Warn me? What do you mean?’

St. Leger picked up another olive and examined it carefully: ‘Warn you about some of the people you know here.’

Mallory’s voice came croaking down the bar: ‘So I told Butcher O’Brien to get knotted — told him he had a touch o’ the sun!’ Someone laughed.

Winston St. Leger said gently, without looking at Neil, ‘You can trust me and Hudson here completely. What I want to tell you is for your own good.’

Hudson was leaning forward, his worried face creased into a forked stick. The brandies came; Neil and Van Loon sat in silence and waited. St. Leger twirled the stem of his pink gin. ‘I’ve been in this city a number of years,’ he went on, ‘and I hear quite a lot of things that aren't always for the record.' He turned and looked Neil in the eye: 'Somebody told me that you arrived in this hotel yesterday with a French secret agent called Charles Pol.'

Neil nodded and drank his brandy. So he was in for a second interrogation, this time from his own colleagues. He said, 'Well, what of it?'

'What of it!' cried Hudson. 'Look here, Ingleby, you must know the score in this place. You arrive here with a man who just about tops the Secret Army's black list. Did you know that? He's seen coming into this hotel with a journalist! Where do y'think that puts the rest of us? We don't like these Secret Army boys, but we got to live with 'em!'

St. Leger nodded: 'I'm afraid he's right, Ingleby. This man Charles Pol could be very dangerous for us all. I don't know how he picked you up, but I do know that he must have had some very good motive.'

'He picked me up,' said Neil, with an edge coming into his voice, 'because he wanted someone to help him cross from Greece in a small boat. The Secret Army know all this, I've already explained it to them this morning.'

'Who did y'see?' asked Hudson.

'I can't tell you that.'

'You can trust us,' St. Leger said again.

'I trust you,' said Neil, 'I just think it would be safer for us all if I didn't tell you.'

St. Leger nodded solemnly and there was a pause. Neil felt that he had won the discussion. He disliked being criticized by his colleagues for what amounted to professional ineptitude.

Then St. Leger said, 'It wasn't by any chance a gentleman called Colonel Le Hir whom you met this morning?'

Neil stared at him in shocked silence: 'How did you know?'

'I guessed,' said St. Leger, 'if you went to see anyone, he was the most likely person. He deals with what is politely called counter-espionage.'

Hudson had drawn in his breath and gave a little whistle: 'You saw the Colonel! O Jesus!'

'You know him?'

'I know of him,' said Hudson, 'did he tell you to get out of the country?'

'No,' said Neil, 'he was very civil to me, we had coffee together, he asked me how I knew Pol, I told him, and he left it at that.'

St. Leger smiled: 'My dear fellow, if you imagine that Colonel Le Hir was prepared to "leave it at that", as you put it, then — if you'll excuse my being blunt — you must have a very simplified view of what is going on in this city.'

Neil flushed but said nothing. Van Loon just stared at his empty brandy, hoping to be bought another. St. Leger was studying another olive, his face old and delicate and relaxed. 'If Colonel Le Hir did not call you this morning in order to expel you,' he went on, 'then it's not difficult to guess what he really wanted. Certainly not his picture in the paper.'

'He wanted an explanation of how I came to know Pol,' said Neil, 'that was all.'

St. Leger shook his head: 'No, Mister Ingleby, that was not all. I think Colonel Le Hir asked you to get him information about Pol.'

Neil said nothing. St. Leger continued, 'And yesterday Pol asked you to get information for him — information about people you meet here in the course of your work. Isn't that so?'

'No,' said Neil, 'all he did was ask me to ring him this afternoon. He said he might have something to tell me for my paper.'

'In exchange for what?'

'For nothing — as a simple favour.'

St. Leger had taken out his toothpaste tube and was sucking it thoughtfully. 'Monsieur Charles Pol is a very deceptive man,' he said at last. 'I knew him in Barcelona in 1936. He was a leading Anarchist then, quite a flamboyant character. Among other escapades he organized the kidnapping of one of Franco's generals. Then during the last war he became one of the Allies' most successful double agents, working for the Vichy Government and spying for the Free French. He's come out here to help break the Secret Army. And the fact that he arrives in a private boat with a well-known British journalist doesn't strike me as altogether a coincidence. The Secret Army won't think so either.'

Neil finished his brandy and stared glumly at the bar: 'So what do you suggest I do?'

'Leave the country — before you get yourself, and perhaps the whole Press Corps, into serious trouble.'

CHAPTER 5

Neil lay on his bed smoking. It was now 12.40. He had one hour and twenty minutes left before telephoning Pol and finally committing himself.

All morning he had worried over what action he should take. So far he had not been directly threatened; all he had been asked to do was to make a phone call and report on it. It was possible that Winston St. Leger had been wrong. Neil knew from experience that journalists are essentially creatures of temperament, enjoying a world of melodrama often of their own making, and often given to irresponsible judgments. St. Leger and Hudson had perhaps been in this city too long. What happened to luckless Moslems in the street was one thing; as Pol had said, the Secret Army did not harm distinguished members of the foreign Press. On the other hand, if Pol and Le Hir were seriously intending to use Neil as a pawn between them, then clearly he should swallow his pride, take St. Leger's advice, and get out.

Later in the morning he had gone to the offices of Agence France-Presse and studied the teleprinter reports. Several hundred new security troops were being flown in from France during the next twenty-four hours. That meant the airport would remain closed to civilian traffic until at least tomorrow night. All other means of escape — ports, road and railways — were still sealed off. The decision had been made for him. He would have to stay.

A fat fly lobbed about on the ceiling, then whined away under the blinds. Twice the air shuddered with the shockwaves of plastic bombs set off in Arab shops in the European quarter.

He was low in spirits. He did not have the bloody-minded resilience of a Tom Mallory who in similar circumstances would have got steadily drunk and profited from the intrigue and danger. In Greece, Neil had fancied himself as an adventurer, a man of action; but now that it was happening to him, he found he was not enjoying it. He had drunk a number of Pernods downstairs, but they had only depressed him more, and made him randy into the bargain. He thought longingly of Caroline, wanting to talk to her, touch her, fold her between clean sheets: smooth flat belly and breasts like lemons, pinching her soft buttocks to make her squeak.

At noon he had booked a call to her London office, person to person. If the lines to Paris were not too busy he might get through before one of the executives took her out to lunch, to Prunier's or Simpson's in the Strand.

To avoid thinking about her he began planning a colour piece for Sunday morning's paper. The deadline was tomorrow evening. He knew he could not safely describe his meeting with Le Hir without risking a deportation order, even the closing of the paper's Paris Bureau; and to write about Pol ('France's answer to James Bond') would invite sure recriminations from the Secret Army. He would have to content himself, and about half-a-million of the better educated of Britain's Sunday newspaper readers, with a bill of fare consisting of pretty girls, bombs, bright cafés and men kicked to death in broad daylight. Like Nice in a nightmare.

The telephone was ringing by the bed. It was not Caroline, but Anne-Marie: 'Monsieur Ingleby! *Ça va bien?*' There was a lot of shouting and laughter in the background. She sounded excited and rather tight: 'Have you had lunch yet? We're eating at a restaurant called Le Berry — corner of the Rue de la Liberté. It's only a few minutes from your hotel. Come and join us! I've got some friends who want to meet you.'

The militant determination of this morning had gone: now she was just another good-time girl like Caroline, enjoying herself in a restaurant. Neil said, 'I'm waiting for a call to London.'

She sounded disappointed: 'Can't you take it later?'

He looked at his watch. It was almost one o'clock, time for Caroline's lunch hour. He said, 'I'll be with you in about a quarter of an hour. Can I bring my Dutch friend?'

'Certainly! And you call the fat man at two o'clock from the restaurant. Then we go down to the Casino de la Plage. It's very chic, you'll like it!' The voices and laughter swelled suddenly and she shouted, '*À bientôt!*' and the line clicked.

Down in the bar the Press Corps were still buying one another rounds of drinks on their expense accounts and telling anecdotes about the Congo. In the corner Tom Mallory slept in an armchair, snoring with a noise like a bath running out. Van Loon was sitting alone over a chilled Alsace beer, looking bored.

Neil said, 'Pieter, we've been asked to lunch by Anne-Marie and her friend.' He tried to sound flippant: 'So no horseplay! There's a lot of Corsican blood round here.'

Van Loon nodded wisely: 'I don't fool around, old fellow. These girls here are pretty hot, I think? I know what to do.'

Neil ordered another Pernod, waiting a few more minutes for his call to London. He wondered if lunch would be on the Secret Army. St. Leger came over and said gravely, 'I suppose you've heard that the airport's staying closed? Have you registered at the British Consulate? I should do that as soon as possible.'

'And what sort of protection will they provide?' said Neil wryly. 'Are they armed?'

St. Leger looked offended: 'I don't know. But they'll have the support of the British Government, if anything happens to you.'

'Yes, of course,' said Neil. It was a quarter past one and his call to London had still not come through. He decided to cancel it. Van Loon and he were just leaving when they heard the shots. They seemed to come from just outside the hotel. The bar emptied as the whole Press Corps stampeded into the foyer.

An old Moslem who sold cigarettes at the hotel entrance was dead. He lay sprawled under the palms with his tray of French and American brands scattered round him near the base of the fountain. Neil had bought a packet of Chesterfields from him only that morning. Blood was oozing out of his head into the flinty gravel, and his hands were flung out beside him, thin as chicken claws. He had a wooden leg.

The journalists stepped gingerly round him. The receptionist with the yellow moustache pointed up the street. 'They shot him from a car,' he said casually, 'just two shots, straight in the head.' St. Leger looked away from the body, pulling a face of disgust: 'Poor devil! It was bound to happen — I told him several times to keep away from here and stay in the Casbah.'

Mallory had stumbled up, roused from his sleep more by instinct than the actual sound of the shooting: 'What's happened? Killed a man with a wooden leg, have they? Sods! I could have killed him with a tennis racket.'

Van Loon tugged at Neil's arm. 'Come on, nothing to do here. We go for lunch with Anne-Marie.'

'I don't think I want to have lunch with her, or her friends. Bloody savages!'

'If we do not go, she will be fed up with us,' said Van Loon, 'and she is an important girl, I think.' They began to walk down the street, keeping to the margin of shade under the walls. 'Don't talk about that dead man,' Van Loon said after a pause, 'I don't think they will like it.'

Neil had no wish to talk to anyone about it, least of all to Anne-Marie and her friends. He had no appetite, no wish to finish up with his head broken open with a pistol bullet. And in less than an hour he would have to ring Pol.

Le Berry restaurant faced the Front de Mer and the bay. There was a crowded café with wicker chairs and Dubonnet umbrellas out in front. The restaurant was behind a glass porch, hot and noisy, with the fans whirling and the people packed along tables under high gilt mirrors. Anne-Marie's party was at the back of the room, at a table stacked with seafood and white wine in ice buckets.

There were five altogether in the party: Anne-Marie, and a slim, pretty girl with hair the colour of red Burgundy, called Annette, a broad man in a khaki shirt with sunglasses that curved round his face like black goggles, who was introduced as Lieutenant Carlos Morin. He sat beside a sensuous dark girl who reminded Neil of a bad-tempered starlet, her rampant breasts pointing like fingertips through her flimsy dress, who was introduced simply as Pip. And at the end of the table sat a solemn big-boned Jewish boy with a coal-black crewcut, in a grey flannel suit with a chalk pinstripe. He was Louis Rebot, leader of the city's main student organization.

Apart from Pip, whose bosom was lolling dangerously close to her lobster soup, they all greeted Neil and Van Loon with smiles and broad gestures, squeezing up to make room and pushing glasses of wine at them. Neil was beside Anne-Marie, with Van Loon wedged between Annette and Lieutenant

Morin. Anne-Marie gave Neil a glass of Pouilly Fuissé and cried: '*à votre santé!*' sweeping her own glass round in a wide arc above her head and draining it off in a gulp. Neil asked her if they were celebrating something. She smiled slyly, then pounced out and kissed him on the cheek: 'We are celebrating victory, mon cher!' She lifted her glass again, and turning towards the whole restaurant, shouted in a ringing voice: '*Vive Guérin! Guérin au pouvoir!*'

Her words were greeted with a roar like an echo, followed by the brutal banging of cutlery on the tables to the rhythm of '*Guérin au pouvoir!*' For a moment the restaurant was bedlam, like a school dining-room gone berserk. Neil had always loathed mass demonstrations — stamping, chanting, slow hand-clapping — and he sat cowed over his wine, feeling that the primeval barbarism of Man had suddenly been released to invade this smart French restaurant and provoke within these apparently civilized beings a savage hysteria.

Van Loon thought it rather amusing and even joined in the demonstration, using his knife and fork like drumsticks. When the noise had died down Neil asked Anne-Marie what had happened. She put a hand on his shoulder and said, 'We've won! Two battalions of Army reservists have come over to our side. By tomorrow perhaps the whole Army will be with us, and Metz and his Gestapo, the Gardes Mobiles, will be running for their lives. Then we can go in and smash the Casbah and get Ali La Joconde and his murderers!' She spoke with a gay ferocity as though discussing the prospects for the 'Tour de France'.

'When did this happen?' said Neil.

'Forty minutes ago, we got it through Louis Rebot there.' She nodded towards the Jewish student leader, who lifted his glass in a toast.

Neil drank deeply. The Right-wing Revolution was about to triumph. He wondered whether Pol and his team had anything left up their sleeves. It should have been a sad moment — a military junta on the point of seizing power and overthrowing the French Republic: Broussard's mob of paratroopers and degenerate legionnaires ready to go on the rampage through the Casbah.

He felt vaguely ashamed that his own worries should overshadow what might be a tragedy for Western civilization. But he was scared. He deplored everything that Anne-Marie and her friends stood for, yet in a curiously perverse way he felt more secure with them than he had with Pol, or even the Press Corps in the hotel.

Anne-Marie ordered him scampi and fat tournedos on cushions of toast with bearnaise sauce. She put her arm round his shoulder and announced to the table: 'Monsieur Ingleby is a famous English writer — he is going to tell the people of England what is really happening here.'

They began asking him his opinions about the revolt. He tried to be shrewdly neutral, remembering the dead Moslem and the stump of leg frayed at the end like an old walking-stick. He felt no enthusiasm for talking to any of these people, noticing that Anne-Marie ate and drank with an appetite so healthy as to be almost coarse. Once during the discussion she grabbed his arm and pointed at Louis Rebot. 'In France people call us Fascists!' she cried; 'but Louis there is with the Secret Army and he is a Jew! How can a Jew be a Fascist, Monsieur Ingleby? It is impossible, ridiculous!'

He nodded tactfully, and Rebot answered from the end of the table, 'All the Jews here are one hundred per cent behind the Secret Army. It is a struggle for survival against Arab nationalism. It is simple: if we do not win, we will perish.' He spoke with the melancholy passion of his race, an echo from generations of persecution, a new Moses leading an army of paratroopers to defend the Promised Land against the invader.

Van Loon was talking noisily to the slim red-headed girl Annette, who was giggling and feeling his blond beard. He was swallowing a great deal of wine, rolling his blue eyes, suddenly finding Borneo a long way off. When Lieutenant Morin asked him what he thought of the situation in the Protectorate, he grinned and said obscurely, 'I make no trouble for anyone, I just like drinking and good food and nice girls!' — he gave Annette a lewd wink — 'but if someone makes trouble for me, I break him with my hands!'

They all laughed except Neil, and Lieutenant Morin clapped him on the back: 'I can see you are one of us, Dutchman!'

Van Loon said, 'I would like very much to be one of you, with all these girls around!'

Anne-Marie touched Neil's elbow and whispered, 'It is two o'clock. You have to telephone the fat man.'

Neil felt a sinking in his stomach; he had hoped he was free of this. What could he say to Pol? That he'd met Le Hir behind the barricades and was lunching at Le Berry with one of the Secret Army student leaders?

Anne-Marie said, 'The telephones are through past the toilets. They'll give you a jeton at the cash desk.'

Inside the padded booth he pulled the door firmly shut and dialled the number Pol had given him. He wondered if there were an extension in the restaurant which could be listened in to. Perhaps that was why she had asked him to lunch in the first place. The line the other end did not give the normal ringing tone; there were three pips and a woman's voice repeated the number he had dialled. He said, 'Monsieur Pol, please.' There was a click, silence, then Pol's voice came on — warily, Neil thought, 'Who is it?'

'Ingleby.'

'Ah Monsieur Ingleby, *comment ça va*?' His voice cooed and chuckled deafeningly down the line, he was in his expansive mood. Neil wondered how many bottles of Johnny Walker had already been brought into the heavily guarded High Command headquarters.

'Are you enjoying your stay here?' Pol went on, with a trace of irony: the line was probably being tapped his end by the Sûreté.

'I'm fine,' said Neil, feeling the sweat itching down his nose in the heat of the booth.

'*Bien!* Now where are you speaking from?'

Neil hesitated a second: 'A tobacconist's — near the hotel.'

'Very well, now listen carefully. This is very important.'

Neil wedged his toes and buttocks between the narrow walls; the receiver was growing wet under his hand. Pol spoke with slow emphasis: 'Tomorrow morning at ten o'clock you will walk out of your hotel and turn right into the rue Victor Hugo. At the end of it is a cinema called le Roxy — at the moment it is showing "Spartacus" with your English actor Laurence Olivier. Next to this cinema, down a small turning, is a place called "La Cintra Café". It is very small and is usually empty at that time. You will go in and order a drink. At a quarter past ten a man will come in. He will be wearing a white shirt with no tie, and will carry a light blue linen jacket over his left arm. He will come up to your table and address you by name, but you will have no time to buy him a drink. Instead you will leave together and drive away in his car. Is that clear?'

Neil changed the dripping receiver from one hand to the other. He would have been amused had he had any sense of humour left. Pol had now descended to traditional amateur dramatics: secret assignations in cafés, men with no ties, coats over their left arm. Even the stage directions were absurdly gauche: 'He will come up to you, but you will have no time to buy him a drink!' Surely he should buy the man a drink! It was supposed to be a casual meeting. He was surprised that Pol had not included a password for good measure — something like '*Il pleure dans mon coeur, comme il pleut sur la ville*' — with perhaps the reply … 'Spartacus!' He wondered again, with a sense of dull resignation, whether the line was being tapped at his end. St. Leger and Hudson had been right of course, he was now hopelessly involved.

He said wearily to Pol, 'Where will I be taken?'

'I would prefer that you find out tomorrow. It is a little delicate — from my point of view.' There was a pause. 'Just in case you decide not to turn up.'

Neil nodded at the receiver. So Pol was playing his own little game and was giving nothing away. If I had any sense, he thought, I should try to get out with the 'Serafina' this afternoon.

Pol said, '*Entendu? Au revoir*, Monsieur Ingleby!' and rang off, and Neil went back to the brandy and coffee that Anne-Marie had ordered while he was out. The Secret Army was paying.

She smiled up at him and said, 'Well, what did he say?' There was nothing in any of the faces round the table to suggest that they knew what Pol had said. Rebot and Van Loon had lit up cigars and were both talking to Annette who was shaking her head and laughing; and Lieutenant Morin had his sunburnt jowls sunk in the neck of Pip the sulky starlet. They did not look a menacing gang.

Neil clasped his fingers round the tulip glass of brandy and said, not looking at Anne-Marie, 'He didn't tell me anything at all. He said he was too busy. I have to call him again tomorrow.'

He turned and looked at her. There were narrow streaks of bronze in her hair and her lips looked lighter than her face, drawn in a long curved line that did not smile.

She lifted her brandy and nodded. She spoke softly, but it was as though her voice were on a different wavelength that sounded clear above the noise of the restaurant. 'I hope you will not lie to me, Monsieur Ingleby.'

CHAPTER 6

The white Simca drop-head was out in front, shrieking round the steep camber of the Corniche, past the sun-baked rocks on which the Arab bidonvilles grew: a rash of mud and corrugated-iron huts climbing up the raw earth to where the twelve-storey tenement blocks stood against the sky like mouth organs turned on end.

The car belonged to Anne-Marie; she was driving, with Neil beside her and Van Loon up in the casual seat buffeted by the hot salt wind. Lieutenant Morin and Pip were following in a red Austin Healey. Louis Rebot had had to leave them after lunch, taking — to Van Loon's dismay — Annette with him into the Cité de l'Université behind the barricades.

Van Loon now sat with his meerschaum jammed between his teeth, glowering out at the lines of Army trucks rattling up the Corniche towards the city. Anne-Marie cheered and waved at them, and most of the troops waved back. It was not clear whether they were Guérin's latest recruits from the dissident reservist battalions, or reinforcements belonging to General Metz. Probably many of the troops were not even sure themselves. They sat in tight rows facing inwards, craning their heads round to catch a glimpse of the pretty girls speeding past towards the beach.

Neil leant over and shouted to Anne-Marie above the slipstream, 'Shouldn't you be back behind the barricades too?'

She flashed her teeth at him, hair swirling across her face: 'We have time to enjoy ourselves first, don't worry!' Time to finish her game of bowls, Neil thought: with the white sands curving into the horizon and the oiled guns coming up the road under the palms.

The Casino de la Plage was at the end of a private beach protected by barbed wire to keep the Arabs out. It looked like a Georgian mansion done up by Oliver Messel for the Shah of Persia, surrounded by a screen of bleached palms. There was a dance hall, a restaurant and gaming rooms and a terraced bar built out of bamboo poles where waiters in Mexican-style shirts shook up genuine mint juleps and daiquiris in frosted glasses at up to nine Nouveaux-Francs a time. Paths of coconut matting ran out across the scorching sands to the sea edge.

At this hour the place was quiet. The thé dansant did not begin for another hour. Neil and Van Loon hired bathing trunks and joined the other two under a sunshade on the sands. Anne-Marie wore strips of white bikini which showed up her dark body until Neil had to look away almost in pain. Pip lay provocatively on her front with her feet in the air, smoking Philip Morrises which she offered to no one while Lieutenant Carlos Morin, a polished muscular brown, rested his head on her splendid buttocks and read a back number of *L'Equipe.* He had brought a transistor radio with him which later in the afternoon played a pirate broadcast by General Guérin: long and metaphysical, promising France a renaissance of dignity and self-respect. It finished with Le Chant des Africains, followed by the thundering drumbeat of the Marseillaise. The sea was warm and calm and they swam and raced each other down the sands, while Van Loon sat like some Nordic seer, sucking his meerschaum and casting looks of haunted desire in the direction of Anne-Marie and Pip.

Neil swam out beyond the barbed wire barricade and called Anne-Marie after him; together they walked along the edge of the breaking sea, their bare feet pressing the spongy brown sand into pools of whiteness. The beach here was deserted. They came to a line of black rocks that ran out to sea, sheltering the sands from the scum of the city harbour. There was an abandoned pillbox higher up the rocks, its concrete wall scrawled with the words '*Vive Le Front Arabe!*'

Anne-Marie stopped: 'Come on, let's get away from here! The Moslems come to this part of the beach sometimes.' She took his arm and they started back towards the barbed wire.

He looked down at her body: at the swelling breasts and deep fold in the rounded belly, and her long thighs streaked with threads of salt. He put his arm round her, and her skin felt like hot silk in the sun. His emotions were confused, blunted by the heat and wine and events of the morning. His moral indignation at the slaughter he had seen earlier was beginning to ebb away. He found he could not judge these people by civilized standards. They were cruel and physical, they killed their fellow beings as a farmer kills rabbits. But they were friendly and attractive, and their simple passion for life was infectious. They believed only in the sun and health and the beauty of their own bodies. He wondered what would happen now if he kissed Anne-Marie.

They sat down on the wet sand with the surf curling round them, and she told him that she was an only child and that her father had been killed in Indo-China. Her mother had gone to France until the crisis was over, and Anne-Marie lived with her stepfather in a flat that was now behind the barricades. She was a student in her second year at the university, studying economics and political theory.

He looked at her, sitting there in the slanting sun with her knees drawn up under her chin and the sea-foam clinging to her toes and the edges of her bikini. Studying for Tripos Part

One, he thought: Right-wing Revolutionary Theory: practice, terrorism and murder.

She did not discuss her love life and he did not ask her. She had been to France once, for a summer, to Paris and Tours, and for a weekend on the Riviera, but had not liked it. 'They are all snobs over there,' she told him, 'they look down their noses at us — they think we are just stupid colonialists. Do they think the same thing in England?'

'Most people in England don't know about it,' he said carefully; 'this country doesn't mean much to them.'

'But what about Rhodesia?' she said. 'It will be the same there, with all those Africans attacking women with knives and trying to take over the country. I heard that in Kenya the blacks used to cut open pregnant women and eat their babies.'

He gave a shudder: 'No, Anne-Marie, those are atrocity stories, they are made up by one side against the other. Things like that may have happened occasionally, but they're very isolated incidents.'

'Isolated!' she cried; 'you should see what happens here. Almost every day. When they catch a French soldier or a European farmer in the Bled, they tie him down and cut off his manhood.' She looked pointedly between his legs: 'How would you like that to happen to you?' But without waiting for him to answer, she sprang up and ran leaping into the waves. He followed her, feeling the hopeless gap of understanding between them as they swam past the barbed wire to join the others on the beach.

Lieutenant Morin's transistor was twanging out canned jazz; it stopped for an official Government bulletin declaring the situation 'normal'. There was no mention of the reservists going over to Guérin. 'They are frightened to tell us about it,' said Anne-Marie, 'never believe anything the Government says, they tell only lies.'

Van Loon came prowling along the beach, his hair stiff with salt and his eyes scouring the sands for lone girls. He slumped down on the towel beside Neil. 'Those bloody girls,' he muttered, 'all completely monopolized! You are lucky, old fellow. You have Anne-Marie. You take her back to the hotel — one bottle of wine and you are O.K.'

Neil lay in the sun and tried to drive out memories of Caroline on the beach at Ostia last summer: motoring back into Rome for a lazy dinner at Alfredo's.

They dressed and went into the Casino. There was a dancefloor not much bigger than a card table, with a five-man band in sombreros playing a vigorous repertoire of Twist, Cha-Cha, Madison and Twist again. It was crowded and dark, even at five in the afternoon, and Neil and Anne-Marie danced for a long time. She moved beautifully. When the music stopped they stood with their fingers curled together, listening to the ivory ball clicking round the roulette wheel.

Later they went down and played: he cautiously, betting only on columns of dozens, and she with reckless panache, placing ten N.F. plaques on single numbers, quickly losing the equivalent of nearly twenty pounds. He had won about three. She came away in a black temper and he bought her a half-bottle of champagne on his winnings. Their table was empty, stacked with Coca-Cola bottles and piled ashtrays. Lieutenant Morin and Pip had gone back to the city in their Austin Healey; and Van Loon was at the bar drinking elaborate cocktails he could not afford.

'We ought to go,' said Neil, 'in case something happens.'

She shook her head: 'If something is going to happen, Monsieur Ingleby' — she still called him Monsieur Ingleby — 'we will know about it.'

'Supposing the Army tries to break the barricades?'

'We will know that too. Our intelligence service is very good. Nothing is going to happen today.'

They finished the champagne and wandered through to the terrace where they caught a glimpse of Van Loon bent over a glass full of fruit and green leaves. 'He seems very sad, your Dutch friend,' she said, as they walked out on to the cooling sands.

'His girl left him back in Holland,' said Neil, 'he needs someone to console him.'

She smiled: 'He should be able to find someone here. There are thousands of girls! We are a very warm-hearted people, Monsieur Ingleby — we don't have hearts of stone like you Anglo-Saxons!'

She gave his arm a squeeze that might have been just in fun, but sent a quick needle of excitement up his spine.

'Are you married?' she said suddenly.

He turned and saw the sly whites of her eyes smiling at him. He shook his head.

'You ought to get married,' she said; 'you are a nice man, I like you. Why haven't you got married?'

He laughed without humour: 'I haven't found anybody.'

The sun was hanging low and the sea broke lazily along the sand. She stopped and took out a packet of cigarettes. She gave him one and bent forward till he caught the scent of her hair. There was no breeze. He struck the match and held it to her cigarette. He could hear the thump of music from the Casino: 'Twist! Twist! Everybody's doing the…' The tip flared and went out. The cigarette flicked from her mouth and the box of matches was torn from his fingers. He stared at her and her face jerked out of his vision and was gone, reflected only in his memory. The music and the sea had stopped and the setting sun had turned black and the air was beaten with thundering waves of noise that pressed his head like an orange about to burst.

His mouth was full of sand. His back ached against the beach which was rocking under him, and all round him was a red darkness pierced by a wailing sound, rising and falling, growing louder, till he recognized the scream of an ambulance siren.

He crawled on to his knees and looked up at the Casino. There were dim figures jerking about in a fog of brown smoke. Anne-Marie had gone. He was alone on the beach. He began walking lamely up the coconut matting towards the splintered bamboo shoots and the shrieks and smell of burning. His shoes crunched on glass and torn palm fronds; a young man bumped into him yelling; two soldiers hurried past carrying something on a stretcher. The doors into the gaming-room had been smashed like matchwood. He went through into the choking smoke and sound of weeping and groaning and men shouting orders. The roulette table had sunk down at an angle and vomit dribbled over the red and black diamonds of impair and manque with the wheel broken loose, propped up on the sleeve of a dinner-jacket white with plaster. There was a face under the table and Neil's foot slipped on something wet; then a fierce light cut through the chaos, swinging over the wreckage and rising dust, and he saw at the end of the room, where the orchestra and dance floor had been, the ceiling sagging down in a canopy of plaster and lattice-work, splashed in one corner with what looked like squashed grapes.

He picked his way through a forest of table-legs and smashed bottles and jagged strips of flooring and half a double bass, the torn wood a bright naked colour against the varnish. He came to the edge of the dais where the orchestra had stood. Through the settling dust, which shone in the searchlight beams like falling snow, he could just make out odd shapes lumped together against the wall. He stopped and thought about Anne-Marie, and about Van Loon who had been at the bar behind the collapsed ceiling. Just in front of him, next to a table, lay a woman's leg severed above the knee; the bloodied stocking trailed away under the table like the skin of a liver-sausage. The carpet was scattered with spilt cigarette butts, many of them marked with lipstick.

Neil turned giddily away, tripping over a fallen chair. He put out his hand to stop himself falling and touched the wall. It was sticky with a red stain that extended from the floor to above his head. A French officer was standing beside him, steadying him by the arm. Neil stared at the smear on his hand and heard the officer mutter, '*Ce nest pas du vin rouge, Monsieur!*'

CHAPTER 7

'They must have used two or three hundred kilos of the stuff,' said the doctor; 'I've counted twenty-seven dead already.' He turned to Neil, speaking with quiet fury: 'Monsieur le journalist, you write it all down — all of it!' He swept his arm round the wrecked hall. 'This is what the Arabs do to us! This is what the United Nations are asking us to put up with! — to live with these people! — these assassins!'

Neil looked down at Van Loon, feeling a sudden anger against the doctor. What right had he to start ranting about politics now? The Dutchman lay on the floor with his head resting against a corner of the bar, his arms folded in his lap. His eyes were open and he grinned at Neil with a glazed blue look. He was very drunk. When the bomb had exploded he had been at the end of his seventh Bacardi cocktail. He had woken up on the floor with one of the bamboo poles through his back. The doctor had given him a jab of morphine; the bamboo had pierced his intestine.

He gave a hoarse giggle: 'Hey, Neil, I did not pay for any of those bloody drinks!'

'Try not to talk,' said Neil.

The doctor said, 'I'll speak to one of the ambulance men. You're both staying at the Miramar, aren't you?'

'Hey, give me a drink!' cried Van Loon.

'You mustn't drink,' said Neil. He leant down and looked sadly at the Dutchman; there was blood seeping out of his mouth into his beard. 'How do you feel?' he said.

'Oh I would like a drink, old fellow!' he muttered, 'I would like some ouzo.' He smiled: 'I should have gone to Beirut. I would have found lots of girls in Beirut.'

Neil tried to smile back, then hurried off to fetch the doctor again. He found him standing near the smashed roulette table, giving orders to some stretcher-bearers. The man turned impatiently; he was middle-aged with a grey-chopped head as round as a football. 'What do you want?' he snapped.

'My Dutch friend,' said Neil, 'he's bleeding badly.'

The doctor threw up his hands: 'What do you expect? He has an abdomen wound. Everyone is bleeding.' His face was exhausted, miserable. 'I'm sorry,' he added, 'but there's nothing I can do until we get him to hospital. There are more than a hundred as bad as him.'

'Can I give him something to drink? Some cognac?'

'If you want to kill him,' said the doctor.

Neil went back to the broken bar and found Anne-Marie bending over Van Loon. He was smiling up at her and asking her for a drink.

'Don't give him anything,' Neil whispered; 'the doctor's already seen him. They're taking him to hospital.'

She nodded. Her face was a dull white under her suntan, her eyes round and wild.

'Are you all right?' he said.

'Yes, I'm all right.' She looked round the room and her face quivered. 'This is the work of Ali La Joconde,' she said softly, 'this is the sort of thing he does — then they call a patriot like General Guérin a traitor!'

Neil grabbed her arm. Van Loon had closed his eyes again and his face had suddenly turned the colour of a mushroom. 'Peter!' he called, grasping one of his huge limp hands. Van

Loon opened one eye and muttered, 'I must have another bloody drink.'

'You can't, you crazy Dutchman. Just lie still. The ambulance is coming.'

'Bloody ambulance,' Van Loon growled, 'where is that girl Annette? I want her.'

Anne-Marie took his other hand and said gently, 'We'll find her. She'll come and see you in hospital.'

He smiled, his eyes closed, and they both sat with him waiting for the ambulance until he died.

Neil went out to see the doctor, feeling numb and baffled and wanting to cry. He passed a magazine rack near the door full of back numbers of *Paris Match* and *Elle* and *Ciné* with lumps of red meat stuck between the crumpled, blasted pages. The vendeuse was lying under the counter. He did not look. In the twilight outside the grasshoppers had started up.

PART 4: THE KILLERS

CHAPTER 1

Neil poured out two glasses from the bottle of Hine, just as he had done twenty-four hours ago for agent-extraordinary Charles Pol, a dangerous naked man spilling talcum powder on the carpet. This time it was for Anne-Marie; he could hear her slow splashing behind the bathroom door. Her crimson dress lay over a chair caked with dust and plaster.

The perfect host, he thought: impartial, easy-going, handing out drinks to both sides. He sat on the bed staring at his bare feet. He had put his shoes outside for the Moslem floor waiter to clean. They had picked up a lot of blood.

His skin burned taut with the sun, his back was bruised and aching, he felt weak in the legs and needed a drink badly. He tried not to think about Van Loon. They had waited at the Casino till the ambulance came to take the body to the Municipal Hospital; then he had driven Anne-Marie back in the Simca. She had wept silently all the way, with the moon coming up and the palms sighing past along the twisting edge of the Corniche. They had only just arrived before the curfew fell; it had been advanced to nine o'clock to prevent riots following the Casino bombing. The news had already spread through the city and large crowds had formed, roaming the streets waiting for something to happen. But nothing had happened. The Gardes Mobiles and CRS troops had been slightly strengthened; the barricades stood firm; there were small outbreaks of shooting in the suburbs; and a rumour was about that two of the colonels commanding the reservists had been arrested.

For the fourth night of the revolt a sullen calm lay over the city.

Neil sipped his medicinal helping of brandy and waited for Anne-Marie. He had booked two telephone calls to London: one to his office to give the story of the bombing while the impact was still fresh in his mind, the other to Caroline, to be put through after midnight, trusting that she was not out at Brad's or The 400. Calling her now seemed a superfluous, egotistical gesture, but he needed somebody to talk to — somebody removed as far as possible from this butchery and madness. He knew Caroline could be relied upon to say something utterly irrelevant and frivolous, but it was better than listening to the dismal passion of the doctor at the Casino, or even to Anne-Marie. With Caroline there was something very refreshing about her silliness.

Anne-Marie came in from the bathroom wearing a towelling robe and sat beside him on the bed, not too close. He gave her the glass of brandy, and she took it without looking at him, her face quiet with sudden translucent purity. After a pause she murmured, 'I shouldn't be here.'

'You can't get back behind the barricades now,' he said, 'we can order cold supper up here. They do very good chicken and salads. And we can have a bottle of wine.'

She nodded, still not looking at him. 'I want to get drunk,' she said, 'in the bath I washed myself all over three times, but it didn't seem to make any difference.' She looked round at him, her eyes sad, without violence or passion: 'You don't like the Secret Army, do you? You don't know what it really stands for, what it's trying to do?' Her glass was almost empty; he poured her some more. She went on, 'Can you imagine what it's like for us here? For five years the Government tells us we are French — that they will defend this country. Then one day they turn to us and say they are going to hand us all over to people like Ali La Joconde and his friends. Can't you understand what we feel — what it will be like for us when men like that get into power?'

He stared back at his feet, not knowing what to say, and she went on: 'You don't like us, do you? You think the same about us as everyone else?'

He looked up at her and frowned. 'This morning,' he said, 'your people murdered an old man with a wooden leg outside this hotel. Can't you understand what sort of impression that makes on us? How can we like you when you do things like that?'

'He was probably an Arab Front spy.'

'Oh for God's sake!' he cried. 'He was selling cigarettes to keep himself alive!'

'Many of their spies do that. It's one of their favourite tricks. They find old beggars with wooden legs and send them down here to report on us.'

He said nothing; he could no longer be bothered to argue. It didn't seem to matter anyway, something had gone tragically wrong in this country and there was nothing he could do about it. It only worried him to realize that in a funny way he liked Anne-Marie and her friends. He wondered whether they would receive the same hospitality if they were to arrive suddenly in England. He tried to imagine her and Lieutenant Morin and Pip putting up at the Dorchester and seeing some old man selling the *Evening Standard* shot in Park Lane.

He poured more brandy, and she slid her hand along the bed and touched his with her cool brown fingers. 'Try to understand,' she said, 'I was brought up a Catholic. My father was not born in this country — he came from France. He was a very good man. He believed deeply and I used to go to church every Sunday. That was when I was a little girl. Then he was killed and my mother married again. My stepfather is very strong and brave but he is not such a good Catholic. He is one of those people who doesn't know whether God exists or not.'

'An agnostic,' said Neil.

'Yes, that's right. After he married my mother I stopped going to church so often. In this country we are not very religious, and when I went to the university I began doing things that are not allowed. I mean, sometimes I went to bed with other students. I don't think that is really wrong — not if you like them.'

He looked at her quickly: her face was pale and absurdly earnest. She went on: 'My stepfather is with the Secret Army. He is very serious about it. But when we started killing the Moslems last year I was worried. I felt like you did this morning. I was shocked. I went to the priest and he told me that the only way to defend ourselves and to defend the Christian faith was to fight the Moslems. He was right, because all we are doing now is what they are doing to us. There was never any trouble until they started killing Europeans — like they did at the Casino today. We didn't start the terrorism — they did!'

'The priest told you all this?' said Neil.

She nodded: 'He said what my stepfather says — what everybody here says. Even the Archbishop is with the Secret Army.' Her glass was empty again. He began refilling it, but she held his arm: 'You're trying to get me drunk?'

'You said you wanted to get drunk?'

'Not yet. Let's eat first.' Her face was almost touching his. He turned away, picked up the telephone and ordered consommé, chicken and lobster-in-the-basket for two, with a bottle of Chablis. As he spoke she squeezed his arm. Her eyes had a dry glitter in them. She suddenly smiled. He bent forward and kissed her on the cheek. Her skin was cold and she did not move.

He sat back feeling awkward, frightened to go too far, desiring her with the fumbling, heart-thumping lust of an adolescent. He realized that he found the prospect of making love to a member of the Secret Army faintly terrifying.

She sat crouched forward beside him, holding her glass in both hands. He poured her a small drop: 'As an aperitif,' he said.

She nodded. There was a pause. 'I'm sorry about your Dutch friend,' she said, 'he was a nice boy. It must be terrible to see someone you know die like that. Did you know him well?'

'Not very. We met about a couple of weeks ago going round some monasteries in Greece.' He said it idly, without thinking, and for a moment did not realize the effect his words had had on her. The glass stopped at her lips and her whole body stiffened. He turned and looked at her. There was a shocked, bleak look in her eyes. The bathrobe had fallen carelessly open and he saw, with distracted interest, that she was naked.

They stared at each other and Neil gulped down his drink.

'So you were on Mount Athos?' she said, almost in a whisper.

Neil said nothing; he leant back against the pillows, seeing the dark curves of her body under the white towelling. She put her glass down on the table, and with a slow deliberate movement stood up and faced him, drawing the edges of the bathrobe round her.

'I don't understand,' she said, 'you're an Englishman — you have no reason to interfere in our affairs. Why are you working for this man Pol? Why have you chased us from Greece? And why do you play the fool with me, giving me cognac in your bedroom when you know…?' Her voice caught and he thought she was going to cry.

He said: 'You're wrong. I'm not chasing you. I was on Athos for a holiday and they arrested me in Athens because they thought I was somebody else.'

'That's not what you told Colonel Le Hir.'

'I know it's not.' He realized that it was hopeless to lie to her now, she knew too much. He began telling her about his meeting with Broussard; he had reached the incident of the lost coin at Zographou when she bent forward, her hands on his shoulders, and cried, 'Oh God, I don't know what to do! Please, tell me what to do? I don't want all this killing!' Her voice now had the cracked edge of hysteria. He put his arms round her and looked into her face, saying, 'It's all right, it's all right,' patting the small of her back as though placating an overwrought child.

She drew closer to him, pressing her belly against his cheek, and said again, her voice trembling with unshed tears, 'I don't want all this killing! But they will kill you if they find out!'

He pushed her away and stood up: 'Find out what?'

She still clung to him, her face turned aside: 'Everything! Everything you've just told me!'

'But I've explained. I met Broussard on Athos — it was a coincidence.'

'No! No!' She shook her head violently; her whole body shuddered against him: 'They are very suspicious. They won't believe you. You are mad to have come here. Oh please go away! If they find out you were on Athos they will know you are a barbouze working for the fat man.'

'But can't you tell them I'm not?' He tried to keep the fear out of his voice. This was worse than he had expected: 'Can't you tell Le Hir and Broussard?'

She looked at him, her fingers digging into his shoulder blades: 'It won't do any good. He won't listen to me. He never listens to me. If he finds out I am here it will be terrible for me!'

'Who? Le Hir?'

She shook her head and began to sob.

'Broussard?'

She gave a choking cry and let go of him, sinking down on to the bed with her face in her hands.

'Broussard?' he repeated, almost savagely.

She turned her face up to him, crumpled, desperate, shouting, 'Go away! Go away, please, before they kill you!' — then suddenly reached out and touched his hand: 'You are very *sympathique*! I like you very much, but go away!'

He turned and poured another brandy. She was sobbing hysterically now, curled up with her face to the wall. He gave her the brandy, but she pushed it away. He drank it himself. There was something here he did not understand: something she was frightened of, and was hiding from him. Perhaps he was not the only one who was in danger.

Telling her about Mount Athos had been a serious error. The only thing he could now do was to wait until she was calmer, then try to persuade her to keep the information to herself. He assumed that she was only a minor figure in the Secret Army: a pretty public relations girl specializing in the foreign Press. He hoped that, like most public relations people, her loyalties could be corrupted.

There was a knock on the door. The same Moslem from yesterday bowed himself in, grinning with gold tusks, and put the dinner tray on the table by the bed. Anne-Marie stirred round and saw him and gave him a venomous look, pointing towards the chair. 'Take that dress downstairs,' she ordered, 'and have it cleaned! I want it by nine o'clock tomorrow morning.'

The man bowed again and collected the dress off the chair. '*Sale umbe!*' she said, as the door closed. Neil knew the futility of trying to convert her, of trying to defend a hapless servant who was likely to be shot because he stayed at work to keep his family from starving. Nothing he could say would measure up to the gang of Moslems who had hidden three hundred kilos of plastic explosive under the bandstand, fused to go off at the height of thé dansant.

They sat side by side and started on the consommé. 'You caught the sun today,' she said, 'your nose is red.'

He smiled and poured out the Chablis. There was a strained silence between them. The wine had a chilled iron taste, and after the third glass he said, 'Anne-Marie, you will have to trust me. You will have to believe me — even if your leaders won't.'

She said nothing, chewing a lump of white lobster meat.

'I cannot leave this city until the airport opens again. That may not be until tomorrow night — even later. And you realize that if you tell your people about Athos before I can get on to a plane —' He paused. 'Well, you know even better than I do what'll happen.'

She nodded, her black eyes slightly dimmed with wine and cognac. 'That was a good meal,' she whispered, pushing the tray away.

'Anne-Marie, you haven't answered me. Are you going to tell them about Athos?'

She took a deep breath and stretched out her legs, wriggling her toes: 'Let's discuss it tomorrow. I don't want to talk about it now.' She looked at him and her mouth turned down into a shy smile: 'Let's drink some more wine.' She leant out and brushed her cheek against his, sliding her mouth round till her tongue touched his teeth.

'Anne-Marie,' he murmured, 'do you really believe I'm a barbouze?'

She drew up her legs, pressing her thighs against him, her face tilted back: 'I don't know.' Her voice had begun to thicken: 'I don't want to think about it. *Je m'emmerde des barbouzes.*'

He pulled her up to him and her mouth opened wide and her body closed against him, his hands rubbing down the rough towelling to the fold of her buttocks. But she broke from him and cried, 'No, wait, wait! Take away all this food first.'

He carried the tray outside the door. When he came back she was walking naked to the bed. The bathrobe lay over the chair where her dress had been, and she slipped under the single sheet and lay looking at the ceiling. He sat beside her, lit her a cigarette, not very steadily, and passed it down to her, wondering, with a vague sense of dismay, whether this too was part of the Secret Service ritual.

He poured himself another Hine and waited. After a moment she said, 'You know, if I loved you I would let you do anything to me. Anything you liked.'

He wished he could enjoy this scene more. In less than an hour he would have to dictate 500 words to his office in London, while on his bed lay a beautifully naked girl who needed to say only a couple of sentences to have him shot. She pushed back the sheet and curled against him, and he said, with a sense of tactics, 'You don't love me, Anne-Marie.'

'No.' She reached up and grabbed him by the neck, pulling his face down clumsily against hers. He remembered her taunts about Anglo-Saxons and kissed her on the mouth, then took hold of her breasts, transparent bluish-white against her dark shoulders and belly, and kissed the hard brown nipples, carefully, till he felt her tremble. He wondered again, with a closed part of his mind, whether she were acting on the orders of Le Hir or Broussard.

'You are very sensuous,' she said, 'I think I am rather drunk. Is there any more cognac?'

'A little.' He picked up the bottle. 'I've got some work to do,' he added.

'All right, you do some work.' She lay with her eyes closed, knees drawn up under her chin. He poured her another brandy and went over to the table to type his 500 words on the Casino bombing. When he had finished she was already asleep, the empty glass still in her hand. He lay on the bed beside her and began checking through his story, then rang down to Hudson, having the call put through to the hotel restaurant.

'Hello — Hudson? This is Ingleby.'

'You still here?'

'I can't get out — the airport's closed.'

'Oh yeah, I heard.'

'Can you give me the latest official casualty figures from the Casino de la Plage?'

There was a pause. 'A.F.P. put over between thirty-eight and forty-five. There's nothing definite yet. What have you heard?'

Neil hesitated. If he announced that he had been an eyewitness to the disaster, he'd have the whole Press Corps up in his room in five minutes. There was nothing he could tell them except that he was about to sleep with a member of the Secret Army. He told Hudson, 'The Arab Front put a bomb under the orchestra and blew the whole place up.'

'That's what I heard. By the way, are you getting out when the airport's clear?'

Neil said nothing.

'I heard another rumour, that's all,' said Hudson.

'What did you hear?'

'That you'd been meeting up today with some more big noises in the Secret Army.'

'Hudson, are you jealous?'

'What the hell do you mean?'

'Have you got any contacts at all in this place?'

'Listen, Ingleby, I thought I'd tried to get through your thick damned English skull —'

'You keep your contacts, Hudson, I'll keep mine!' Neil slammed down the receiver. Anne-Marie stirred beside him. He lay back and lit a cigarette, picturing to himself Hudson's nervous little face bouncing about, scrapping for information, always eager to scare his colleagues. Perhaps it was the cognac and Chablis, but he had decided he would not just tamely obey the windy advice of Messrs. Hudson and St. Leger. He remembered his rendezvous the next morning at ten o'clock at the Cintra Café and wondered what would happen if he didn't turn up. If he did turn up, of course, he was jumping right into the fire. But the Hine was warm in his belly and the prospect of that café was not as fearful as perhaps it should have been. He still had twelve hours in which to make up his mind.

Anne-Marie stretched out along the bed and laid her hand casually, innocently, between his legs. 'Get undressed,' she said.

He put out his cigarette and switched off the bedside lamp. The moon was bright over the balcony. He undressed quickly and lay down beside her, and her mouth crept down his chest, over his stomach, lips fluttering against his raw skin. She said nothing; but with the dexterity of her race, a pairing of competence and delicacy, began caressing him, as he lay back and felt himself harden with her touch, watching the cubes of moonlight on the ceiling.

The telephone rang. It was London via Paris; the Fleet Street operator came on the line. Anne-Marie shifted slowly, like a smooth dark animal, her back curving away along his line of vision as he switched on the light again and settled himself ready to dictate.

Foster, the Foreign Editor, was on the line: 'Must have been pretty frightful. Reuters say it's the worst atrocity since the troubles began.'

'Sounds about right,' said Neil; 'There are no definite figures, but I've heard there were more than forty dead.'

'Reuters give forty-seven. We'll go on that for the moment. What sort of reactions have there been?'

The connection was not good, Neil had to shout into the receiver: 'Very quiet so far!'

'Right, bang over everything you've got! And I've had a hundred pounds sent to the Credit Lyonnais to keep you going. Are you all right otherwise?'

'I'm all right!' Neil yelled, and Anne-Marie muttered, *'Tu cries comme un fou!'* — and went back to caressing him beautifully as Foster said, 'Putting you over to copy!'

The memory of the afternoon became a dull emptiness. Later, with the light out, she murmured, 'What a funny language English is! All in your nose.' And as he splayed her arms wide across the sheet he thought guiltily of his second call to London, booked for midnight. He remembered how Caroline mewed in the dark like a kitten, and he tried to shut out her face, not asking Anne-Marie again if she loved him, but going into her savagely till she cried out and whimpered against the pillow, and later lay folded warm and wet against him, the sheet over them and the windows open, listening to the sounds beyond the balcony: the booms and sirens and the soft chatter of gunfire and grasshoppers.

CHAPTER 2

Neil sat with a black coffee and croissant, alone in the café except for the waiter wiping down the zinc bar beside the expresso machine. The time was 10.12. He had left Anne-Marie in the hotel combing out her hair in front of the balcony windows. At exactly nine o'clock her dress had been returned by the Moslem, faultlessly washed and ironed. She had not paid him.

Neil had pressed some money into his hand outside the door, and before leaving had telephoned the Dutch Legation and told them he wanted to attend Van Loon's funeral. He had arranged to meet Anne-Marie for lunch in Le Berry restaurant at half past one. He had then left the hotel, followed the street round to the Roxy Cinema, and entered the Café Cintra.

He knew, with a sense of perverse pleasure, that in the next few minutes he would reach the point of no return. To have slept with Anne-Marie might be one thing: to deceive her in this ugly game of fratricidal strife was almost certainly fatal.

He sat over his coffee with a sensation of having been drugged against the effects of acute physical pain. At this moment all he wanted was some means of immediate, violent escape: something to get him through the next few hours, days, to stop him thinking, stop him remembering what he had heard in the early hours of the morning. He had come here to find adventure, and he was going to get it.

His midnight call to London had come through at a quarter to three. The number had taken a long time to answer. When it did, Caroline was yawning with sleep, telling him she was going to marry Tommy Drummond next Saturday. He had started to yell at her, and she had said drowsily, 'No darling, I'm serious.' He had bawled into the mouthpiece, 'You must be mad!' and she had said, 'I'm very fond of him, and you haven't written to me for over a month.'

'I was in a monastery!' he had protested. 'I'm stuck in the middle of a revolution!' — and she had said, 'Oh darling, it's too late and I'm so sleepy' — and he had tried to plead with her, her voice fading with long-distance whines and hummings, as he fought to change her mind, to postpone it, to make her wait till he got back. And far away, beyond the bay and the barricades, she had said, 'Neil darling, I've made up my mind. Really, I love Tommy.' And so it had gone on, while Anne-Marie slept through it all, the sheet wound round her like a shroud; and all he wanted was Caroline, and in a week's time Caroline would be stepping out in white (in white, if you please!) to be married at Holy Trinity, Brompton.

The man came up to the table and bowed: 'Monsieur Ingleby?' He smiled, holding out a gloved hand: a tall, pale man of about thirty, with rimless glasses, no tie, carrying a raincoat over his left arm. 'I haven't time for coffee,' he added, before Neil had spoken, 'the car's outside.'

Neil left some money on the table and followed him into the street in a state of febrile exhilaration.

'The weather seems to have improved for your visit,' the man said, steering the car along the Front de Mer, 'we've been having a lot of fog lately.' He drove carefully, without hurrying. They turned up from the sea into the main shopping boulevard, past names like Windsor, Guerlain, Mercedes Benz, across a great square and into a hive of dark streets, between arcades peeling with posters, deep in garbage, where Neil saw for the first time Moslems mixing with Europeans — mostly old men with turbans like dirty bandages, shuffling between fruit stalls. This was a fringe area of European and Arab streets just below the Casbah. There were many killings here.

They were stopped by the CRS at a movable barbed wire barricade. The street beyond narrowed into a steep alley. It was very quiet. The driver flashed a plastic disc at the CRS officer who saluted, peering curiously at Neil, then ordered the barbed wire to be rolled back. The car moved forward, its engine growling softly. Steel-shuttered doors stood on either side, bolted down into the flagstones, and barred windows looked down from the swelling walls below a strip of sky far above.

The driver nosed the car along at walking pace, scraped round a corner and stopped with the window on Neil's side opposite an iron door fitted with a Yale lock.

He pointed with his gloved hand: 'You go through there. I'll be waiting here with the car. You won't be more than an hour.' Neil tried to fight down the rising fear: 'Where is this?' His hand tightened round the hot upholstery.

'You have nothing to worry about,' said the driver, 'just knock on the door. I'll be waiting here.'

Neil opened the car door. A cat flicked across the street a few yards away. He stood up and closed the door, not banging it, and something moved behind one of the barred windows above. He thought, in a mad moment, of the crowds at Brand's Hatch: woollen caps and fumes and pretty girls jumping out of Lotuses.

You should see me now, Caroline, he thought grimly, and rapped on the iron door.

It was opened by a man with a complexion like a slice of brown bread. He wore a khaki shirt and his eyes were flat and slanting. He looked at Neil, at the driver, then stepped aside. Neil followed him across a bare stone room like a cellar, up some steps and into an alley that climbed under the mouth of an arch.

The air had a thick musky taste: of charcoal and sweet ripe fruit and mutton fat, and the bitter acid taste of urine and pepper spicing and cheap black tobacco. The ground shelved upwards over sloping stones, wet and slippery, into a web of turnings and steps and tunnels under the baked mud, past miniature doors and arabesques smooth with age and sudden corners of shining white against a patch of sky.

Tiny sounds pierced the stillness: whispered voices, quick quiet movements, chimes like water dripping in a cave. A radio twanged and wailed somewhere behind the maze of walls. The alley widened and they walked on earth strewn with palm fronds. Spears of light filtered through the latticed roof, on to men in brown jellabahs sipping mint tea and chattering peacefully. Young men in khaki watched from the shadows; children peered at them, boys with shorn grey heads and girls with hair stained copper-red.

They ducked down into another tunnel where water moved in the darkness: through a door where Neil had to bend almost, double, and up four flights of stairs into a wooden room with a Coca-Cola calendar and a big dark girl behind an old-fashioned typewriter that looked like the ribcage of a dead bird.

The guide led him across the room and shouted something in Arabic through a closed door. A face of smooth brown leather jerked round, examined Neil, and held the door open. The guide did not follow.

Neil went into a high room with latticed windows that shut out the sun. An oil lamp in a glass bowl hung from the ceiling, there were low couches along the walls draped with handwoven rugs. Three men sat round a table drinking mint tea off a tray of hammered brass. They rose together and bowed to Neil. One of them, a graceful man in a pale flannel suit with hawk's eyes, made room beside him on the couch.

'I am Dr. Marouf,' he said, handing him a glass of tea. He turned to a plump man on his left: 'This is Mohammed Abdel Boussid' — a moist face behind green pebble-glasses bobbed forward, unsmiling — 'and this is Mohammed Sherrif.'

A sallow man with a pointed head of knitted hair, sitting on Neil's left, bent forward with a sad smile and said, in almost a whisper, '*Enchanté, m'sieur!*' His eyes were like pools of oil that caught strange prisms of light. He was dressed in a threadbare blue suit with a faded pin-stripe and a grimy shirt with no collar or tie. His hands were thin and dry, with a papery whiteness.

Dr. Marouf opened the conversation. He explained that he and Boussid were members of the Arab Front Political Bureau in the Casbah. Mohammed Sherrif was responsible for 'defence and security'. 'We are not famous men,' he added, with self-effacing modesty, 'we are small people working for the good of our nation.'

Neil thought hard: Marouf, Boussid, Sherrif. Whatever the elegant doctor might say, Neil knew that the first two names had been on most of the French security police files for the last five years. He remembered that Dr. Marouf had escaped twice from prison, and rumour had it that he had been tortured by the paras. He looked at Neil now like a Harley Street surgeon discussing a diagnosis.

The one name that puzzled Neil was Sherrif. The man sat with his thin hands clasped between his knees, smiling with deep sadness at the brass tray.

Marouf said, 'We are greatly honoured to have a famous journalist from England to visit us.'

'Thank you,' Neil said, bowing and wondering what the hell Pol was playing at — Pol was a French agent: and these men were as much wanted by the French Government as were the leaders of the Secret Army — especially after the Casino bombing.

They talked gently, at great length, in wide spirals of thought, touching only obliquely on points of political passion, as when Marouf complained that the hospitals in the Casbah were hopelessly overcrowded and medicines destined from outside were seized by Secret Army commandos. They talked of patriotism and the unity of the people and the honour of manual work, like monks discussing faith and the Holy Spirit. Occasionally Marouf or Boussid would pause and ask Neil, with fierce earnestness, what he thought would happen in the country — did he think the Secret Army had any chance of winning? And if they did, would the British and Americans send in troops to help the Arab Front?

There was something oddly naive about them which both disarmed and rather worried Neil. He sipped his sweet green tea and said judiciously, 'I don't think the Secret Army has one chance in a million of winning. But nor do I think they can be beaten so easily. They are as much a popular movement among the Europeans here as you are among the Moslems. They are only saying what you are saying — that the country belongs to them. These Europeans are determined to fight and kill in order to hold on to what they honestly believe is theirs.'

Boussid pursed his moist lips and replied, 'This country is not theirs. It is not France. It belongs to us. And one day the Europeans are going to understand that!'

The leather-faced man by the door refilled the little cups and Neil thought of the twin snakes of blood running down the boulevard: a woman's severed leg in the darkness, and Van

Loon groaning for a drink, dying with a pole through his guts. He said, in a feeble outburst of liberal righteousness, 'Killing innocent people will do no good — it will make no one free.'

'That is true!' Sherrif blurted suddenly on his left. 'But if killing does no good, what can we do to be free?' His eyes widened into great pools of sorrow and his lips, smiling their perpetual sad smile, began to quiver.

Neil thought he recognized the symptoms of a paranoiac. He said cautiously, wondering again why he had been called to this meeting, 'There are surely other methods besides killing and terrorism? You are only using the same methods as the Secret Army, and the Secret Army is going to lose.'

'But what else is there, m'sieur?' cried Sherrif. 'We are poor men — we do not have tanks and atom bombs!' His dry white fingers rustled together in his lap like dead leaves.

'There is world opinion,' Neil suggested, dubiously, 'that is on your side.'

'World opinion is one thing,' said Boussid, focusing upon Neil his tiny cod's-eyes behind their pebble-lenses, 'but alone it does not make us a free people. If we ever win our freedom it will be because we have used the weapons of war. There is no dishonour in that.'

Neil looked at the plump pouting lips, the unblinking eyes, and said recklessly, 'Was there no dishonour in what happened yesterday at the Casino de la Plage?'

From beside him came a whine like a wounded animal. He turned and saw Sherrif staring at him, the smile frozen on his lips, tears flowing like a child's down his yellow cheeks. Neil realized that the smile was the result of partial paralysis of the mouth.

'M'sieur, croyez-moi!' Sherrif cried. 'When I heard what had happened to those poor people in the Casino I wept — I

prayed for them, I could not sleep, I wept all night at the thought of them!'

Neil looked at him in dismay; a dreadful suspicion began to creep over him. 'I was there,' he said, 'I went in just after the bomb went off. I had a friend who was killed there — a Dutchman. He had nothing to do with this country. He and about forty other people who were enjoying themselves dancing in. the afternoon, harming no one, were murdered in cold blood. Do you really think that is how you are going to free your people?'

Sherrif put his hands over his ears and moaned: 'You call me a murderer! They all call me a murderer! I am not, m'sieur, I am not!' He stared at Neil with his dead smile and Neil stared back with a curious thrill of horror. This man was Ali La Joconde.

'If you were responsible for what happened at the Casino de la Plage,' Neil said, with a boldness that even astonished him as he spoke, 'then you are a murderer, Monsieur Sherrif.' He sat back, gripping his brass teacup, waiting. The polite preamble, the eastern ritual of barter, was over. There was a dead silence. It was broken by the sobbing of Ali La Joconde. Neil found the sound slightly obscene. He turned at last to Marouf: 'Doctor, why have I been asked to come here?'

The directness of the question upset Marouf; he looked awkwardly at his hands and made a little coughing noise. It was as though the Harley Street surgeon had been asked to perform an abortion.

It was Boussid who answered. He squinted through his green bifocals and said, 'In the last three days we have lost two hundred and forty dead — murdered by Fascist thugs in the streets on their way to work, on their way to buy food for their families. This is senseless slaughter, m'sieur. The Secret Army are foolish. They do not understand that their struggle is not with the Arab Front — it is with the French Government. Why do they send their terrorists against us — killing innocent working people, when their true enemies are sitting in Paris, in the High Command headquarters on the hill?'

Neil said, 'I cannot answer for the Secret Army. But it seems to me that they believe in terrorism for the same reasons that you do — to demoralize the population and destroy the rule of law.'

'That is so,' said Boussid, 'but the Arab Front are not the rule of law. We are peaceful people, we want to live in peace with everyone, including the Europeans in this country. We do not wish to go on killing Europeans, if they will only stop killing us.'

He spoke fluently, without the passion of Ali La Joconde. More tea was poured, and Boussid's words flowed in the smooth patter of a political PRO. Neil looked into the small cod's eyes, at the impassive Dr. Marouf and the sad smiling face of Mohammed Sherrif. 'Do I understand, messieurs,' he said slowly, 'that you wish to stop the terrorism?'

None of them around the brass table moved, except Sherrif who gave a little shudder. Boussid went on as though Neil had not spoken: 'The Secret Army is not our problem — it is an internal French problem which must be solved by the French. The Paris Government may soon grant us our independence. Then we will have no more quarrel with France. All we want is peace and freedom. Let us have peace with the Secret Army, and the Secret Army can be left to work out its own problems with the High Command and with Paris.'

'So you desire to make a truce with the Secret Army?' said Neil.

Boussid was silent. Dr. Marouf pressed his fingertips together and nodded. Ali La Joconde went on staring at the table, shuddering.

'The Secret Army don't know this?' asked Neil.

'No,' said Marouf.

'Does the French Government know?'

'We have no relations with the French Government,' said Marouf, 'that is why we have asked you here today.'

Neil paused, controlling his excitement. Boussid began to speak, softly, urgently: 'Monsieur, we are told that you are a man of some influence. You are British — you are not involved in the problems here. You can meet with the Secret Army, you can meet with us. If you can contact the leaders of the Secret Army, talk with them, explore their feelings, tell them that we wish to spare the innocent, then perhaps we can prevent a repetition of what happened yesterday at the Casino de la Plage. We cannot do this ourselves. The French will not do it for us. It must be done by someone like you.'

Neil sipped his tea and contemplated the role of Ingleby the Peacemaker. It satisfied most of his ambitions and a few of his fantasies. Secretly he had always hankered after fame, although the fame enjoyed by most public figures rather appalled him. He wanted to be seen as a remote romantic figure, aloof from publicity, going down in history as a lone force who called halt to murder and terrorism.

He liked the role. The only thing that worried him was Pol's part in it; but he did not bring this up now with Marouf or Boussid. It was a problem that could be tackled later. It was 11.52. He had been in the Casbah for nearly an hour. He remembered the car waiting outside and said, 'You want me to contact the Secret Army and tell them you are prepared to call a truce? Then what?'

'You will hear from us,' said Marouf.

Neil produced the packet of Chesterfields he had bought from the murdered Moslem outside the hotel, and offered it round. They hesitated; Marouf said, '*Ah, ce sont de vraies cigarettes americaines!*' Shyly he took one, followed by Boussid. Ali La Joconde shook his head, grinning tearfully at the table.

'We haven't seen American cigarettes here for nearly four years,' Marouf said, bringing out a Zippo lighter.

CHAPTER 3

The Yale lock snapped shut behind him. Neil was alone. The car was not outside. He felt a spasm of terror and looked up and down the alley.

It was about fifty yards away, near the corner, parked at a clumsy angle against the steel-shuttered doors. The man had promised to be waiting directly outside; perhaps he had gone away and got the doors confused when he returned.

Neil started up the alley, walking fast. It was the right car — a black Aronde. As he came closer he noticed that the offside wing had been crushed against the shutters. The driver sat with his head resting on the back of the seat. Neil came level and looked in.

The man's throat gaped open like a shark's mouth, bulbous and wine-red, with the severed cords glistening like dark streaks of bubble-gum. His rimless glasses had dropped into his lap and his eyes stared at the roof. Both hands were thrust out along the seat, fists clenched; and a sheet of paper splashed with blood was pinned to his shirt, with the scribbled words in biro: '*JE SUIS UNE BARBOUZE*'. Neil thought for a second, how odd the word should be feminine. The blood was still thick and wet.

Then he turned and ran. He reached the right-angled corner, slipping on a lump of squashed fruit, catching himself with his hands: stumbled up arid raced down the narrow street, his feet clattering between the high walls: feeling the sweat prickling on his face, his palms chafed raw with his fall, running on towards the CRS roadblock.

He took a second turning, dizzily, his bearings gone, seeing only another stretch of black arcades: dented dustbins and rinds of fruit and dreadful cats thin as wire, watching him, ready to flee.

He dodged back, trying frantically to remember where the CRS had been. He thought the car had taken two turnings, perhaps three. There were some railings on his left. They led to a long flight of steps into a little square far below lined with trimmed palms.

He started down, four steps at a time. There was a fountain in the square tinkling over mossy stones. He ran into another street heading down towards the sea. There was barbed wire in front of him; it stood six feet high, sunk into concrete blocks and riveted into the walls on either side. There were no CRS here, and no way out.

He doubled back into the square and tried a second turning. The street was crooked and ended on a plot of wasteland. He caught glimpses of the sea as he began leaping down the steep slope, loose tins and stones rolling away in front of him. Traffic hummed by in the street below. There was a wire fence about four feet high under a faded poster for Source Vittel. He clambered over the wire, ripping the inside of his trouser-leg.

There was a café on the corner. It was full of Europeans in blue overalls drinking wine and eating calimares. He went in and asked for a brandy. The barman seemed to look at him for a long time, scooping a dishcloth round the inside of a glass. He nodded slowly and turned to the bar. Neil could see himself being watched in the mirror as the man poured the drink. He looked at his own face, and it seemed to belong to someone else.

The barman came back with the brandy. '*Un franc dix*,' he said, looking Neil in the eye. He was a bald man in a soiled apron. Neil gave him the money and gulped down the drink. He put the glass on the counter and saw several people watching him. One of them moved forward. He turned, walked quickly towards the door. A voice shouted, '*Eh — monsieur.*'

He began to run, through the door and round the corner, into a lane crowded with orange barrows. He tried to think clearly, to keep his mind under control, imagining that he was a long-distance runner. He must not look back. Just keep running, steadily, without panic, dodging between the barrows, heading down towards the sea. Faces swept past: suspicious European faces, stubble-black and fanged with cigarette butts, turning to watch him. Someone backed out in front of him with a tray of oranges. They collided and the tray crashed to the pavement.

He ran on, with the oranges bouncing down the street beside him, hearing shouts behind him, as he turned off at the back of a covered stall, down a flight of steps that led into the main shopping boulevard. He came out by the Air France building and knew at last where he was.

No one followed him out of the opening up the steps; and gradually he began to relax, dragging himself down into the next street and along the last stretch to the Miramar.

The armoured cars were out, the iron-faced Gardes Mobiles behind their heavy weapons, and he felt suddenly reassured, protected. They couldn't chase him here.

He went into the Miramar, up in the cage-lift, along to his room. He wanted a shower and a cold beer, and it would be time to meet Anne-Marie for lunch at Le Berry. He unlocked the door and went through into the bedroom.

A face grinned at him from the window: 'Come in, have a drink!'

CHAPTER 4

He was a big man of about forty-five with beige hair going grey, and bright piggy-blue eyes set close to a wedge of broken nose. He sat with his back to the window, holding a glass of brandy in one hand and a long-barrelled pistol in the other. His fingers were thick and blunt with knuckles like doorknobs. On the floor by his foot lay the bottle of Hine which Neil and Anne-Marie had been drinking the night before. It was almost empty.

The second man lay on the bed, also drinking. He was young, very good-looking with a square blond crewcut and sly, arrow-shaped eyes. His mouth was long and thin. He wore jeans and a silver-blue windjammer.

The big man lifted his glass. 'Come in, have a drink!' he said again, in guttural French, the gun lying across his knee pointing at the floor.

Neil said, 'Help yourselves.' He leant against the wall, feeling very tired. The young man looked lazily at him and said in English, with the sort of American drawl that Americans never have, 'You're a bad guy, Englishman.' He shook his head theatrically.

'How did you get in?' said Neil.

The young one looked at his elder, and they grinned at each other like dogs. 'We got in,' said the big blond man, 'we have friends in the hotel.'

'All right,' said Neil, 'what do you want?'

The big man began to swing the pistol between his knees. The young one said, '*Er is ein dummer lump, glaub'ich!*' He looked back at Neil, still grinning: 'You been up in the Casbah?' He took a drink of brandy: 'What yer been doing up there?'

'I'm a journalist,' Neil began.

'We know you're a journalist,' said the young one, 'what you think we been doing in yer goddam room for half an hour?'

'It's my job to go into the Casbah.'

'Not with the guy you go in with, it isn't,' said the young one, turning his glass round in his hand, 'you go in with a barbouze. You know what happens to barbouzes!' The big blond man finished his drink and stood up: '*Geh'wir los!*' He waved a hand at Neil: 'Good cognac, this! Must have cost you a bit!' He came across the room, his thick arms bent like an ape's: 'Come on, Englishman, we go downstairs.'

'I've got to meet somebody,' said Neil, 'at half past one.'

They both laughed. The young one swung himself off the bed and mimicked in French: 'I have to meet somebody!'

'I'm meeting somebody from the Secret Army,' said Neil.

'You are not meeting anybody,' said the big blond man, taking him by the arm and turning him round. Neil felt the pistol prod against his kidney.

The young one opened the door and they walked down the corridor, taking the stairs instead of the lift. The big man put the pistol away when they reached the foyer. Neil looked round him hopelessly, trying to find a face he knew — Hudson, St. Leger, Tom Mallory drunk or sober. The only person in sight was a tall stringy man with yellow hair, standing at the reception desk with a Gladstone bag and typewriter in a waterproof case. Just as they were crossing to the entrance the man picked up his luggage and turned. For an instant his eyes met Neil's. It was a pleasant, dried-brown face the colour of an old leaf with very pale blue eyes. There must have been something about the way Neil looked at him, for the man gave a faint, confused smile.

'Are you a journalist?' Neil asked loudly, desperately, as he passed the stranger. It was his only hope. He felt the big blond man's hand press into the small of his back, hurrying him towards the plate-glass doors.

The newcomer stopped: 'Yes, I am indeed.' He spoke English with a slight accent. 'I am Nielsen,' he went on, holding out a hand, 'Carl Nielsen, *Svens Dagblatt.* I only just arrived now.'

Before Neil could take the man's hand, the young one behind him said, 'Sorry, sir, we got business! See yer later!' He pushed Neil towards the entrance, past the receptionists who kept their eyes carefully averted. The Swede looked puzzled, waving a hand: 'I will see you then. Goodbye!'

'Goodbye!' chanted the young one as they went through the plate-glass doors, then laughed, squeezing Neil's arm: 'Not much help, was he?'

Neil said nothing. They took him across the gravel to a black Citroën DS. A huge man who looked like a Corsican, with a square face and heavy moustache, sat behind the wheel; his brown suit bulged under the elbow. The blond man pushed Neil into the back and climbed in beside him. The young one sat up in front, and they drove away.

'May I ask where we're going?' said Neil.

'You find out,' said the young one.

They passed two jeeps, an armoured car, guns and men in steel helmets. Neil stared out at them, and none of them looked back.

The young one turned suddenly: 'You got a British passport?'

Neil nodded, trying to swallow; the inside of his mouth felt like scuffed leather.

The young one took out a cigarette. 'You from London?' he went on, sounding almost friendly.

'That's right,' said Neil, his voice far outside him. The big man had the pistol lying against his knee again.

'I know plenty journalists,' the young one said, lighting his cigarette, 'here — in Saigon — all full o' shit!' He sat there looking like a well-scrubbed American college boy. 'You bastards know nothing,' he added.

'You must have been very young to have been in Saigon?' said Neil, hoping to keep the conversation as polite as possible.

The young one nodded. 'I was legionnaire first at seventeen years old in Saigon. I lied to 'em — told 'em I was twenty.'

'Where do you come from?'

'From Dresden. Now under the Bolsheviks.' He smiled broadly: 'For fifteen days I was a Werewolf in the Hitlerjugend. *Ach, das war toll!* Crazy days!' He nodded towards the big blond man: 'We two, we are in the Premier R.E.P. — Foreign Legion paratroopers. Best regiment in the world!'

The big man said, 'Thirteen years I am in the Legion. *Vetminh, Araben, alle Scheiss!*' He grinned with teeth like peanuts and spat on the carpet of the car.

'Arabs, all shit!' translated the young one, grinning too, proud of his English.

Neil knew that the Premier R.E.P. had been disbanded after the last putsch. 'What do you do now?' he said, trying to keep his voice steady.

'You heard of "Gamma Commandos"?'

Neil nodded.

'That's us,' said the young one, winking at the big blond man, 'anybody fooling around, we put a bullet in his head. You see us driving past a bus stop — Moslems standing in a row with their veiled fatmas. We drive past — twenty-five, thirty kilometres an hour, wam-wam! — we get four, five Moslems in the head. The fatmas we leave standing. Good for *bordels militaires!*'

Neil suppressed a surge of nausea. He tried a new tactic. 'I know your chief, Colonel Le Hir,' he began, 'I met him yesterday morning.' They said nothing. Neil went on: 'I'm supposed to be meeting one of his adjutants for lunch at half past one.' It was ten past now.

'You meet nobody,' said the young one, 'what you think we're here for? You know Colonel Le Hir? O.K., you think you're a big shot? Now shut your mouth!'

They drove on in silence, climbing into a hot, bleak street which Neil recognized as being near the place where he had crossed behind the barricades yesterday. The car stopped outside a café. The big man ordered him out and the young one followed, leaving the Citroën at the kerb.

The café was crowded with young men in blue shirts and leather jackets slamming pin-tables. A giant jukebox, like the control panel of an airliner, screamed out a number by Helen Shapiro. The record had a flaw in it that made a sound like tearing paper.

The big man pressed the pistol back into Neil's kidney and the young one said, '*Wir machen es hinten!*'

Neil understood enough German to know what they meant: they were going to take him into the back of the café. They were going to kill him.

He felt a loosening in his bowels, blood pounding in his head, and an empty pain flowed through him, as the three of them began to walk down between the bar and the rows of flashing, clicking pin-tables. People turned and watched them: swarthy faces, sleek hair with Roman fringes, cowboys and smiling blondes in frilly panties lighting up along the tables behind them. The young legionnaire led the way, and some of the men in leather jackets smiled and joked with him as he passed. One of them jabbed him playfully in the solar plexus, and they both stopped for a moment, shadow-boxing with faces of mock pain. The legionnaire finally grabbed the man by the neck and called to the barman, 'Give him a beer, Georges!'

Somebody said close to Neil's ear, 'Who's the goose?'

'Don't ask questions,' growled the big blond man, walking behind Neil with his ape's arm dangling, the gun now at his side.

Helen Shapiro clicked off; there was a whir and clatter and a voice sang, 'When I see you standing there — with the sunlight in your hair!' Aren't there any French pop songs? Neil thought.

The young legionnaire opened a door at the back of the café. Neil was pushed into a bare room with crates of bottles stacked along the wall. From behind him he heard laughter, the jukebox calling, 'When I see your big blue eyes...' The door slammed, shutting out the howl of the bar. The big man said, 'Up to the wall!'

Neil started to turn and the man pushed him on the shoulder so that he lost his balance. 'Up to the wall!' he yelled.

Neil straightened up. The wall was white-washed and empty. There was a window to the left looking into a yard. Suddenly he felt quite calm. He was never going to see Caroline again. That didn't matter, he'd lost her anyway. He was never going to sleep with a girl again, never have another drink, another meal, see another film, spend any more money, write another word, talk to anybody, drive his car onto the air-ferry at Lydd, off for a sunny Continental holiday. He felt like a little boy who is being kept in during school Sports Day. The treat was over. He was going out like Van Loon: stretched naked on a slab in the municipal morgue. He remembered that he still hadn't registered with the British Consulate. He began to walk towards the wall. Without turning round he said, 'This isn't going to do you any good. Colonel Le Hir is a sensible man — he's not going to like the publicity of killing a journalist.'

He was two feet from the wall. God what a waste, he thought. The Foreign Office would kick up a bit of a fuss. They'd catch these two eventually. They might even get the guillotine. The young one came up behind him and hit Neil twice, once in the kidney, with a burst of pain that spread through his gut to his groin, then hard across the back of the neck.

The white wall went red and black and broke up into sparkling fragments. Neil waited for the noise: the crash of the gun, the bullet boring through flesh and bone, out the other side into the white plaster. But there was only a roaring like wind, then nothing.

PART 5: THE PEACEMAKER

CHAPTER 1

Pol wiped his face and neck with a handkerchief soaked in sweat and looked wearily across the desk at the Sûreté man. The whisky bottle stood at his elbow three-quarters empty next to a dirty glass. The Sûreté man was not drinking. He was stout and balding, with damp patches under the armpits of his sand-coloured shirt. He looked back at Pol and shook his head. 'No, Charles, I'm sorry. There's nothing I can do. The plan is impossible — a fantasy!'

'A fantasy, perhaps,' said Pol, 'but it might work.'

They were on the eleventh floor of the High Command headquarters, an ugly concrete building on the wooded hills above the city. The room was stifling and stank of latrines. Two days earlier the plumbing, lift-shafts and generating plant had been destroyed by plastic bombs smuggled in by some of the three hundred employees. The incident had amused Pol when he first heard of it. The explosives had been secreted on the girl secretaries in places which even the CRS were too delicate to search, and the detonators had been brought in disguised as biros. The engineers estimated it would take at least a week to repair the damage. A mobile generator was supplying emergency current for telephones and lighting. There was no sanitation, no air-conditioning; and eleven flights of stairs to be climbed twice a day, were beginning to destroy even Pol's sense of humour. He was obliged to wash and shave in cold Vichy water, and the Venetian blinds had to remain drawn all day. This was because somebody in the building had taken the trouble to paint white crosses level with a man's chest on the windows facing the hills, where a sniper would have little difficulty using a telescopic rifle. Pol did not know whether it were meant simply as a gesture to intimidate him; but twice the crosses had been scraped off, and twice they had reappeared. He now drew the blinds and tried to ignore them.

The Sûreté man was saying, 'The Department is quite definite about it. The final veto even came from Paris. We can't go along with you, Charles.'

Pol lunged out and pounded his fat fist on the desktop, his eyes sore with sweat: 'But we're halfway there! Two more moves and we have them in the bag!'

'I'm sorry,' said the Sûreté man, turning his eyes to the floor. His hands shook with the effect of too many black coffees: 'Your plan has been given every consideration, but the Department cannot sanction it. It's too dangerous.'

Pol splashed an inch of whisky into the dirty glass, drained down half of it and sank back breathing hard: 'I'm not suggesting a simple police exercise. Of course it's dangerous! The people we're dealing with are dangerous. Everything we do in this city is dangerous.'

'But this is dangerous in a special way,' the Sûreté man said patiently, 'it could embarrass the Government and the local administration, that we cannot afford. Commandant Duxelles said so himself this morning.'

'Damn Duxelles! He's just a thick-headed policeman,'

'He's head of the Sûreté here. One should not speak too lightly of him. His decisions have to be accepted.'

'Duxelles doesn't make decisions,' said Pol, 'they're made for him in Paris by a bunch of diplomats who know nothing about what's really happening here.'

'That may well be,' said the Sûreté man, 'but Duxelles is still responsible for the Department. I couldn't possibly offer you my support without his authority.'

Pol grunted and relapsed into a moody silence. The Sûreté man went on looking at the floor. 'And what about this Englishman?' he said at last. 'Supposing he gets killed?'

'He won't get killed.'

'You're taking a chance on that.'

'It's a chance worth taking. They wouldn't shoot an Englishman.'

'I hope not,' said the Sûreté man, 'we've got enough troubles without the British Government standing on our feet. What sort of fellow is he?'

Pol shrugged: 'Insular, over-educated, rather stupid.'

'I heard he was intelligent. He's quite a well-known journalist, isn't he?'

'Well, intelligent perhaps, but not clever. *Pas une fine mouche.* These English don't have a very catholic view of the world, you know. But at least he's a genuine Englishman, not one of those people with Commonwealth passports. He's a true gentleman.' He used the word with a certain old-fashioned reverence. 'That is the beauty of it,' he added, 'everyone still trusts an English gentleman.'

'It's as well they trust someone,' the Sûreté man said grimly, 'but your plan, Charles, is still out of the question. General Metz and the other commanders have political obligations here. If we go into something at this stage involving the Arab Front, we could swing the whole Army against us. It would be tantamount to political recognition.'

Pol roared and slammed the desk: 'But we won't have anything to do directly with the Arab Front!'

'Perhaps, but if the full story ever leaked out it could precipitate a political scandal.'

Pol made a crowing noise and glared up at the motionless fan on the ceiling. 'Political scandal!' he muttered. 'That's all you policemen worry about! You've got a full-scale military revolt on your hands! Isn't that a political scandal? What difference does it make if you get one more dirty editorial in *Le Monde*, when you have the big fish in the net? Is it going to spoil your chances of promotion?' He swallowed the rest of his drink and poured himself another, licking the sweat off his upper lip: 'I'm going ahead with it, anyway, whether I get your support or not.'

The Sûreté man nodded: 'And who will you use?'

Pol gave a despairing shrug: 'I shall use the barbouzes — those that are still alive. I have to do something to justify my salary.'

The Sûreté man shook his head and stood up: 'It won't work, Charles. And when it fails, understand that everyone involved — including this wretched Englishman — will get no help from any of the Departments. I have Duxelles' word for that.'

'*Entendu*,' said Pol, finishing his whisky.

CHAPTER 2

Neil's eyeballs felt like smooth heavy stones, and when he tried to open them the pain raced from his head to his spine, making him retch.

He could make out a white ceiling with patterns of shadow. From somewhere behind him came the clonk of ice cubes, the mewing of clarinet. He was lying on a sofa. His shoes and jacket had been removed and the front of his shirt was wet with vomit. He turned his head slightly and tried to sit up: there was a stiff ridge of muscle across the back of his neck. He raised himself on one elbow and peered across the room.

A girl in tight trousers stood at a table against the wall shaking a silver flask. At the end of the room windows opened on to the balcony where three men sat under sunshades drinking.

The girl turned and looked at him. He recognized the Jewish girl, Nadia. She went on shaking the flask and called out, 'He's awake!'

One of the men came in from the balcony: it was Colonel Le Hir. He came across the room in easy strides with a cut-glass tumbler in his hand. He stood in front of Neil, his pale-brown eyes flecked with yellow, and said, 'Are you ready to talk?'

Neil put his stockinged feet on the floor and murmured, 'Give me a drink.'

'Nadia, one martini!'

'I don't want a martini,' said Neil feebly, 'I want a glass of water.' He felt ashamed of the vomit down his shirt. 'Is there somewhere I can wash?' he added, as the girl came over with his drink. He felt sick and dizzy and half-asleep. The girl handed him a tumbler of water with a proud sneer and walked sinuously away towards the balcony. He saw now that the other men outside were the two legionnaires.

'You can clean up later,' said Le Hir; 'first we're going to have a little talk about what you were doing in the Casbah this morning —'

Neil was beyond subterfuge now. He was alive, on a sofa, not on a slab in the morgue; and the water was ice-cold, clearing his head, making him feel almost happy. He began telling Le Hir about his telephone call yesterday to Pol and the meeting that morning in the Cintra Café. Le Hir looked like a schoolmaster listening to one of his pupils confess to a serious misdemeanour.

'I decided not to go,' said Neil, 'I didn't want to get involved with Pol. That's not what I'm here for.'

Le Hir nodded gravely.

'But I changed my mind. I went after all. A man came and drove me up to the entrance into the Casbah. I can't tell you where it was, except that it was behind a lot of fruit markets.' He sipped the iced water: 'When I came out the driver had had his throat cut, and your two boys were waiting for me at the hotel. Nice morning.'

'What made you decide to keep this appointment?' Le Hir's face was suddenly tight and nasty; he was trying to scare Neil, but somehow Neil was filled with a tired, dreamy feeling and the only thing that really troubled him was the mess on his shirt.

'Well, last night,' he said, 'I rang up my girl in London and the bitch told me she's getting married next week to a racing motorist.' He looked at Le Hir and shook his head sorrowfully: 'Ridiculous, isn't it? Here am I, gainfully employed, full of fine prospects, getting heroically beaten up by Foreign

Legionnaires, and she goes off and chooses a racing motorist!' He laughed into his glass of water.

Le Hir sat and stared at him.

'You think I'm a bit touched?' said Neil. *'Que j'ai des araignées au plafond?'* He ran his fingers over the back of his neck: 'That young lad of yours hit me rather hard, I'm afraid.'

Le Hir blinked. 'I'm in no mood for jokes, Monsieur Ingleby.'

Neil drained down his tumbler of water: 'It's no joke, I can tell you! You wanted to know the reason why I changed my mind and kept Pol's appointment? I've told you. Because of my girl —'

'It's not a good enough reason.'

'Perhaps not for you. It is for me.' Neil glanced across at Nadia, who was leaning against the wall sneering at him. He tried to imagine her and the Colonel in bed together.

'What did you do in the Casbah?' said Le Hir. The welted scar from his mouth to his ear seemed to grow more pronounced, like a strip of macaroni.

Neil said, 'I met three men called Marouf, Boussid and Ali La Joconde.'

Le Hir sprang up and hit him across the mouth. The blow made a dry smack that cut across the room and brought the two legionnaires to the door of the balcony. Neil put his hand up to the hot pain and said apologetically, 'I thought you wanted to know what I did in the Casbah?'

Le Hir grabbed him by the collar, pulled him a foot off the sofa and hit him again, hard with the back of his hand, then dropped him on the cushion: 'Repeat what you just said!' His words made a hissing sound between his square teeth: 'Repeat it!'

The two legionnaires were coming across the room with their drinks. Neil's eyes misted with tears, his mouth tasting of salt and blood as his lips began to swell like rubber. Le Hir stood over him flexing his fingers. His face had turned oyster-white: 'Go on! Tell us again what you did in the Casbah.'

The young legionnaire came round and stood close behind Neil's left ear.

Neil began, 'I went into the Casbah. I was taken up to a house where I met three men. They were Dr. Marouf, Abdel Boussid, and Ali La Joconde who was introduced to me as Mohammed Sherrif.' He waited for the blow, from in front or behind, but none came.

'Describe them,' said Le Hir.

Neil did so, in laborious detail, right down to Ali La Joconde's fluttering white hands and Boussid's pouting lips.

'Very well,' said Le Hir, 'now tell us exactly what you talked about.'

Neil took his time, almost beginning to enjoy himself. He described the foothills of political small talk, leading up to the discussion on the ethics of terrorism, and finally Ali La Joconde's tears and Dr. Marouf's offer of a truce.

When he had finished, without being interrupted once, Le Hir sat back and nodded: 'So you had quite a little session up there.' He turned to the two legionnaires: 'What do we do with this clown?'

The girl Nadia leant against the wall and said lazily, 'Kill him.'

Le Hir ignored her. The young legionnaire went round and whispered something to him. He frowned and looked down at Neil, then nodded: 'Nadia, give the Englishman a drink — a proper drink. He's going to need one!' He went over to the telephone and dialled a number, speaking for several minutes. Neil could not catch what was said. He sat sipping a strong chilled martini with a sliver of lemon; it gave him a pleasant glow as he watched, with relief, the two legionnaires return to the balcony.

Le Hir at last put down the telephone and said, 'Nadia, show him the bathroom.' He turned to Neil: 'Clean yourself up. Nadia will give you a new shirt. We want you looking smart.' He went back to the telephone.

The girl took Neil into a bathroom lined with black mirrors and shelves of perfumes and toilet preparations which must have been worth more than a hundred pounds. An elaborate exercising machine composed of springs and pulleys hung from the ceiling. While Neil bathed he could hear the incessant murmur of Le Hir's voice on the telephone,

He cooled his swollen lip and put on a fawn-coloured silk shirt that Nadia had given him. It had a label from Cervi's, Rome. He returned to find Le Hir strapping on a polished gun holster under a white sporting jacket. The legionnaires led the way out, down to the same Citroën DS with the moustached Corsican at the wheel. Neil sat in the back between the two legionnaires.

'Blindfold him,' said Le Hir.

The driver took a black cloth from the glove compartment; the young legionnaire bound it tightly round the upper half of Neil's head, and they drove smoothly and fast, upwards, round steep bends, the driver using the horn in aggressive blasts.

They stopped suddenly and Neil was hurried out across the pavement, up several flights of stairs. A bell tinkled; there was a pause, and a door creaked open. Le Hir's voice said, 'All right, we've got him.' Neil was led forward, round a coiner, and pushed down into a chair. The cloth was untied.

Facing him across a polished table sat Anne-Marie. She gave him a brief nod, as though they had only just met. He opened his mouth to speak but she flashed her eyes at him in warning, and he fell silent.

Le Hir and the two legionnaires took up their positions against the wall. The black-moustached chauffeur disappeared through a door at the end of the room. There was a tense silence.

The flat was small and overcrowded, typical of the French provincial bourgeoisie: heavy, dark-stained furniture, ornate wall lamps, old brown photographs. There was a smell of floor polish and coffee beans.

The door at the end of the room opened again. Anne-Marie looked up, and the two legionnaires stiffened as though coming to attention. The chauffeur stepped through and held the door open for a tall man in uniform the colour of dried mud. He wore no decorations. He walked in, nodded round the room, then stood staring at Neil. Neil stared back, and a little shiver passed through him. He was looking at Colonel Pierre Broussard, alias M. Martel, second-in-command of the Secret Army.

CHAPTER 3

'Good afternoon, Monsieur Ingleby.' Colonel Broussard pulled up a hard-backed chair and seated himself beside Neil: 'You smoke, I believe?' He pushed a rose-wood box along the table, full of fat Turkish cigarettes.

'Thank you,' said Neil, taking one.

Colonel Broussard turned to Anne-Marie: 'Perhaps Monsieur Ingleby would like something to drink? Some coffee?'

'Thank you,' said Neil again. She stood up without looking at him and went into the passage. Broussard turned back to Neil. His face was drawn and tired, and the eyes held that familiar luminous glare, sunk under his bony brows, which Neil now recognized as a symptom of the opium-smoker.

'So we meet again,' Broussard said, with the hint of a smile, 'first on the Holy Mountain, and now here. It seems that our ways cross by destiny. Or is it by design? I should like to know.'

There was an oppressive pause. The door opened and Anne-Marie came in with a tray of coffee. Neil cleared his throat, took a cup, thanked her, and began once again to explain about his arrival in Athens and his meeting with Pol.

Broussard held up his hand: 'Monsieur Ingleby, I do not know why you should suppose that I am the last person in this city to have heard of your exploits. My intelligence service is not inefficient,' he added dryly. 'However, I confess that when you were summoned here today I did not realize that you were the same Englishman I met on Mount Athos.'

Neil glanced at Anne-Marie. So she had kept his confidence after all. He gave an inward sigh of relief; at least there was one person here he could trust.

Broussard continued, in a flat, quiet voice, 'I am prepared to accept that our meeting on Athos may have been fortuitous. Your presence in this city is not. You are here for some purpose devised by Monsieur Charles Pol, and it is my intention to find out what that purpose is. I suggest that you begin by repeating to me what you have already told Colonel Le Hir about your visit to the Casbah this morning. Our patience with you, Monsieur Ingleby, is beginning to run out.'

Neil repeated the account of his meeting with the Arab Front leaders. It took him nearly a quarter of an hour to complete. Throughout he felt Broussard's eyes on him like two points of radium, burning ice-cold and deadly. Le Hir and the legionnaires watched him from the wall, contemptuous, hating, with the laconic hate of trained killers; and Anne-Marie watched him across the table, her face grave, expressionless. While he talked, he worried about her — about why she was here. When he finished, Broussard began to question him about his impressions of the three Arab leaders.

'What makes you think they were being sincere?' he asked finally.

Neil hesitated: 'By their manner. They certainly seemed sincere.'

'You have little experience of the Arab race, Monsieur Ingleby. Their manner can be very deceptive and they are brilliant liars. Did they give you any positive reason for thinking them sincere?'

Neil paused: 'Well, Ali La Joconde wept when I mentioned the Casino bombing. He seemed genuinely upset.'

Broussard sunk his mouth in a snarl: 'You're not going to stir my sympathies for Ali La Joconde! Those people are not sentimentalists. Did they give you any political reasons for offering a truce?'

Neil thought hard, trying to remember their exact words. At last he said, 'Boussid told me that the killing had become senseless. He said the struggle was no longer theirs — it was now between the Secret Army and the French High Command. But I think his real reason,' he added, searching in vain for a safe way of phrasing it, 'is that he believes the Arab Front may have won.'

A frozen look came over Broussard's face, his body stiffening visibly, and Neil saw a terrible anguish rising inside the man. Ali La Joconde and his friends had their reasons for a truce. Perhaps even at this moment Broussard believed they were right — that the cause of the Secret Army was already doomed.

He stared at the table for nearly a full minute before fixing Neil again with his grey glare, saying, 'How much money is this man Pol paying you?'

Neil started. 'Nothing! Not a penny — except for the trip over.'

Broussard's eyes narrowed: 'If you were to work as an intermediary between us and the Arabs you would be running certain risks. You realize that? I assume you would expect some material reward.'

Neil was silent, his heart thumping wildly, realizing how useless it is to pretend that even men of integrity can easily resist an offer of money — at least the chance of finding out how much it is to be. He was on the point of asking Broussard, when the man said, 'We might be prepared to offer quite a large sum, Monsieur Ingleby — payable in whatever currency you choose.'

'Does that mean that you agree to Boussid's offer?'

'I did not say that. I asked if you were interested in money.' Something about the way he said it — perhaps the inflexion, the unobtrusive emphasis on the conditional — warned Neil that Broussard was not really concerned with offering him money.

Neil was being tested. He said boldly, 'I am not interested in money, Colonel. I am interested in saving innocent lives.'

Broussard's face relaxed just a fraction; he glanced round at Le Hir, then nodded. 'Monsieur Ingleby, I must discuss this matter with my colleagues before we can take a decision. It is, of course, possible that between them Boussid, Ali La Joconde and this man Pol may be laying us rather a crude trap. They would have to be very naive to think that we would fall into it. However' — he looked at his watch — 'if they are serious, we might find room for at least a discussion. You have my authority to arrange with Pol to return to the Casbah tomorrow, when you will tell Boussid and his friends that while the revolt continues we might be prepared, under certain conditions and with certain guarantees, to call off our commandos, if they will call off theirs.' He turned to Le Hir: 'Monsieur Ingleby will not be returning to his hotel, Colonel. You will arrange for him to be put up in comfort.' Le Hir nodded. Broussard looked back at Neil: 'I apologize for the inconvenience, but for the moment it is better that you do not leave the barricades.' He stood up, paused, then added, 'I am glad to find a man who is willing to do more than sell his services for money.' He nodded round the table and left the room.

The gathering broke up quickly. The two legionnaires came over to Neil and began to hurry him away, without blindfolding him this time. As they reached the door he found himself for a moment pressed against Anne-Marie. He started to speak to her but she turned her head, trying to escape. He whispered: 'Anne-Marie, what are you doing here? Please, tell me!'

'*Komm, du fauler Hund!*' roared the big legionnaire, throwing him out on to the landing.

She ran after him suddenly, shouting over the banisters, 'I'll see you — at Colonel Le Hir's!' Then someone called to her and she darted back into the apartment.

CHAPTER 4

During the next four days Neil made five visits to the Casbah. He was taken in each time by the same route as before: one of Le Hir's men — sometimes the young legionnaire from Dresden, sometimes another of the 'Gamma Commandos' — would accompany him from behind the barricades to a rendezvous arranged the day before by telephone with Pol. Here a car would collect him and drive him past the CRS roadblock to the little iron door with the Yale lock. His discussions with the Arab Front were conducted from now on exclusively through Boussid. He did not meet again with Dr. Marouf or Ali La Joconde. There were the endless glasses of mint tea, the sweet dry pastries, the moist face and pouting lips arguing, haggling, picking up each little point, prodding Neil into a state of nervous exasperation.

Neil had only a rigid set of terms on which to negotiate, dictated to him before each visit by Le Hir. The Secret Army would agree to no verbal truce; they insisted on meeting the leaders of the Arab Front in person and discussing the precise terms of the truce face to face. This would mean a deputation of Dr. Marouf, Boussid and Ali La Joconde.

Boussid deferred and bickered and drank more tea, insisting that the Arab Front would only negotiate with General Guérin. No deputy leader of the Secret Army, even Broussard or Le Hir, would satisfy them.

Le Hir refused. On no account would General Guérin agree to meet any member of the Arab Front in person. The discussions broke down.

At the fourth meeting, at noon on the third day, Boussid appeared to be losing his aplomb: he was tetchy and fidgeted, drinking more tea than usual and shouting angrily at his subordinates in Arabic. If Guérin did not participate, he told Neil, then the Arab Front would be represented only by a minor official.

That afternoon Le Hir also relented. General Paul Guérin was prepared to discuss a formal truce, providing he met only the three leaders of the Casbah and in a place which he would name.

The last meeting, which was also the most arduous, settled the place where the talks would be held. After several hours of arguing, Neil persuaded Boussid to accept the spot chosen by General Guérin. It was a farmhouse eighteen miles outside the city, set back on a plain between the mountains and the sea. It had been deserted since the owner, a colon farmer, had left for France three months earlier. The place could only be approached by two roads across open fields which removed any serious risk of an ambush; and it had the vital advantage of lying beyond the urban areas controlled by the Secret Army, and also outside the mountainous territory infested by Arab Front guerrillas. Each delegation would produce an escort of six men, armed only with machine-pistols; and Neil had to convey in turn to Le Hir and Boussid that if there was any breach of the agreement by one side, the other would retaliate with massive reprisals.

Except when he was beyond the CRS roadblock, Neil was under constant watch by Le Hir's commandos; and all his telephone calls to Pol were tapped by Le Hir himself. During these calls Pol did not discuss the talks with Boussid. Their conversations were short and to the point, concerning only the various appointments with the men who were to drive Neil into the Casbah. Once, on Le Hir's instructions, Neil asked Pol whether the French Army had any part in these plans. Pol replied, 'I can promise you that neither the Army nor the security forces have anything to do with this matter. You have my solemn word for that!'

This startled Le Hir. He had assumed, as an ex-member of Military Security, that the Sûreté and the Deuxième would work in close collaboration. His military training did not admit to independent agents. To him Charles Pol was just another fat, overpaid Government employee. But Neil remembered that Pol had been a double-agent in the war and was a former Anarchist. He was not — as he had been at pains to explain in Athens — an ordinary policeman carrying out the instructions of his superiors. Pol was an idealist, a man with dynamic views on how the world should be run. The idea that he might be acting entirely free of the French authorities did not strike Neil as far-fetched. Le Hir considered it, but shrugged it off. The only idealists he knew were in the Secret Army.

During all this time the possibility of treachery by either side occurred constantly to Neil. He would lie on his bed in the spare room put at his disposal in Le Hir's flat and weigh up the probabilities. Always he was reassured by the same process of argument: that it was in the logical interests of all sides — the Secret Army, the Arab Front and the French Government — to put an end to indiscriminate murder. Furthermore, it seemed to him that men like Colonel Broussard, Le Hir, Boussid and Ali La Joconde were far too canny in the ways of terrorism and counterterrorism to allow themselves to be caught out by an elementary ruse.

At first the thing that worried him most was his being unable to contact his office in London. It was one of Broussard's conditions that not a hint of the proposed peace talks should reach the Press. Neil had been allowed merely to cable Winston St. Leger at the Miramar to say that he was leaving the city for a trip into the Bled for a few days. He had missed the Saturday night deadline and could send Foster no final report on how the crisis had looked at the weekend.

The situation in the city remained ominously stagnant. On the Friday evening a cruiser had sailed into the harbour and anchored. By next morning it had been joined by two destroyers, and there were now rumours of a naval blockade. The frontiers and the airport stayed closed during the whole weekend; and reinforcements, rushed from the French zone of Germany, had continued to pour in until Saturday night. On Sunday afternoon helicopters had droned over the barricades, dropping leaflets which appealed to the rebels to surrender honourably and not to obey 'dissident, treacherous officers whose names are a disgrace to the French nation'.

For these four days Neil was kept virtually under house-arrest. He was brought excellent meals prepared by Nadia, but was allowed to leave the flat only to make his visits to the Casbah. His relations with Le Hir were remote and formal. They met only to discuss the progress of his discussions with Boussid. The flat was used as a permanent headquarters for Le Hir's operations in the capital, and a continuous host of visitors — most of them ex-Army officers and Legion deserters — filled the large salon, often for hours on end. Neil's presence in the flat was never mentioned; nor was he allowed to meet any of Le Hir's callers.

Anne-Marie had come to see him on the first evening and they had dined together in his room. She had been quiet and reticent, refusing to discuss her presence that afternoon in the flat with Colonel Broussard, and had left early, kissing him quickly on the lips and promising to call again some time the next day. He had resisted the temptation to ask her to stay the night, knowing by her manner that she would refuse.

The intervals between her visits and his own trips into the Casbah began to hang heavily, making him nervous and irritable.

He had too much time to ponder the many possibilities and perils of the venture. The worst moments were always just before entering and leaving the Casbah, with the walk through the narrow alleys, the tall dark walls and the memory of the pale man in the Aronde with his throat gaping open. Le Hir promised that he would not be harmed by any member of the Secret Army; and Boussid supplied a regular escort inside the Casbah. But there was always the chance that someone — a pistol-touting European teenager or a Moslem fanatic — might decide to take a shot at him from one of a thousand black corners. He would return from each trip exhausted, the back of his neck itching with an overdeveloped instinct for danger, and try to distract himself with Le Hir's meagre selection of reading matter: cheap magazines and *romans policiers*, and a few popular novels. He slogged through *Angelique et le Sultan*, fighting away the thought of Caroline which stabbed at him systematically with a physical wrenching of his stomach.

Occasionally Nadia would wander in and sit on his bed, smoking and chatting in a desultory way to pass the long hours she herself spent cooped up in the flat. Neil decided to forget that she had volunteered her opinion that he should be killed. She had a sulky, sluttish charm, but she was not a bad girl. One afternoon she began to tell him that she was fed up with the revolt: she wanted to get out of the city and travel, to go to Paris and New York. He ventured to ask her, as tactfully as possible, about her relations with Le Hir. She shrugged: 'Perhaps we get married one day — when his divorce comes through. He has an Italian wife, you see. She's gone back to Rome, and there are terrible troubles with the Church.'

He nodded. She stared glumly at her cigarette and said, 'It's not much fun being kept in this flat all day long. Just serving drinks for his men when they come up. I've had no fun since all this trouble started. I never go out — never go dancing.'

'Do you love him?' he asked, with sudden curiosity.

'*Ah, moi je n'sais pas!*' She pulled a sad ugly face: 'It would be all right if I could get out of here. We have terrible rows stuck in this place. Sometimes he beats me. Last night he really whipped me! I think he enjoys it. I told him that if he does it again I'll leave him. Only I haven't anywhere to go.'

CHAPTER 5

On the last evening — Tuesday — Le Hir gave a party. The final details for the truce talks had been agreed in the afternoon: Paul Guérin was to meet the three leaders of the Arab Front in the farmhouse soon after dawn tomorrow.

The afternoon had grown heavy, with sullen purplish clouds rolling down from the mountains; and a thundery light filled the city, setting up an electric tension, a sense of malaise and impending crisis. Brown-bellied helicopters chugged overhead like fat dragonflies; shops began to close early; troops roamed the streets, slowly, purposefully, as though responding to the gathering storm. In an outlying European suburb a car full of Moslems had driven past a cinema queue and machine-gunned eight men and three girls before tossing a grenade into a flower stall and killing an old woman.

Up in his flat, ten floors above the city, Le Hir was in high spirits. He had laid on pink champagne and Beluga caviar, and Neil was called in to enjoy the festivities. Anne-Marie was there, with the two German legionnaires and half-a-dozen ex-Army officers, and a couple of polished middle-aged civilians who looked like well-to-do businessmen. One of them was the proprietor of an extreme right-wing newspaper in the city which had been suspended by the authorities.

They drank champagne and laughed and talked cheerfully; and Neil had a long academic conversation with the newspaper proprietor who spoke English and had the studied good manners of the French commercial classes who have entered the ranks of society. Neil imagined him playing golf at Le Touquet and skiing above Marrakesh. As though by conspiracy they did not mention the crisis, let alone the plans for the peace talks tomorrow; instead, the man boasted to Neil of how he had met Lord Beaverbrook several times at Cap d'Ail.

Nadia served the drinks, while across the room Anne-Marie sat morosely sipping her champagne, taking nearly half-an-hour to finish one glass. Neil was now not only puzzled by her behaviour — the radical change from the wild lithe creature he had met at Le Berry, to this solemn girl who sat at the right-hand of Le Hir and Broussard — but was now also worried by her. He managed at last to extricate himself from the company of the newspaper proprietor and went over to where she sat alone by the windows.

As soon as she saw him she stood up and finished her champagne. 'I must go,' she said, 'I have an appointment at nine.' She refused to stay for the buffet supper prepared by Nadia. He saw her to the door, bewildered and a little angry: 'Anne-Marie, what's the matter? What's happened?'

She looked unhappily past him to where Le Hir stood joking with a couple of handsome young officers attached to the 'Gamma' murder squad.

'That night at the hotel,' she said, not looking at him, 'it was exceptional — it was after the bombing. I was alone — I wanted someone. Anybody. I was a little mad that night.' She turned her dark eyes to him: 'I'm sorry, but things change. There are many things here — things happening now — that I cannot tell you about. Goodbye.' She did not kiss him, but turned quickly and he watched her go with a small twinge of longing, a sense of wounded pride. Behind him Le Hir was laughing lustily, feeling none of the tension and malaise.

Tomorrow was another day, Neil thought. His head was aching, and he went over to Nadia to have his glass refilled.

CHAPTER 6

Dawn broke yellow out to sea, with the city lying dim under a tropical rain. Neil was called by Nadia at half past five with a pot of black coffee, croissants and fresh orange juice.

He shaved carefully, like an actor before the first night. This was to be his day of triumph. In the salon Le Hir was already waiting in a belted khaki raincoat, carrying a briefcase. He was to head the escort of six armed men responsible for General Guérin's safety. He nodded to Neil: 'Would you like a glass of aquavit before we leave?'

Neil accepted, and they drank a stiff toast to each other, swallowing the thimbles of firewater in a gulp.

At five to six the two German legionnaires arrived. They also drank an aquavit; and at exactly six o'clock the four of them went down the street.

They crossed the ring of the barricades through the back of the same building that Neil and Anne-Marie had used on that first morning five days ago. The street below the barricade was almost deserted, with an oily grey shine in the morning drizzle… There was a mobile canteen parked by the kerb and two paras in camouflaged capes sat smoking inside the machinegun nests.

The black Peugeot 403 was waiting outside; the driver was the same big man in a denim shirt they had had on the first morning. In spite of the rain, he still wore his sunglasses.

It was 6.11 when they drove away. Timing was now of crucial importance. Neil had worked out and memorized the schedule to the nearest minute, aware that if either party reached the appointed place too early or too late the whole scheme could collapse. He now experienced the concentrated anxiety of a film director who has sweated long hours on a hazardous production and now watches the result begin to unfold, detail by detail. It gave him a satisfaction that was two-fold: the sight of men like Le Hir and the two legionnaires behaving under what were virtually his own orders helped restore his ego, badly mauled by Caroline, and also gave him a vainglorious sensation that he was positively helping the cause of humanity.

The driver took them on a route carefully prepared by Le Hir, in Neil's presence, to avoid the concentration of Gardes Mobiles and CRS troops in the centre of the city. They drove for seventeen minutes, turning into a long drab street with wilted palms growing crookedly down the pavements, and stopped outside a bistro with a bead curtain and a couple of iron chairs standing out in the rain.

No one spoke inside the car. The time was 6.28. At precisely 6.30 two Citroën DS's turned into the street with a sizzle of tyres and drew up at either end of the Peugeot. The timing impressed Neil. He nodded to Le Hir: 'I hope the Arab Front are as punctual as this.'

Le Hir made no reply. The legionnaires opened the doors and they climbed out into the drizzle. There was only the driver in each of the Citroëns. Together with Le Hir and the two legionnaires they made up five of the armed escort of six. Neil and Le Hir got into the first Citroën, the legionnaires into the second. On the floor lay a couple of machine-pistols and a pair of new number plates. The doors snapped shut and the two cars drove away simultaneously, leaving the Peugeot still outside the bistro.

Neil watched the speedometer needle creep round the dial and pass the 100-kilometre mark. By the feel of the car he guessed that it must be supercharged. He noticed that the back of the driver's neck was pitted with tiny slit-like scars.

There was little traffic. Once they passed a line of Army trucks driving into the city with motorcycle escorts; then they turned into a broad dual-carriageway that curved away into the rolling mists, with the suburbs giving way to white farms scattered across flat brown tobacco fields. There were no roadblocks.

Neil relaxed into the soft-sprung seat and said conversationally, 'The weather seems to have changed for the worst. It's like England.'

Le Hir stared stonily ahead, gripping the briefcase in his lap. 'The weather's fine,' he murmured.

Neil said no more. Le Hir was obviously not in the mood for small talk.

The speedometer needle now wavered on the 180-kilometre mark, the air passing in a long high scream; and Neil watched nervously for some lone Moslem with donkey and cart to loom up suddenly in their path. But the road was empty, sweeping out of the mists like the mouth of a smooth white tunnel; and they drove on at more than a hundred miles an hour, keeping well within Neil's careful schedule.

After fifteen kilometres of dual-carriageway the two cars drifted out of the right-hand lane on to a side road leading up towards the mountains. Neil had studied the road plan round the farmhouse from contour maps. The ground was open, rising slightly, but the mist was closing in, hiding almost completely the dark slopes of mountain ahead. He remembered that the spot had been chosen because it was exposed and free from ambush. He now began to wonder how much the weather would affect security arrangements. He looked at Le Hir, who sat grim-faced and quiet.

Neil said, 'I don't much like this mist. Is it going to make things more difficult?'

'Never mind the mist,' said Le Hir, still staring ahead, 'the plan will proceed as before. You will be protected.'

As he spoke, the Citroën pulled off the road into a layby. Ahead of them stood a sand-coloured Mk 10 Jaguar.

The Citroën crunched up beside it and stopped. The driver leapt out and held the rear door open, and Neil and Le Hir stepped out. The second Citroën, with the two legionnaires, had drawn up behind the Jaguar.

Neil had heard about this car. Yellow Venetian blinds were pulled down over the side and rear windows, which were of bullet-proof glass. The coachwork had been reinforced with armoured plating and the tyres were self-sealing. It had been built specially for Guérin while he was Commander-in-Chief in the Protectorate, as a safeguard against assassination attempts by Arab Front terrorists. It was one of the General's conceits that he still dared use it as his personal car, although it was well known to all the security forces.

Le Hir opened the rear door of the Jaguar, saluted and spoke to someone in the back, then stood aside. Neil stooped down and climbed into the sudden darkness of the car which had a brittle smell of pinewood. The driver had turned to watch; he sat behind a glass partition, holding a machine-pistol in his lap. He made up the full escort of six.

Neil looked along the wide leather seat at the man in the corner. He looked smaller and older than in his photographs. His hair was thin with a transparent silvery shine, combed straight back from his tall brow, making him look almost bald. He had a strong jaw and a good profile, but there were pouches of chicken skin sagging under the eyes which had the jaundiced look of a man who does not sleep well. He sat with one elbow on the padded armrest between them, peering at Neil in the dim striped light from the Venetian blinds. 'So you are Monsieur Ingleby?' he said at last, in a slow pleasant voice.

Neil replied, with a natural reverence of which he was rather ashamed afterwards, 'I am honoured to make your acquaintance, mon General!'

Paul Guérin looked at his watch. The time was 6.44. 'We are a minute in advance,' he said, and stirred forward in his seat, adding, 'I am pleased with the way you have handled the negotiations in the last four days, Monsieur Ingleby. You have shown tenacity and intelligence. My opinion of journalism as a profession' — he slid back a pane in the glass partition — 'has risen considerably. Drive on!' he snapped at the driver.

The engine hummed with quiet force, and the great car moved out into the road between the two Citroëns. They drove fast, with the mist growing thicker, the road beginning to climb, turning and heading into the brown darkness that was the mountains. Neil tried to recall the details of the contour map. He remembered the two straight roads that led up to the farm, and the octagonal design of the outer walls: sheds and barns along three sides, the farmhouse and courtyard in the middle, with the gate leading out to where the two roads met. The mountains began to rise about a quarter of a mile behind; and towards the sea the land was flat for more than three miles of rank maize fields.

General Guérin did not speak again during the drive; and Neil, tense and watchful, did not attempt to break the silence.

At 6.57 the leading Citroën slowed suddenly. Neil saw the rear lights of the car in front flash on and off three times. He thought they were the brake lights. He did not know that the driver was flashing the yellow high beam at a point somewhere in the mountains.

The leading Citroën now turned off the road on to a rutted dirt track. Neil presumed that this was one of the two roads to the farm. After less than twenty yards the convoy stopped. Le Hir came round and opened the Jaguar door. Guérin said quietly, 'Monsieur Ingleby, you will now verify that the enemy has honoured their agreement. We shall wait here until you return.' As he spoke, his eyes were old and worried, one slender grey hand stroking the seam of his immaculate dark flannel trousers.

Neil got out. Le Hir closed the door after him, standing there in his khaki raincoat, huge and menacing, with the briefcase grasped to his chest, and said, 'It is less than a kilometre up the track. When you get inside make sure that all three of them are there, and that they have brought no more than six men.'

The engines of the three cars had been switched off. Le Hir looked at his watch: 'Right! It should not take you more than thirty minutes at the most.'

Neil turned and began to walk up the track into the swirling mist. The air was damp and close. He began to sweat. After a few minutes he stopped to take off his jacket. Behind him the shapes of the three cars grew dim and vanished. Ahead he could now see the white outline of the farm, with a watchtower jutting up like a tooth from the blur of walls and outhouses.

Around him the silence was total, with a deceptive whining in his ears that strangely unnerved him. He quickened his step over the rough track, keeping his eyes on the wall of mountains and on the growing shape of the farm. He thought he could just make out the blob of a man's head above the wall of the crenelated watchtower.

It was hard to calculate distances in the mist, and the building rose suddenly over the last fifty yards. It was designed like an old-fashioned fort. The walls formed a stockade round the farmhouse and courtyard, with low embrasures like the mouths of a pillbox. The only entrance was through the heavy wooden gates overlooked by the tower. To have abandoned such a formidable stronghold, Neil thought, the colon who had owned the place must have been sure the end was coming.

Neil breathed slowly, deeply, trying to keep his heart steady, as he walked over the last few yards to the gates. He could now clearly see the man in the watchtower, with two others peering at him through the embrasures on either side. They had small dark faces under khaki forage caps, and the muzzles of their burp-guns were trained on his head.

The gate was of broad timbers clamped together with rusted bolts. He pushed, and it swung inwards with a wooden creak, showing a whitewashed passage leading into the courtyard. He stepped inside, past a couple of bald tyres propped against the wall. There was a dead silence in the building that made him want to shout and run and show himself, like a child playing hide-and-seek who longs to precipitate the inevitable shock of discovery.

For this was no ordinary silence; not the silence of solitude, of no sound, but of a crowd, of sounds suppressed, of silent breathing and watching and waiting: a fearful, furtive hush, as he walked almost on tiptoe, through the passage, out into the yard.

They were there by the wall, sitting in the open behind a green baize table laid with notepaper, carafe of water and upturned tumblers, like three people waiting to make up a bridge party.

Dr. Marouf rose and bowed; beside him Abdel Boussid gave his pouting, fish-eyed smile, while Ali La Joconde simpered frozenly at the table.

Three Moslems in grubby, makeshift uniforms and forage caps stood beside the table holding their burp-guns at the ready. Neil looked carefully to make sure they were not also carrying pistols or grenades. Three on the walls, he thought, three down in the yard. Dr. Marouf said, 'We welcome you, Monsieur Ingleby, and trust everything is in order?'

Neil looked round the yard. 'You have only these six men?'

'That is correct,' said Marouf.

'I should like to look round for a moment,' said Neil, taking a sudden officious pride in his task, determined not to skimp any final detail. Marouf's face remained pleasantly inscrutable; he said, 'You have our word, Monsieur Ingleby.'

The dull light of the yard shone on Boussid's upturned pebble-glasses. He said gently, 'There is not much time, m'sieur. We cannot wait here all morning. You have seen our escort — they are armed as we agreed. There are no more of them. So if General Guérin's delegation is ready, let them come in and we can begin our discussion.'

Neil hesitated. There was something that worried him about the silence of the place. He remembered Colonel Broussard's words: 'They are brilliant liars.' And what were they doing sitting outside as well as at the preposterous green baize table? Why weren't they inside? He looked round at the windows of the farmhouse. They were opaque with dust, and several panes were cracked and boarded up with newspaper. There was an outside staircase up to the rampart round the walls. Both the Moslem guards in the embrasures, as well as the one in the watchtower, were still covering him with their guns.

He turned to Boussid: 'If I am to trust you, tell your men to take their guns off me.'

Boussid gave a guttural order, and the three men moved back to their places overlooking the plain.

Neil began to walk over to one of the ground-floor windows. Behind him Dr. Marouf called, 'I must warn you, monsieur, that you are wasting our time!'

Neil peered through the window and saw a bare room with an iron stove against the wall. He moved on to the next window, ignoring Marouf. A few inches beyond the grimy panes he found himself looking down the funnel-shaped barrel of a Douze-Sept machinegun. The room behind was full of men.

He stepped back and dodged sideways, flattening himself against the wall by the window. The Douze-Sept did not fire. Across the yard both Boussid and Dr. Marouf were on their feet, and the three guards by the table were coming forward with their guns up, pointing at Neil's stomach. Only Ali La Joconde seemed unaware of what was happening, crouched forward staring at the green baize.

Neil drew in his breath and yelled in English, 'You damned traitors! You bloody little —!'

Marouf snapped an order in Arabic and the three guards stopped. Neil, in fury and confusion, went on swearing at them in English.

A door opened beside him and someone laughed, shrill and lilting like a woman's laugh.

CHAPTER 7

Pol stood there in the doorway swaying on the balls of his tiny feet, smiling his cherry-lipped smile, with the kiss curl pasted down in an elegant loop across his shining brow and an outrageous mauve hibiscus flopping from the lapel of his rumpled suit, with tie askew.

He thrust out his short little arms and walked up to Neil, clucking like a hen: 'Ah, you look surprised, my dear Ingleby! I gave you a bit of a turn perhaps?'

Marouf and Boussid had sat down again, and the guards had lowered their guns, watching. Pol stopped in front of Neil and began patting him on the arm, grinning sublimely.

'You bastard!' said Neil, under his breath in English. 'You fat French bastard!'

'*Qu'est-ce qu'tu dis?*' Pol crooned, still grinning and patting his arm.

'You're not going to get away with this,' Neil said, this time in French, 'I don't know what you think you're trying to do here, but whatever it is, it's not going to work.'

Pol was still grinning, but his eyes now had a cold sly look. He flapped his hand towards the gate: 'Is he out there?'

'He won't walk in here,' said Neil. 'I'm keeping my word, even if you're not.'

The cherry-lipped smile set tightly at the edges: 'He's in the Jaguar, then?'

Neil said nothing. He nodded at the farmhouse windows, 'Your men won't be able to take him. If I'm not back in a few minutes, he'll drive away. He won't come here until I give him the word.'

Pol began patting Neil's arm again, and his smile now became sad and wistful: 'I've been counting on you, Monsieur Ingleby.'

'And I on you,' said Neil, 'and you bring along half the French Army!'

Pol laughed: 'Half the French Army! My dear Ingleby, they wouldn't even spare me one conscript!' He turned and kicked open the door. Inside were about a dozen men, all Europeans in civilian clothes, crouching along the walls and round the Douze-Sept that pointed at the window. They wore machine-pistols and grenades. Pol closed the door and looked at Neil, 'Barbouzes,' he said, 'riff-raff, dregs of the nation.'

'I thought you said you were a barbouze!' Neil murmured, his anger weakening to a sense of futility.

Pol shrugged: 'Ah, the status of the barbouzes has very much declined, I'm afraid. We don't get the material we used to.'

'What were you hoping to do?' said Neil.

'Kill Guérin when he came in.' He nodded towards the watchtower: 'There's another Douze-Sept up there, and a bazooka. I was counting on them coming right up to the gates. Of course they're out of range now — even with the Douze-Sept.'

'You won't get them anywhere near the gates,' said Neil, 'unless I tell them to come. And I'm not going to tell them.'

Pol nodded, holding Neil gently by the elbow. 'The man out there in the Jaguar,' he said, speaking with quiet intensity, 'is a Fascist — a terrorist, Monsieur Ingleby. He is not an ordinary criminal, he does not merit ordinary personal loyalties. He threatens a great nation, a whole democratic tradition. We are at war with this man. You must understand that!'

Neil thought of Le Hir, the German legionnaires, the serpents of blood and flaying feet and the crowds smiling at death: and of the man who was responsible for it all, waiting out there in the Jaguar behind the Venetian blinds, old and tired, threatening the French nation. He said wretchedly, 'What can I do? I gave my word!' He looked over at Marouf, Boussid and Ali La Joconde: 'They gave me their word too.'

'Sometimes one is obliged to break one's word,' said Pol; his fat little fingers tightened round Neil's arm. 'Go back, Monsieur Ingleby, and tell General Guérin that all is well here.'

'And then what?'

'You will be protected.'

Neil laughed savagely: they were the same words Le Hir had used as the cars approached the farm. 'As soon as you try to take Guérin they'll kill me on the spot — and you know it! No, Monsieur Pol, you take Guérin any way you like, but not here — not while I'm around.'

Pol nodded and pulled out a pistol. 'Monsieur Ingleby,' he began, with studied formality, 'I shall have to force you to do as I say.' He poked the blunt barrel into Neil's chest.

'You can't force me to do anything,' said Neil, 'and put that ridiculous thing away! You're not going to kill me.'

Pol took a deep breath, looked down at the gun, sighed, and finally put it away again inside his rumpled jacket, shaking his head: 'You are lucky I'm a humane man! It wouldn't be difficult to have you shot. We could always say it had been done by the Secret Army.'

'If you kill me,' said Neil, 'you lose your last chance of getting Guérin. If I don't walk back out of that gate in a couple of minutes, Guérin will know something's wrong. Your only hope is to let me go.'

'Will you tell them it's clear to come over?'

'I don't know,' said Neil, 'I haven't made up my mind yet.'

Pol's eyes flashed with sparks of rage: 'Monsieur Ingleby, don't play the comedy with me! I might shoot you just out of irritation. And you are being very irritating at this moment!'

Neil realized that he was not joking. The six armed Moslems stood all round, waiting for the order. Pol was angry: somehow Neil had touched him on the raw. Perhaps he had been too offhand, or too scrupulous. Why should Pol give a damn about 'keeping one's word' when it came to catching a man like Guérin? For that matter, why should Neil?

He knew that if Pol thought he was going to walk out of here and tell Guérin that there was a trap waiting, he would be shot dead before he got beyond the gates. 'All right,' he said, 'I accept. I'll go back to the car and tell them to come.' He nodded and turned and began to walk across the yard, down the whitewashed passage with its two bald tyres and the gates standing half-open. He had been in the farm for more than fifteen minutes. He would have to hurry.

Behind him he could feel Pol watching him, the pistol inside his coat, his eyes hard and thoughtful. Pol waited until Neil was past the gates, then turned and went up the outside staircase to a room on the first floor where a radio-transmitter stood with an aerial trailing out of the window like a fishing rod.

One of the barbouzes followed him: a slouching oaf of a man who had been thrown out of the national gendarmerie after a prisoner in his charge had died of a brain haemorrhage. Pol felt dejected and ashamed at having to deal with such men.

'So what happens now?' asked the barbouze.

'We wait,' said Pol, 'the Englishman is going to tell them it's all clear.'

'Supposing he warns them? He's under their orders, not ours.'

'If he warns them, it'll be just too bad!' Pol growled, switching on the transmitter.

'We could still shoot the cars up.'

'They're out of range.'

'For the bazooka, perhaps, but we might get them with the Douze-Sept.'

Pol shook his head: 'The car's got armoured plating. Anyway, even if he does warn them and they try to get away, they won't get far.'

The radio came on with a high swooping moan.

CHAPTER 8

Neil walked away from the farm at a brisk but controlled pace, resisting the urge to run. He knew he had not convinced Pol; but he also knew that Pol would have to take a chance on him. He would not dare shoot him now. Nevertheless, as Neil walked on, he was conscious of that over-sensitive itching at the back of his neck, just below the cranium. He felt more at ease when he was a few hundred yards away, out of range of the Moslem guards' burp-guns.

The mist was beginning to lift, and he could see the three cars standing just as he had left them — the pale slender Jaguar as impressive here as in its showroom in Piccadilly.

He slogged over the last stretch of dirt track, and the silence was again total. He remembered that in four days and about four hours, Caroline would be a married woman. He now noticed that the number plates on the two Citroëns had been changed. It was Le Hir who appeared first, slamming the car door. 'Where the hell have you been?' he yelled. 'You were in there nearly twenty minutes!'

Neil took his time before answering. He walked almost past Le Hir, towards the Jaguar, and said, 'I had to make sure everything was in order.'

'Well, was it? Are the three of them there?'

'Yes, they're there,' said Neil.

'And their escort? How many men have they got?'

'Six men,' said Neil, 'they're armed with machineguns — as we agreed.'

'Are they waiting?'

'Yes, they're waiting. They told me they don't want to waste any time. They want to get on with the talks.'

Le Hir nodded, with a curious secret smile; and Neil opened the door of the Jaguar.

General Guérin sat with his hands folded in his lap, his face strained and grey, preserving a deceptive calm. He looked eagerly at Neil, but Le Hir thrust his head in first and said something that Neil did not catch. Guérin leant forward and rapped on the glass partition. Neil saw the driver flick down the headlamp switch twice, dipping the beam with each flash with his foot.

Three seconds later there came a series of quick rasping sounds far off through the fog, like iron scraping on iron, followed by a thudding echo. Neil looked in the direction that General Guérin was looking towards the farm.

The mist was rising swiftly now, and he could see the white outline of the walls, which shimmered and seemed to break up like a smudge of smoke across the fields. At the same time there came a rapid *clonk! clonk! clonk! CLONK!* — and as he stood by the car door, the sound waves bounced through the mist and seemed to touch him like lapping water.

He heard the rasping *WANG! WANG!* from the direction of the mountains, and the shape of the farm now collapsed visibly, like a card-house going down, the speck of the watchtower suddenly gone.

Guérin was out of the Jaguar, getting into the second of the Citroëns, its engine roaring, and Le Hir was pushing Neil through the other door, climbing in afterwards, as the car, began to turn off the track, followed by the other Citroën, with the Jaguar behind.

The explosions now followed fast: the rasping of the mortar fire and the bombs exploding with thick clonking bursts, in a field of fire measured to a couple of feet.

Le Hir was giving orders to the driver. At the turning into the dual-carriageway, Neil saw the Jaguar streak off towards the city. The two Citroëns bumped over the centre verge and screeched round, facing down the coast. In the first car Guérin, Le Hir and Neil were thrown back as the driver accelerated, foot flat on the floor, with the lead-grey road climbing towards them, as the hydraulic springs lowered the chassis to within a few inches of the shrieking tarmac.

Le Hir began to laugh. He turned to Neil: 'They weren't expecting that! Where were they, by the way? In the farmhouse?'

'They were in the courtyard,' said Neil, 'they had a green baize table out, with a carafe of water, glasses, everything.'

Le Hir shook his head, still laughing: '*Ah, c'était vraiment trop facile.*'

Neil stared out at the maize and tobacco fields, watching the mist rise into the pale sun, experiencing an odd, abstracted sensation, like the weightlessness that follows a night of heavy drinking. He no longer cared about Guérin or Pol or Ali La Joconde. What had happened back in the farmhouse seemed suddenly unreal, unimportant. He wondered where Caroline would go for her honeymoon. He said to Le Hir: 'I suppose you consider it a pretty good operation?'

'Five mortars,' said Le Hir, 'four for each corner of the yard, and one for the centre. Twenty shells, with an expanding arc of fire!' He laughed again.

'It might have gone wrong,' said Neil.

Guérin was not listening; he too sat watching the fields swing past the windows.

'One has to take risks,' said Le Hir cheerfully, 'but why should it have gone wrong? After all, they trusted us!'

CHAPTER 9

The driver had hidden the machine-pistols in a rug under the front seat. They were driving again at more than one hundred miles an hour, heading for the bridge across the Oued Zain and the highway south into the mountains to the town of El Mansour.

It was twelve minutes since they had left the road up to the farm. The second Citroën, with the two legionnaires, was fifty yards behind, as the road began to spread out like a slender hand into three, four, five lanes, sweeping into the clover leaf or flyovers just before the Oued Zain Bridge. White arrows flashed out across the tarmac, south to El Mansour, to the mountains and the desert, and west, back towards the capital.

The Citroën slowed with a sigh, as they came in sight of the bridge: a single span of concrete like a white bone reaching across the parched bed of the Oued Zain. The sun peered through the mists, a silvery yellow shining on the stony channels that forked towards the sea.

There were several cars approaching them in the oncoming lane, as they swooped into the booming darkness of the underpass and rose into the steep bend that looped up to the head of the bridge.

The driver braked hard. They had not been able to see the road block from below the clover leaf. There were squat concrete pillboxes at either end of the bridge, and a convoy of Army trucks was lined up on the far side. A couple of jeeps and a mixed unit of three soldiers and three CRS was guarding the entrance to the bridge, turning back the traffic.

A queue of cars stood in front of them. A young NCO was examining papers, and a couple of CRS men strolled round the cars, looking at number plates and poking about in the boots.

The Citroën slowed to a halt before the last car. Le Hir turned to Neil: 'The police will be looking for the Jaguar. The General has papers made out in the name of Maurice Girard, an inspector of waterworks and hygiene in El Mansour. My name is Jean Dubuis; I am a schoolmaster from El Mansour. You, as a journalist, are visiting us to examine social conditions in the town. You understand?'

The first car in the queue was being waved across into the oncoming lane and returning towards the capital. The Citroën crawled forward. Neil looked back and saw the second Citroën about twenty yards behind. Le Hir said, 'Don't worry about them. They have nothing to do with us. Just remember Monsieur Girard and Monsieur Dubuis of El Mansour.'

General Guérin's face was stiff and immobile; he kept his eyes averted from the windows, on a point somewhere on the floor.

The driver of the car ahead was shouting furiously at the young NCO and waving towards the bridge. The NCO shrugged apologetically and beckoned to a CRS officer who sat in one of the jeeps. The boy was young and callow, probably a newly-arrived conscript from France. He left his colleague to deal with the incensed motorist, and turned towards the Citroën. He had the flat red-cheeked face of a Norman peasant boy, with a smudged shaving cut on his upper lip. He came round to the driver's window and said, 'The bridge is closed. You have to go back.'

'What's wrong?' said the driver.

'They're moving troops up to the city. There's something big happening.' He shrugged: 'They've got tanks the other side — but they never tell us anything.'

General Guérin's eyes flickered and met those of the NCO. The boy looked at him, then back at the driver and said, 'Can I see your papers?'

Ahead, the motorist was waving his arms like a bookie laying bets, shouting, '*Malheur pour moi! Malheur pour le France!*' A door slammed and the car drove off with a grinding of gears. The CRS officer came towards the Citroën.

The young NCO had begun examining their identity cards; he looked at Le Hir's, then at Guérin's, and passed them both back while the CRS officer went round and opened the boot.

Neil handed his passport to the NCO. The boy leafed carefully through it as though he had never seen a British passport before, compared the photograph with Neil's face, then walked suddenly back to the CRS officer. Le Hir cursed: 'Is something wrong with your passport?'

'Nothing.'

The CRS man closed the boot and came round to the driver's window. He had a tough intelligent face with very fine eyes, almond-shaped with a bright hazel light in them, and thick eyebrows with a black sheen like horses' hair. He looked round the car and said: 'Are you all going to El Mansour?'

The driver nodded.

'You too?' He looked at Neil.

'That's right.' Neil felt General Guérin sitting very still beside him. Le Hir looked tense, with a taut little muscle working under his cheek just below the white scar.

The CRS man handed Neil's passport back and turned again to the driver: 'Have you got your licence?'

The other two CRS men were now checking the second Citroën. Another car had pulled up behind and was hooting furiously. The CRS officer began studying the driver's licence with exasperating care.

One of the soldiers came over and spoke to the young NCO who went back to the leading jeep. Neil saw him clip on the earphones of a walkie-talkie.

The CRS officer looked at the driver and said, 'You're Michel Rios?'

The driver nodded, and Neil watched the skin on his scarred neck stretch like pitted rubber.

The officer leaned forward, tapping the licence-holder against the door: 'Monsieur Rios, this licence is not signed.'

The driver grinned: 'I never remember to sign anything!' He took out a pen.

Neil looked up and saw the young NCO thrust the earphones at one of the soldiers and start back towards the Citroën. The driver signed the licence, and Neil watched the NCO talking excitedly to the officer, glancing at the Citroën, then at the jeep.

The officer turned, put his head through the window and said to Neil: 'Would you please get out for a moment, monsieur?' He opened the rear door. Nobody in the car moved. Neil looked at General Guérin, then at Le Hir, and their expressions betrayed nothing. The officer held the door open and said again, 'Will you please get out?'

Neil climbed from the car and stood up, feeling the morning sun warm through the mist, and the officer said quietly, 'Follow me, please.'

They began to walk towards the two jeeps. 'You're the English journalist, Ingleby?' said the officer.

'Yes.'

'Those men in the car — you know who they are?'

Neil said nothing.

'Stand behind the jeep, please,' said the officer, 'don't move.' For a moment his eyes met Neil's and their brilliant hazel light held a dangerous glitter. Neil nodded and stood behind the back of the jeep. He could just see the two Citroëns. Still nobody had moved in either of them.

The officer walked back towards the first car. He went round the bonnet until he was on the side where General Guérin sat, then shouted something and raised his machine-pistol. The two CRS men who were checking the second Citroën turned and ran forward, and the three of them, joined by the NCO, closed round the first car. Doors were pulled open and there were two bursts of gunfire.

The CRS officer slid forward against the rear door of the car and went down on to his knees, his machine-pistol crashing on to the road. The young German legionnaire was coming round the side of the second Citroën, his gun jumping in his hand, and Neil saw the little spurts of flame as the NCO shivered and grabbed at his stomach, then sat down and began to scream and vomit on to the tarmac.

The CRS officer was on his knees, groping for the door handle of the first car, when the driver came out with one of the guns from under the rug and slammed the steel butt across the back of his head.

Le Hir had sprung out of the car with the second gun from under the rug, and was crouching down with the two legionnaires, firing steady bursts from behind the open doors.

General Guérin was still inside the car, kneeling on the floor against the front seat.

Neil sat huddled behind the back wheel of the jeep, listening to the shriek and whine of bullets, glass shattering and empty shells rattling on to the tarmac. The young NCO was still sitting in the road, holding his stomach and letting out a horrible panting shriek like an animal. Near him one of the soldiers was lying on his face, trying to crawl back behind the jeeps; and the other soldier was frantically fitting a new clip into his gun, edging back towards the pillbox. The remaining two CRS men had taken cover close to Neil, firing at the tyres of both Citroëns.

Neil heard doors slamming and an engine trying to start with a loose clatter. A bullet whined somewhere very near, and when he looked out again he saw Le Hir sinking on to the road. The second Citroën suddenly roared out from behind the first, its doors open, and swung round in the road with a squeal of rubber, both guns firing in a wide arc as the car reached the opposite lane, steadying a dry skid, and began to accelerate. Then the Douze-Sept opened up across the bridge.

Neil watched the blue flashes spitting up along the road as the armoured shell casing peeled off like a banana skin, with lead splashing out across the tarmac; then came the long thundering roar, and the car shook and split and cracked open, pieces flying off it like something seen in an old jerky film.

A column of men began to advance across the bridge. The firing stopped. All Neil could hear now was the steady crash of boots and whistles and words of command.

Le Hir sat against the wing of the first Citroën white-faced and bleeding from the legs. His gun was empty. The driver had laid down his own gun and came round the side of the car, hands above his head, waiting for the troops across the bridge. He had given up when the Douze-Sept started.

The rear door of the Citroën now opened and General Guérin stepped out. He moved slowly, closing the door behind him as though it might break in his hand, then walked to the side of the road and stopped only a few yards from Neil.

He looked neither at Neil nor at the advancing troops, but stood gazing out across the bridge, down the flat bed of the Oued Zain to where it trickled into the sea. He was stooped and old and broken. He did not answer when the officer came to arrest him. They took him to a jeep and sat him up between four armed CRS men, and the officer who arrested him was very respectful, addressing him as '*mon Général*' as he helped him up, although he did not salute.

Le Hir was still sitting against the wing of the Citroën. They had carried the young NCO to the side of the road. His screams had stopped and he was dying. Neil was put in another jeep bound for the High Command Headquarters above the city. The lieutenant in charge of him smiled grimly: '*Une jolie fin de partie!*'

Neil glanced at what was left of the first Citroën. The big blond legionnaire was sitting upright with the top of his head sliced off like a boiled egg, bone and brain spattered over the seats. The body of the young one was lying broken behind the buckled door.

'At least five dead,' said the lieutenant, 'and Guérin and Le Hir arrested. The Secret Army isn't going to like you for this!'

'I had nothing to do with it.'

The lieutenant shrugged: 'You were in the car. That was the only reason they caught them. They got a tip off that there was an Englishman travelling with them. At least, that's what I heard.'

‘I had nothing to do with it,’ Neil repeated, quietly this time as though talking to himself.

The NCO did not pursue the matter. He only wondered how they had managed to get an Englishman to do the job for them.

PART 6: THE FUGITIVE

CHAPTER 1

'Ah, we're both in the soup, my dear Ingleby,' Pol muttered, as his great wounded body was born aloft, straddled like some modern Buddha across the arms of four soldiers who were now sweating past the seventh floor of the High Command headquarters. Neil followed, listening despondently as Pol continued between groans of discomfort: 'All three of them dead — Marouf and Boussid blown to pieces, and Ali La Joconde dying before the ambulances got there. Most of the barbouzes dead too — *ah, merde!*' Pol's sweating face, streaked with dust and dried blood, creased up with agony, and the soldiers stopped.

'How did you get away?' asked Neil, pausing while the soldiers hoisted Pol into a less awkward position. He had two cuts above the eye, a lump on the crown of his head, and the mauve hibiscus was wilting rapidly in his lapel.

'I was in the shed outside,' he gasped; '*Le petit endroit.* Those rich colons still have the habits of peasants. A little stone shed with a filthy sand-hole. Too much mint tea with Boussid — went through me like a drain — and there I was, squatting down with my ankles caught in my trousers when the heavens are blown open and I'm bounced up to the roof and down again on to my arse, then up again and down again, four times before they stopped. They must have used thirty-six-millimetre shells. It was like a knacker's yard outside.'

'Are you badly hurt?' said Neil, as they rounded the ninth floor.

'Damaged my coccyx. Hit my head too, three or four times — but as I told you, I've got a hard head. It's my spine, close to the arse.' He tried to grin but gave a small scream instead, as one short fat leg began slipping again to the floor.

Neil had waited two hours in a room downstairs before they had brought Pol in from the ambulance. 'You're lucky to be alive,' he said.

'I'm not so sure. These damned policemen, they don't love me for this! I've spoilt the Government's precious relations with the Arab Front. They don't love either of us. We're both very unpopular, my dear Ingleby!'

'But they got Guérin and Le Hir. Aren't they satisfied with that?'

Pol shook his head: 'Not the Sûreté, nor the Deuxième. Guérin and his lot were taken by the CRS — on a tip from me, as a matter of fact. But there's a lot of jealousy between the departments. The Sûreté and the Deuxième won't get any credit for catching Guérin, although they'll have a lot of trouble over the Arab Front killings. That's why I can't stand working for policemen. They have the pettiness of children — only less charm!'

They reached the eleventh floor and Pol was laid to rest on his camp bed, a tumbler of whisky placed between his fingers by one of the soldiers.

'So what happens now?' said Neil. The room was stark and fetid; it smelt of excrement and cement dust and police bureaucracy.

Pol said, 'Have a big whisky.'

Neil helped himself from the bottle on the desk and sat down in front of the camp bed.

'Ah, we're in the soup!' said Pol again. '*Dans la purée noire!*' He rolled his eyes at Neil and grinned: 'You have to get out of this country quick, Monsieur Ingleby. They'll all try to get you now — both sides, after what happened this morning.'

Neil felt a cold lump harden in his stomach, and his fingertips were minutely corrugated like lizard's skin. He said, 'Both sides?'

Pol nodded glumly.

The door opened and a square man with a large head of reddish-blond hair walked in, smoking a leather-bound pipe. He glanced contemptuously down at Pol, then at Neil and said, 'You're the English journalist, Ingleby?'

'Yes.'

'I am Commandant Duxelles, Sûreté Nationale.' He pulled up a chair and sat down facing Neil. He wore a tweed suit with an open-necked white shirt, and his forehead and the backs of his hands were mottled with large pale-brown freckles like tea stains. He studied Neil with shrewd yellow eyes, pulling at his pipe. At last he said, 'You were responsible this morning for the death of almost a dozen men, Monsieur Ingleby. That does not include the incident at the Oued Zain Bridge. Do you consider this part of your duties as a journalist?'

Neil opened his mouth to speak, but Commandant Duxelles jabbed his pipe at him like a pistol and said, 'You have behaved with criminal irresponsibility. You deliberately conspired with the Secret Army to assassinate the leaders of the Arab Front. This, as you know well, will gravely endanger all our efforts to obtain a ceasefire with the Moslem rebels.'

Neil felt his blood rise, the cold dry feeling melt away, and he shouted, 'I acted on the instructions of the Arab Front to try and stop the terrorism! Both sides betrayed me!' He glanced furiously at Pol, reclining Roman-style on one elbow with the whisky in his hand, 'I did what I did in order to stop this endless, meaningless killing!'

He paused, shaking a little, while Duxelles scowled into the bowl of his pipe. The Frenchman lifted his head and his lips turned down into a mean little smile: 'You must be a very stupid man, Monsieur Ingleby.'

Neil flushed and stiffened: epitaph on a bright young pundit who, at the tap of a typewriter, could make politicians writhe over their Sunday breakfasts or snigger in the bar of the House of Commons. He had done what he believed to be right, in keeping with his liberal principles, only to be insulted in a hot stinking room by a member of the French secret police.

'You should leave that sort of work to the professionals,' Duxelles added, taking out Neil's passport and a typewritten document. 'This is your expulsion order. You have until midnight tonight to get out of the country.'

Neil looked at the document. It was stamped by the Department for External Affairs, the Department for Internal Security, the Bureau for the Ministry of the Interior, and bore the seal of the Garde Républicaine de Sécurité. Neil decided it would look rather impressive framed in his flat. He said to Duxelles, 'How do I get out of the country?'

'The airport should be reopening later today.'

'Do you guarantee that?'

'I guarantee nothing,' said Duxelles. 'It is up to the airport authorities. What I can guarantee is that if you're still in the country after midnight you will live to regret it. That is, if you live at all!' He gave Neil a sharp narrow look over his pipe, which he sucked slowly with a crackling of spittle.

'Will you give me an escort to the airport?' said Neil.

Duxelles shrugged: 'I don't have any men to spare. One of our cars will take you back to the hotel. You can get a taxi from there to the airport. And I advise you to spend as little time in the hotel as possible.' He stood up, nodded to both of them, stuck his pipe back in his mouth and strutted out.

Neil turned to Pol: 'You've got to help me. That man has no interest whatever in whether I get killed or not.'

'He'd prefer you killed,' said Pol evenly. 'You're a very dangerous witness to what happened this morning — and a journalist on top of it.'

'Will he try to get me killed?' The cold lumpy feeling came back; and Neil stood there with a sense of nightmarish unreality: he under sentence of death and Pol with his damaged coccyx, drinking whisky together surrounded by the stink of lavatories and memories of white telephones and green figs in Athens. And Neil heard Pol saying, 'Commandant Duxelles is too subtle to have you killed. He relies on someone of the Arab Front or the Secret Army doing it for him.'

'Then you must help me,' said Neil again, now desperate. 'You got me into all this — now get me out of it! I want an escort to the airport and a safe-conduct on to a plane.'

'The airport's still closed,' Pol muttered. 'My dear Ingleby, I can do nothing. I am in a very bad odour here.'

'Can't you persuade them to give me protection in this place?'

'I'm sorry, but you heard what Duxelles said. They want you out of the country.'

'But supposing I can't get out of the country!'

Pol's eyes closed with pain. 'Give me another whisky,' he murmured.

Neil splashed some more into his glass and said, 'I helped you in Athens — you must help me now.'

'Things have changed. My own position' — he waved his hand round the grim concrete room — 'has become very delicate. I haven't any influence left.'

'You must have some influence!' Neil cried. 'Surely they're not just going to leave me here to be killed, are they? Can't you contact Paris and get them to do something?'

Pol cleared his throat and spat on to the linoleum close to Neil's foot. 'The only thing you can do,' he said, 'is go to your Consulate. Perhaps they can bring pressure to bear. I can't do anything.'

'You did plenty earlier this morning!'

Pol nodded, sipping whisky.

'I suppose you planned it all back in Athens — using me as bait?'

Pol looked up at him, and for a moment Neil thought he saw tears forming in his eyes. He realized that the man was in considerable pain. 'Yes, I got the idea in Athens,' Pol said feebly, 'I thought it might work. The situation was getting desperate. We had to catch Guérin somehow, and I wasn't particularly concerned about who did it. I'm not like these policemen — I don't mind who gets the credit.'

'Or who gets killed!' said Neil, glaring at him as he lay there propped on his elbow, with the hibiscus drooping like a soiled napkin from his lapel. 'You great fat lout!' he snarled. 'If you weren't so fat, and could walk, I'd kick you down those eleven flights of stairs!'

'Ah, you have an unkind tongue, Monsieur Ingleby!' said Pol miserably, in pain.

'I'm not feeling in a kind mood,' said Neil. It was becoming like some preposterous lovers' quarrel. 'It's a pity Peter Van Loon didn't let Jadot kill you on the boat,' he added, and Pol's eyes rolled upwards, sad and swimming with tears: 'Ah, don't talk like that! I didn't want to see you in danger, but you did ask for it.'

'Ask for it!' Neil yelled; 'what the hell do you mean?' He clenched his fists and took a step forward.

Pol flinched slightly, took a gulp of whisky, and said. 'This morning you told Guérin that I was waiting for him, didn't you?'

Neil stopped and gaped at him. The anger had suddenly gone: now he just felt tired and frightened and desperately in need of help. 'No, Monsieur Pol. I told General Guérin that it was all right to go into the farm. I told him that the three Arab leaders were there and that the escort was in order. You convinced me. I broke my word.'

For a moment Pol did not speak. The two of them drank in silence.

'Very well,' said Pol at last, 'I will do what I can for you. I can talk to a couple of CRS I know here — they may be able to arrange to get you on to a plane. Or perhaps send an escort to your hotel. I can't promise much, but it may help you.'

At that moment a man came in to tell Neil that the car was waiting outside. He went without another word to Pol, down the eleven flights and past the three lines of CRS guards and the sandbags in the courtyard, with more troops and mounted machineguns, and down the steps to where the armoured cars waited facing the road into the capital.

In the distance he could hear gunfire: not the sporadic crackle of small-arms, but a continuous rumble, slow and heavy, rolling through the humid air like thunder.

The car was a small Renault and the driver a nervous-looking corporal who saluted as Neil got in and muttered, 'It's a bad time — they've started attacking the barricades.'

'When?'

'About half-an-hour ago.'

Neil looked at his watch. It was 10.35. They had told him nothing about it at High Command headquarters. At nine o'clock, the corporal said, the radio had announced that General Guérin had been arrested and was on his way by military Caravelle to Paris. The rebels had been given one hour in which to surrender. They had stood firm; now 5,000 Gardes Mobiles, supported by fresh troops from France, were moving in to break the barricade.

The corporal shook his head with dismal ferocity: 'Ah, that it should come to this — French against French!'

They passed long lines of troops in battle order and armoured vehicles along the road out of the hills into the city. There were roadblocks now at every corner and the troops grew thicker, colour of mud and olives, with guns on tripods up the boulevards, shutters down and cafés empty, jeeps sprouting radio antennae like squat brown insects.

The streets up from the sea cracked and popped and stuttered with obscure echoes; then came the tearing crash of heavy artillery that made windows rattle, and the corporal cried, 'That's a cannon Trente-Six — they must be murdering them in there!'

They turned into the wide curving boulevard towards the Front de Mer and looked down on the truckloads of troops below, helmeted, like wedges of green caviar. The corporal was pale and began crashing his gears, and Neil thought: perhaps this is how Duxelles wants it done. One Englishman, and one French corporal to spare, shot in action.

There was a tank in the middle of the street outside the Miramar and a line of troops stretched away under the arcades opposite. The corporal pulled up in front of the hotel and cried, 'Hurry! I want to get out of here!'

'Could you take me to the airport?' said Neil. 'I've just got to pick up my luggage.'

The corporal smacked the wheel with both hands: 'You think I'm mad? — risk getting shot down by my own countrymen? No! I'm getting out of here!'

Neil sat and said, 'I'll give you money. Plenty, just take me to the airport. The road there'll be as safe as the one we've just come on.'

The corporal pointed up the street: 'That's where the shooting is! Up there — the way to the airport! Go on, get out of here!'

Neil got out and said, 'Go to hell!' slamming the door, and the little car bolted away like a frightened colt.

At the desk the silver-haired receptionist gave him an odd, dead-eyed look as he handed him his key and a couple of telegrams. Neil said, 'Can you call a taxi?'

The receptionist shook his head: 'You won't get a taxi on a day like this, sir.'

Neil went through into the downstairs bar. It was empty except for the sleek-haired boy who was putting out salted nuts on the tables. He could hear Hudson's muffled voice bawling from one of the nearby telephone booths: 'Yeah, it's started — tanks, bazookas! No jets — yes. O.K.!'

The first telegram he opened read '*No reply explanation absence must assume serious situation Foster.*' It was dated the day before. The second telegram had been sent three days ago, late on Saturday night. '*No copy or follow-up stop other correspondents filing stop where the devil are you reply immediately Foster!*'

He screwed the cables into little blue balls and bowled them across the bar at a spittoon against the wall. Both missed. Hudson's voice bellowed out, 'Yeah for Christ's sake — G for

George — U for Uncle — E for Edward — yeah, the big boy! — arrested this morning…'

Neil went through and said: 'Hudson, I've got to talk to you!'

A hand waved angrily, head into the mouthpiece: '"After fierce gun battle" — not now, for Christ's sake!'

There was something about the way that receptionist looked at me, Neil thought. He would go up and pack, then find one of the other reporters. He started down the passage and met Tom Mallory coming from the lifts.

'What a bloody din!' Mallory's hair rose like flames round a dark sun.

'Have you been outside?' said Neil.

'Hell, I was trying to get a bit of kip! Woken up by those bloody guns. Let's have a drink.'

'You're not going out to have a look at the fighting?' Neil said, following him into the bar.

'What's the point? You can't get near the barricades. Most of the Press boys are up on the roof. There's nothing to see — just a lot o' stupid buggers shooting at each other.'

The sleek-haired barman poured two Scotch-on-the-rocks. They could still hear the crash of gunfire outside, but it seemed to be slackening now.

'I heard you were down in the Bled,' said Mallory, 'anything doing?'

'Nothing much.' Neil was trying to decide how much he could safely confide in Mallory; for if he were to get out of this country alive he was going to need help. Tom Mallory was hardly a rock of responsibility, but he possessed a certain reckless courage that Neil badly needed at this moment.

'It's all right for you, old boy,' Mallory was croaking over his whisky, 'you don't have to file till the weekend. I have to give the sods a story every evening at six. You heard, by the way, that Guérin's been arrested?'

'Yes, I heard,' said Neil. 'I was there.'

Mallory nodded. He was too old a hand to show surprise at anything anymore. He just said, 'You'd better tell me about it.' Neil gave him the brief outline, and Mallory listened with his huge hairy head down near the bar, breathing like a dog after a run. When Neil had finished he said glumly, 'You're in a fine bloody mess, aren't you? Better have another drink.'

'Officially, I've got till midnight to get out.'

'I think you'd better get out before that,' said Mallory.

Hudson came skidding in, his tight little face forked with tension. 'I heard at least a hundred dead!' he cried. 'They shelled the university.'

'Well done,' said Mallory, 'have a drink.'

Neil said, 'I came in by boat. It should still be down at the dock.'

'We'll try that first, then the airport. But the last I heard, it was still closed when the fighting started.'

'What is all this?' said Hudson.

'You'll find out,' said Mallory, 'best story of the day.'

'What do you think they'll do?' Neil asked.

'Try and kill you. Both sides think you betrayed them. And these boys don't let you off with just a warning.'

Neil took a long drink and Hudson whined, 'Hell, Tom! What's all this?'

'You're not drinking your drink, Hudson,' Mallory growled. He turned back to Neil: 'Did reception see you come in?'

'Yes.'

'When?'

'About a quarter of an hour ago.'

Mallory nodded his great mane and said slowly, 'They're not likely to try anything before dark — at least not until the city quietens down. That gives us a bit of time. All the trains have stopped and the roads are closed. You might just manage to get out by boat. But your best bet is still the airport — if it opens in time.'

Winston St. Leger came in, groomed and urbane as though it were Boodle's. 'I heard they've just packed it in, surrendered,' he said, placing his homburg on the bar and popping an olive into his mouth.

'That official?' snapped Hudson.

'I gather so.'

'Have a drink, Winston,' said Mallory.

'Thank you, pink gin.'

'We're having a little talk about our friend Ingleby,' Mallory went on, 'he's in a spot of trouble.'

The drinks and the company made Neil feel better. He told his story again, in more detail this time, to Hudson and St. Leger. Hudson scribbled furious shorthand throughout, and at the end said knowingly, 'Well, we warned you! Now you're right in it.'

'Drop dead,' said Mallory, without venom. He turned to Stu Leger: 'What do you think?'

'It seems quite astonishing to me,' said Winston, squeezing a blob of toothpaste on to an olive, 'that the authorities refuse to give you any protection. Outrageous, in fact.'

'You get yourself screwed up in this sort of situation, you can't expect help from anybody,' said Hudson. 'You're sure Ali La Joconde's dead?' he added. 'Good! I gotta phone.'

'Don't mind him,' said Mallory, tipping his stool recklessly on to one leg, 'agency man — his ulcers start bursting on a story like this.'

'Have you tried the Consulate?' said St. Leger, sucking the nipple of his toothpaste tube.

'To hell with the Consulate,' said Mallory, 'they can kill you as easily in there as in here. Only here it's bigger and there are more of us.'

Neil remembered Pol's suggestion: 'The Consulate might be able to persuade the French Government to get me out.'

'They might,' said Mallory, 'but not in the time you need. You've got to be out of here tonight — or at the latest, tomorrow morning.'

'Still, it would be a matter of form to contact the Consulate,' St. Leger persisted.

'Matter of form!' Neil mimicked — 'a lot of good that's going to do me when I've got a bullet in my head!'

'Yes, you've a point there, I grant you.'

'Have another drink,' said Mallory.

'I ought to be going.' Neil was beginning to feel drunk. Hudson's voice came trumpeting through, amid a burble of foreign tongues on telephones: 'Yeah for Chrissake, O C O N — French for Giaconda, like Mona Lisa with a J…!'

Mallory held his empty glass up to the barman and screeched, 'Nurse!' His tilted stool suddenly crashed sideways, nearly rolling Winston St. Leger to the floor.

'I saw that was going to happen,' said Winston rather testily, and Neil said again, 'I ought to go — I've got to pack.'

'Stay and have another. Plenty of time.'

'He ought to go,' said Winston, 'to be on the safe side.'

The safe side! thought Neil. Winston St. Leger, sir, you overestimate the power of understatement.

A number of reporters were coming down from the roof. The fighting had stopped altogether now. Neil rode up in the lift and began to walk down the corridor. He met no one and the only sound was the whirring of the air-conditioners. He remembered the last time he had been in his room. They had been there waiting for him. The receptionists had let them in, and they had sat there drinking his cognac, taking their time till he unlocked the door and walked in. If they came to kill him again — somebody other than the two legionnaires now this would be the first place they'd try. They'd be in there waiting. And Tom Mallory and Hudson and the rest would get a good story almost without having to step out of the bar.

He reached the corner of the corridor leading to his room. There was still no one in sight. A sudden instinctive terror warned him to run. He looked up the dim rows of doors to an oblique shaft of sunlight from a window at the end of the passage.

He turned and fled, back to the lifts. The one he had come up in was on the way down. He began to run down the stairs. He now felt very drunk, and once he slipped on the marble and nearly fell. He was sweating and out of breath when he reached the bar.

A crowd of reporters had collected, with Mallory in the middle buying drinks. 'What happened?' he croaked. 'You seen a ghost?'

'Come on, let's go!' Neil said.

'Where's your gear?'

'I didn't get it. Come on!'

Mallory tipped back his drink and heaved himself off his stool, and Winston St. Leger smiled nobly at Neil and said, 'Good luck! Hope you get away!'

Mallory had his Hillman Minx parked behind the hotel. They got in and headed down the Front de Mer. 'You think there might be someone up in your room?' he said.

'There might be. There was last time. Two Foreign Legion boys. Germans. That was the start of it all.'

'Disgusting Krauts,' Mallory muttered, 'all over the bloody place. I heard they've got some ex-Waffen SS boys here leading Jewish commandos in the Gambetta suburb. What would our modern sociologists make of that?'

They had reached the end of the Front de Mer where the 'Serafina' had been moored under the sea-wall. It seemed a long time ago: less than a week. Neil climbed out into the sunlight and thought, God I feel drunk, as he watched the CRS men come forward from under the palms.

'You can't stay there!' shouted the officer. 'Go on, get moving!'

Mallory had produced a reel of international Press passes like a postcard rack, growling at the guards who only shook their heads and waved him on with the muzzles of their machine-pistols. '*Allez, passez, messieurs, passez!*'

Neil stood weakly against the parapet of the sea-wall and watched the 'Serafina' below, bobbing white against the brilliant blue, feeling the glow of whisky dying in him with a flat sour taste as he listened to Mallory croaking at the CRS with mock rage. But the guards only shook their heads again and began to hustle him towards his car. For a moment Neil thought he was going to hit one of them. It gave him a gloomy inspiration: why not assault one of the CRS and get himself arrested?

Finally Mallory relented. He shook himself free and turned to Neil, hair flaming gold in the noon sun, his face like a flaking gargoyle: 'Come on, old boy! Port's closed. Nobody gets in, nobody gets out!'

They climbed back into the Hillman and turned back down the Front de Mer: palms curving sharp against the sun like scimitars, balconies rising layer on layer, shutters clattering up and people coming down into the streets. Some of them might belong to Le Hir: anonymous black-jacketed toughs mixing with the crowds. Or perhaps Ali La Joconde's men. But they'd have difficulty slipping into the European area. They certainly wouldn't get past the receptionists at the Miramar. He wondered about Anne-Marie: was there some way in which he could contact her? Explain to her that he hadn't been responsible for General Guérin's arrest?

'So you left your luggage at the hotel,' said Mallory, 'and you gave your key up, didn't you?' He frowned and thumped the horn at a couple of Gardes Mobiles in a jeep; they threw him a furious look as he swerved round them on the wrong side of the road. 'Cretins can't even drive straight! You know, you ought to have held on to that key. Best thing is pretend you're still in the hotel. Then if the airport's open, just sit tight till you get on a plane.'

'I suppose I'll have to collect the key, then?' said Neil faintly. They were crossing the Place Lyautey. The two burnt-out cars they had passed on that first afternoon were still there, lying beside the statue of France's greatest colonial pioneer, his bronze whiskers whitened with gull droppings.

Another hundred yards and they'd be at the hotel.

'No, forget about the key!' said Mallory. 'We'll fix something for you.' They were driving past the palm-groves at the entrance to the Miramar: 'And even if you do get killed, you'll still make the front pages. Blood and glory, old boy! Your photograph and everything.'

'Where are we going?' said Neil.

'The airport.'

CHAPTER 2

Out on the shimmering tarmac the Caravelles lay like sleeping swans. Neil sat watching them, twisted round on his high stool, drinking Pernod. After a moment he began to imagine that they were silver fish in a vast sunlit tank behind the plate-glass of the airport building. And to escape from the airport he would somehow have to swim into the belly of those fish and rise with them thousands of fathoms, high above the distant mountains, into the purple stratosphere where he would be cool and free, away from the crowds and sweat and danger.

He and Mallory were at the upstairs bar overlooking the departure hall. They had been here for more than three hours now; and Mallory had written, in bold letters with his gold-topped Parker 51, the word 'EXODUS' twenty times down the back of the price-list.

From somewhere in the ceiling came the stereophonic *PING PING!* and the seductive purr of a girl's voice: *'Air France regrette d'annoncer qu'aucun depart est prévu pour Paris'*. The words floated down among the lozenge lamps, past the cases of perfume and silks and over-priced Kabyle jewellery, to the dove-grey couches and parquet flooring packed with scared, crumpled people: women weeping and children spewing and shrieking, squatting nerve-racked and exhausted over the pitiful litter of refugees — bundles wrapped in newspaper, and prams and dolls and strapped-up trunks too heavy to carry.

Airhostesses, in trim tailored blue with sharply shelved hips, tapped across the floors carrying flight schedules. Only there were no flights. It was now 4.15 and no plane had left since the airport reopened shortly after midday.

As soon as the barricades had fallen, the flight of the Europeans had begun. There were now more than two thousand of them inside the airport; and another five thousand waited along the roads outside, where threads of barbed wire and columns of CRS troops guarded the queues of cars and crowds.

The Secret Army had broadcast an order that any European — man, woman or child — who tried to flee the country would be punished with death. The threat had now been extended to crews and ground staff who attempted to man a refugee flight. Shortly after one o'clock most of the airport staff had gone on strike; they had been followed by several of the Caravelle crews who came from France. Each plane was now being searched for bombs; crews, staff and airport officials were being questioned; and everywhere there was slow spreading chaos and panic.

Neil watched the Caravelles and thought of boiled sweets before take-off, hostesses smiling like nurses, frozen lunches, orange streetlamps down the Great West Road. In his pocket next to his passport he had a white card with the number 57. Pol had at least managed to do that much for him. No air tickets were being sold or accepted; instead, everyone who arrived at the airport was given a numbered card, against a list kept by the CRS. Only five hundred numbers had so far been issued, and the list was now closed. The lucky ones might be able to get away that night. Neil's number guaranteed him a place on the first flight.

Mallory was explaining, almost inaudibly, his theory of expenses. As the day had drawn on his voice bad sunk from a croak to a whisper, punctuated by bursts of bronchial laughter that showed a few isolated teeth, like rusted nails at the back of his mouth.

'Always stick to the small items,' he was saying, in a low hiss, 'confuse 'em with little things — thousands of 'em. They mount up. In Leopoldville I got away with "Five pounds, sending bananas to Congolese Parliamentarians".' He opened his mouth wide and laughed with a sound like toast being scraped, 'Never try to make a big coup. I was chasing old Fuchs round the Antarctic. Bought myself a great fur coat — had to, I wasn't going to freeze in a bloody sports jacket. Charged 'em almost what it cost — a hundred and fifty quid from Fortnum's. I also went to town on the little items. You know, "hire of sleigh, hire of huskies, purchase of food to feed the huskies, fee for interpreter to give orders to the huskies, petrol for motorized sleigh when the huskies died". Got most of it through, but the sods in the office wouldn't pass the coat. Said the office never pays for reporters' clothes. So they sent all the expense sheets back — exactly eight hundred and seventy-nine pounds six shillings' worth, and I started all over again — sleighs, huskies, husky meat, interpreter's fee, with purchase of radio transmitting equipment thrown in, adding a few quid to every item. Got it up to exactly eight hundred and seventy-nine pounds, six shillings.' He paused, grinning vilely with his empty gums. 'Then I put a little note at the bottom,' he hissed, 'I wrote: "Find the fur coat in this!"'

His laugh broke into a hacking cough which almost shook him off his stool. Neil stared into his glass. The ice had melted and the dull green liquid was tepid and bitter-sweet and his head was beginning to sing. Mallory had called over one of the airhostesses. She was a delicate-boned girl with ash-blonde hair in a neat helmet-cut. She paused by the bar, head turned, listening as Mallory hissed at her in his abominable French, 'Any chance of a flight?'

'What number do you have, please?'

'Fifty-seven.'

She gave a contemptuous shrug: 'Perhaps. I don't know. The Secret Army say they're going to blow up the planes if we try to take off. You're not from here, are you?'

'Journalists,' said Mallory.

'Ah, journalists!' She nodded, looking suddenly fierce: 'I'm not from here either, I live in Paris. I'm not getting mixed up in this mess. I want to get back alive!'

Mallory cackled at her and she walked away. 'You see, old boy, she's intelligent — she wants to get back to her nice civilized sex-life in Paris. She doesn't want to get blown up. Pity to see a girl like that blown up, don't you think?'

Neil nodded, focusing giddily. His Pernod glass had gently reproduced itself into two glasses, and there were two barmen and two dark faces with flaming hair. He squinted across the bar, watching the airhostess stepping down the shallow stairs, past the rows of refugees, babies on their backs screaming, the CRS prowling with guns at the hip — watching her slim legs and neat little haunches disappear behind one of the departure desks. Air France, TWA, El Al, BEA. Pictures of a beefeater in colour; Manhattan skyline at dusk, patterned with dominoes of light.

He thought, if I don't get out of this place in the next few hours, I'm going to die.

He began trying to tell Mallory about Caroline. Mallory was coughing and spitting into his drink, hissing, 'Well out of it, old boy! Well out of it! Sounds like a bed-and-breakfast girl.' Somewhere close by a baby began a scratchy shriek, followed by other babies, all beginning to howl together with the instinct of dogs barking. Mallory was banging the bar for more drinks. Neil said slowly, trying to get the words out as if they were plums in his mouth, 'She's getting married on Saturday morning to a racing-motorist.'

'Good! You're all right, old boy. You skip your first marriage — get on with your second when you're forty.'

Down in the departure hall a group of CRS were grappling with a burly middle-aged man with grey hair and dark glasses. They had him by both arms, swinging him round with his legs splayed out absurdly behind him, as they began dragging him over to the airport police offices.

The ash-blonde airhostess came out from behind the departure desk and trotted over to a glass partition in the Garderie d'Enfants. Neil watched her mistily, miserably, imagining the brass bedstead and flowered wallpaper in a Paris hotel: her slim body crisp as celery, wearing nothing but seamless stockings. Harmless sex fantasies of an English intellectual about to die. 'Drink up!' croaked Mallory, clinking glasses: two glasses, four, eight, multiplying and dividing, and Neil murmured, 'Do you like sleeping with girls wearing only stockings?'

'Don't mind. With or without.' Mallory looked at his watch. 'I'll have to go soon, old boy. Got to file copy.'

Neil felt a griping panic, a terror of being left alone among these thousands of destitute helpless people. He knew suddenly that he was going to die. Mallory was finishing his drink, saying, 'By the way, I heard you had a nice little bird in your room last week?'

Neil stared at nothing. Mallory went on, 'There was a funny rumour going round. I don't know where it started — there's a lot of gossip in the hotel. Receptionists don't miss much.'

Neil was trying to exercise his stiffening face muscles, while Mallory gave him a rusty leer, speaking now with a crafty look in his eyes: 'Only hearsay, old boy, but the rumour got around. Those bloody receptionists. You want to know what it was?'

'What? What are you talking about?'

'The girl you had up in your room.'

'Oh yes.'

'D'ye know what they've been saying?'

'Who?'

'In the hotel. People in the hotel. Gossip, old boy. Evil gossip.'

'What did they say?'

'Somebody heard that the girl was the stepdaughter —' He broke off with a violent bout of coughing that seemed to send bits of his face flying off in all directions, his whole physiognomy breaking up like a jigsaw puzzle.

'Stepdaughter?' said Neil.

'Stepdaughter of none other than the illustrious Colonel Pierre Broussard.'

Mallory's two purple faces quickly elided. Neil blinked, swallowed drily, tried to think. Mallory was saying, 'Who is she? It would be a bloody magnificent story if it was true.'

Neil held on to the edge of the bar. It made sense: she had been in Broussard's flat, she had been on friendly terms with Le Hir, she had known all about Athos. And she had tried to warn him that night in the hotel; then later, in Le Hir's flat, she had refused to talk about anything. She would have known what was going to happen: the plan for the flashed headlamps and the mortars in the mountains.

Mallory said again, 'Who was she, you randy old lecher?'

'I don't know. Some girl from the Secret Army. She had supper with me. Very innocent.'

Mallory made a gurgling noise: 'There was an American in Leopoldville who managed to lay one of Lumumba's Belgian lady advisers, so-called.'

Neil wondered: if it were true would it make things better or worse? Would she believe that he had betrayed Guérin? Perhaps it didn't matter in the long run. Distantly, through layers of numb brain tissue, he heard a girl's voice calling to him: '*Air France annonce le depart de leur premier vol vers Paris —*'

The atmosphere suddenly intensified. From the main hall came a surging sound like the sea. Mallory was tugging at Neil's elbow, calling for the barman: 'Come on, you're off!'

Neil slid from the stool and felt the floor lurch under him like the deck of a fast ship. He walked carefully, with a slight keel to port, down the shallow stairs behind Mallory, listening to the girl's voice all round him: '*Tons les passagers munis de cartes de police numerotées l'un jusqu'au quatre-vingt-douze doivent se présenter au Guichet Zéro!*'

Numbers One to Four — Twenties-and-Twelve. Ninety-two. And he had number Fifty-seven. It was like the incantation of some sinister lottery.

Across the main hall the crowds were stirring with restless anticipation. Those who were among the lucky numbers were hurrying, pushing, shouting, scrambling to get into the untidy column forming outside Guichet Zéro. An illuminated board had flashed on above the head of a bull-necked CRS with horn-rimmed sunglasses: 'DEPART ORLY 1900 H.'

At the far end of the hall, beyond the main entrance, Neil caught a glimpse of more crowds, and cars jammed three abreast along the dual-carriageway into the city, with motorcycle escorts droning up and down beside them in the dusty heat. Like an August Bank Holiday, he thought, with guns.

Now that he was standing up he realized that he was very drunk indeed, but with no sense of elation or release — only a giddy nausea, accentuated by the feverish sobriety all round him.

Since they had no luggage, they found themselves near the head of the swelling queue which edged slowly, under growing pressure, towards the departure desk. Here the passengers were being examined by three CRS. The first studied each passport, checking names against a list of Secret Army suspects; the second checked the numbered cards, and the third searched the passengers for arms and explosives. The bull-necked CRS man with the sunglasses stood beside the desk covering the queue with his machine-pistol.

Most of the passengers were either old, or very young children. Behind Neil was a fragile man of about seventy with a white waxed moustache, standing next to a pasty-faced woman who looked like a Spanish fishwife. She was laden with a heap of parcels and cardboard boxes, while he struggled with an enormous Empire clock. The pendulum stuck out from under the mechanism like a spear. While they were standing still the old man guarded it between his bow-legs, bending slowly down whenever the queue began to move, heaving it up to the level of his knees. Each time he laid it down his face had turned blue about the lips and his old watery eyes would fall on Neil and Mallory with a look of faint shock.

Mallory's appearance had become fearful, and his bouts of asthmatic coughing were now exploding at regular intervals, between which he kept up a hissing, spluttering conversation. Neil made muddled efforts to follow what he was saying, knowing vaguely that they should be helping the old couple with their luggage. He thought, if I take more than two parcels I may fall over. Mallory'll have to take the clock.

They were coming close to the desk. Neil looked at his watch and saw that it had stopped at twenty past four. 'Have you got your card ready?' Mallory croaked close to his ear. Neil fumbled inside his jacket, got out his passport, numbered card and deportation order.

'All right for money?'

Neil nodded: 'I've got traveller's cheques.'

'You'll be all right,' said Mallory, 'if anything goes wrong and you can't get away after all, give me a ring at the Miramar.'

Neil focused on him with difficulty and held out a hand; 'You've been very good, Tom. Thanks. Thanks for everything.' Behind him the old man was again grappling with his monstrous clock. Neil leant down and murmured, '*Permettez-moi.*' He stood up clasping the edifice to his chest, peering at Mallory's baroque face: 'I'll buy you a drink back in London. Bottle of champagne.'

'Never touch the stuff, old boy. Gives me wind. You can buy me a bottle of whisky at Raymond's Revue Bar.'

'I'll do that,' said Neil.

Mallory shook him by the arm, and Neil watched him shamble away across the hall, walking like an old man whose limbs are not perfectly co-ordinated.

The CRS guard said, '*Passeport! Carte de depart!*'

Neil lowered the clock and handed over his papers. The man studied them, then passed the deportation order to his colleague, who lifted a telephone, spoke a few inaudible words, nodded and hung up. The first CRS man waved his hand: '*Ça va, passez!*' The third man stepped up and patted Neil under the elbows, on his hips and between his thighs and knees. Neil remembered that this was how it had all begun: six days ago at the Piraeus, with the puffy-faced policeman frisking him and

Van Loon. Only this time it was done more gently, almost as though he were being measured for a suit.

He was still holding the Empire clock. The old man and the fishwife were coming through behind him, ready to be searched. Neil took a step sideways and tripped over the woman's heap of parcels. His elbow, sank deep into one of the cardboard boxes which was full of crockery. He heard a soft crunch, and the fishwife shrieked something, and the CRS man glared down at him: 'What's going on?'

He realized that he must be looking conspicuously drunk. He murmured something about tripping: 'Lost my balance — fell over the luggage.' He struggled up, and the little old man grabbed back the clock, touching it all over to make sure it had not been damaged. Neil could hear him muttering to himself, making no effort to thank Neil for his trouble. But Neil felt relieved, his conscience salved; he had carried the old man's clock, and he was through the CRS checkpoint, walking up the sloping corridor to the departure lounge.

From the tall windows over the airport he could see the Caravelles being nosed slowly round, taking up their positions in line at the end runway. Men in blue-and-white overalls scuttled round the planes with flags, and black-helmeted CRS weaved about on motorcycles, while more CRS foot-patrols stood under the wings and near the doors. A caterpillar convoy of Total oil trucks was winding across the tarmac towards the first Caravelle, 'La Princess d'Aquitaine'.

The departure lounge was quiet and restful, except for the burbling of a few infants in arms. The bar and the souvenir counter were open, presided over by a handsome middle-aged woman with a gleaming bell of dyed-blonde hair. Neil went to the bar and ordered a black coffee; and wondered whether it would do any good at all buying Caroline a four-ounce bottle of Balenciaga perfume. Next to him a harassed mother with a small girl was pleading with the blonde woman at the counter. The child was pointing at a doll in Kabyle national costume, whining softly and tugging her mother's sleeve. The blonde woman shook her head: 'I am sorry, madame, but the company does not give away presents.'

The mother had her purse out and was hunting through some loose change. 'I'm expecting some money when we get to Paris,' she muttered.

Neil moved forward and said, with a pronounced slur that seemed to come from behind his left ear, 'Do you want to borrow some money, madame?'

Both women glanced suspiciously at him. The mother looked embarrassed and the blonde woman's face hardened as Neil went on, 'Does your little girl want to buy a doll?'

The mother was confused, tired and pale, glancing at the whining wide-eyed child. Neil took an ironic pleasure in the scene: the floor was still swaying, his head throbbed, the faces blurred, the child went on gaping at him. He realized that he was not a prepossessing character to meet in a crisis; but he persevered, enjoying his philanthropic role, asking the blonde woman, 'How much is the doll?'

The mother cut in hastily, '*Non, monsieur, je vous en prie* —!' Her words were broken off by a loud thud from outside. They all looked at the windows. Men were running across the apron, away from the Caravelles. The CRS motorcycles snarled out from under the wings and two men leapt from the driver's cabin of the Total fuel convoy.

White smoke was drifting along the belly of the 'La Princesse d'Aquitaine', crawling up the sides of the fuselage close to the jets. In the lounge somebody screamed. There was a movement, shouting, pressing round the windows.

Neil was halfway across the floor when it happened: a roaring boom, followed by a crack that shook the plate-glass. The slim silver body of the Caravelle had burst into black billows of smoke that opened into swelling cauliflowers of orange flame, spreading across the runway, covering the second and third Caravelles, while the sirens started up and bells began to ring inside the terminal. The seductive girl's voice purred from the ceiling, unobtrusive, undisturbed: '*Tous les passagers munis de cartes de police numerotées* —'

They were ordered back to the main hall. The little girl was trotting after her mother, still whining about the doll. The mother turned at the door and slapped her, and the child set up a high artificial scream of pain that wailed down the corridor towards the departure desks.

Neil took a last look across the lounge and wondered if he would ever see it again. Perhaps in another hour, two hours, after nightfall. He saw the little old man stumbling across the floor with his Empire clock, at the heels of the black-haired fishwife who led the way with her pile of parcels held aloft, like some ludicrous offering to the gods. To answer what prayer? Neil wondered, walking slowly, drunkenly, wanting to curl up in a corner and sleep.

He passed the three CRS at the departure desk and asked wearily, 'Have you any idea at all when we'll be leaving?'

One of them grinned: 'Next year perhaps — if it goes on like this.'

Neil walked on into the main hall, between the hunched waiting crowds; and he wondered how long the end would now be, and how it would come, and who would do it.

CHAPTER 3

The sun went down and Colonel Broussard sat up in his cramped rented flat, smoking opium and staring at his reflection in the table varnished like a dark mirror. In his left hand he held a long-stemmed pipe of china clay; in his right, in the closed palm, lay the 100-sestertii piece that had once paid off Brutus' troops in Egypt.

Across the table sat two para troop captains, their adjutants, and Broussard's personal bodyguard and chauffeur, Serge Rassini — the big black-haired Corsican with the bandit moustache. They had been in conference all afternoon, passing orders on the heavy transmitter concealed in the metal box that Broussard had carried on Atnos. After Guérin's arrest Broussard had taken command of the Secret Army, organizing first the defence of the barricades, and later the dispersal of the combat units, hiding of arms and explosives, and regrouping of the commando units.

He had first learnt of the surrender of the barricades on a transistor radio inside the Préfecture. The broadcast, seven hours ago, had been shrill and confused, on a pirate channel operating from the Cité de l'Université. The collapse had come almost before any resistance could be given. He had known that the students would be the first to break, but had hoped that the paras and the legionnaires would hold out at least until nightfall, when the Army might come over to their side.

But the Army had not come over. Instead, the students had panicked, allowing the Gardes Mobiles to storm the Cité de l'Université with heavy artillery, battering through whole buildings, leaving lanes of rubble, trailing tram-wires, buckled lamp-standards and bodies bleached with dust and plaster. The assault had taken even the paras and Foreign Legion units by surprise; they had pulled back in confusion, dispersed, fought sporadic gun-battles through cellars and across rooftops, and finally followed the students in a chaotic surrender.

Broussard had fled through the back of the Préfecture and set up headquarters in his flat, where he had sat at first bitter and dejected, cursing the students for their cowardice, cursing the treachery that had delivered up General Guérin, knowing that it was Guérin's arrest, and not the guns of the Gardes Mobiles, which had really broken the barricades. The opium had gradually soothed him. The conference was now almost over. There remained only one thing to be settled: the affair of the Englishman who had betrayed Guérin.

Broussard sucked at his clay pipe, breathing out a sweet smoke that filled the room like incense. The bowl of the pipe was small and shallow as a salt-spoon, holding the shrivelled kernel of burnt opium which bubbled slightly as he inhaled.

The paratroop officers folded their files into briefcases, stood up and saluted, the door held open by their adjutants. Broussard saluted them with his closed fist holding the gold sestertii coin. His mind was dulled, his nerves rested, the machinery of thought working slowly, pleasantly, clear in purpose, knowing precisely what must be done. His power remained, orders and responsibility had been delegated. He smoked in silence.

Only Serge Rassini stayed seated opposite him across the polished table, checking the latest report from the airfield.

Anne-Marie came in with a pot of coffee and placed it on the table between them. Broussard made a faint motion with his hand and murmured, 'Stay a moment!' She sat down beside him, saying nothing.

Serge Rassini read out, 'All the Caravelles were grounded at 1650 hours. One was destroyed, and the rest are being searched for the second time. There's full co-operation from the airport staff, and from most of the Air-France personnel.'

Broussard nodded: 'So there will be no problem. No chance of a flight at least until tomorrow?'

'Absolutely none.'

They sat listening to the wind outside blowing up from the south. Broussard considered the chances, disadvantages and dangers of his decision. Relations between the Secret Army and the foreign Press would be damaged badly; but to Broussard's mind journalists were of little concern. The execution of one of them would serve *'pour encourager les autres!'* He was a mean, morbid man who took a natural pleasure in vengeance. The Englishman had betrayed them and must pay the penalty. The only problem was the hotel. They had put special guards on the door, and the area was full of CRS. Broussard was reluctant to risk his hard-pressed commandos in breaking into the Miramar to kill a squalid English journalist. It might be difficult to get him alone: the man would be certainly on his guard.

Broussard raised his head and spoke to Serge Rassini. His voice was relaxed, his eyes huge and full of a dull white light, almost the eyes of a blind man: 'Who is on reception at the Miramar tonight?'

'Marc-Claude — until curfew.'

'Telephone him every hour to check if the Englishman gives up his key and takes his luggage. He may try to wait at the airport.' He paused, lifting the pipe again to his lips. As he considered the final decision he did not look at Anne-Marie. His eyes were again cast down at his reflection in the polished table, and his thoughts wandered with a twinge of conscience to his duties as a husband and father.

Five years ago he had married the widow of a fellow commander in Saigon who had fallen at Dien Bien Phu. She was Broussard's first wife, and Anne-Marie was her only daughter. She was now living in France until the crisis was over.

Broussard had married her as much out of duty to a dead comrade as from real love; his method of loving was to be faithful and provide her and Anne-Marie with money and material comfort. In return, he exacted from them both an absolute loyalty. For one of them to have disobeyed him would have been as outrageous in his eyes as if his authority had been flouted by a junior officer.

He looked now at Anne-Marie: 'I understand you have met this Englishman several times before he was brought here?'

She nodded: 'Le Hir sent me down to meet him.' She kept her voice under control.

'Have you been to his room in the Miramar?'

There was a tense pause, while the shutters groaned in their frames. Broussard laid down the opium pipe, his fingers drumming restlessly against the table.

'Once,' she said. 'He has Room 274.' She had gone very pale, knowing what was coming, but felt no fear: rather, a sense of painful pleasure. Unlike her stepfather she had an uncomplicated character. Even if she had tried, she would have been unable to analyse her feelings towards Neil on that night in the Miramar. She had been hysterical and lonely and rather drunk, and had enjoyed feeling him stab deep inside her and churn out some of the memories of that ghastly afternoon on the beach, with death coming with the twilight. She had not thought at the time she would ever see him again, and it did not worry her. She was not in the least in love with him.

But with Guérin's arrest her attitude had drastically changed. Now, instead of having passed a pleasant physical night with Neil, she saw herself humiliated, seduced and ridiculed, while all the time he had been laughing at her, plotting to betray both her stepfather's cause and her country; and she hated Neil now with a cold, terrible hatred, and waited for Broussard to speak.

'I have decided that this Englishman must be killed. As far as we know, he has not yet left the hotel. But there are guards there, and the Front de Mer is being heavily patrolled. I cannot spare any regular commandos for the job — they would almost certainly get caught.' He paused and picked up the slender clay pipe. Anne-Marie said nothing. Broussard stared at her with his sunken white eyes, as the pale smoke curled out of his nostrils. When he spoke again his words were ponderous, like stones plopping into water. 'I want him killed tonight — quickly — privately — in his room. You are the only person who can do it.'

Still she said nothing. It was Serge Rassini who replied: 'She can't do it! Send in one of the "Gamma" men —!'

'Shut up!' said Broussard, still staring at his stepdaughter. 'Are you on friendly terms with this Englishman?' he asked her.

She lowered her eyes to the table. 'Yes. He won't suspect me.'

'Very well. You must try to delay him in the hotel tonight. Write him a letter and arrange to meet him in his room just before curfew. I can have the letter delivered this evening. You will leave here at eleven o'clock.' He turned to Rassini: 'Prepare the pistol, Serge. A cloth silencer will be sufficient in this wind.'

Serge saluted and disappeared into the back room. Broussard turned back to Anne-Marie. His fist, holding the gold Roman coin, clenched and unclenched. His mind felt cold, disembodied, a superior force controlling and commanding, detached from the scrambling chaos of the city. He was pleased with how well she was reacting. He had never thought of her as his own daughter: to him she had always been just another attractive spirited young girl to whom he had a special responsibility. As he looked at her now he felt a stirring of pride.

'I want you to be able to fire all six rounds,' he told her, 'if I gave you an ordinary silencer you would be able to fire safely only two before the barrel overheated. And you must make certain of this Englishman.'

He had placed the 100-sestertii piece on the table beside his pipe; and now, to keep his hands from shaking, he took a backgammon board from the side table and began laying out the red and white ivory counters. When he had them all in position, lined up along the bases of the black arrow-points, Anne-Marie came round and stood beside him. She was still very pale; laying her hand on his shoulder, she said gently, 'Don't worry — everything will be all right — after tonight.' She kissed him on the forehead, and he slid his hand round to hers and held it for a moment. '*Merci, ma petite!*'

Serge came back with the small-calibre revolver with the barrel wrapped in a thick bandage. For five minutes he stood with Anne-Marie and loaded and unloaded the gun, explaining the sighting, safety-catch, and firmest firing position — at arm's length, level with the breast. 'You will have no difficulty,' he said, 'there's no kick. But get as close as you can before you use it.'

She watched and listened in silence, and repeated his motions once, without error. Then she took the gun and went through the folding doors into her bedroom. She closed the shutters against the rising wind, pulled her skirt over her head, peeled off her stockings and brassiere, and sat on the bed in the half-darkness, waiting.

CHAPTER 4

The man's blue-black gun, hanging from the greased strap, threw a finger of shadow that swung across the ground till it touched the edge of the fountain. He finished his cigarette and tossed it into the basin where it hissed like a snake among the shadows.

Across the boulevard the windows blazed with the setting sun. The man turned and went into the hotel. A hot wind was blowing up in bursts that rustled the palms and whipped the dust up along the pavements. He took up his place in a chair behind the reception desk.

He was a muscular, greying man of about forty, and had been a CRS territorial reservist for fifteen years. His wife ran a bar-tabac in the village just outside Juan-Les-Pins, and he worked during the summers as a swimming-instructor and life-saver along the coast. He usually did only about three months territorial work a year; but with this cursed crisis dragging on, he saw himself likely to be out in North Africa for the rest of the summer.

He didn't dislike the country, or the people in it — they were very much like the local people in the Midi — but the work was hard, there were riots, continual guard-duties, arrests, house searches, and quite often street-battles in which several of his colleagues had been killed.

Tonight he was on a simple guard job detailed, so he had heard, by one of the barbouze leaders. There was a second CRS man inside the restaurant. They had been told to look out for commandos who might try to kill one of the clients.

He glanced around him and was faintly amused. Almost the entire clientele seemed to be foreign journalists. And very odd birds they were, too! A couple of them were at the desk now. One was tall and elderly, a real English Major Thompson, he thought, complete with homburg under his arm and those extraordinary striped trousers you usually saw only in cartoons of Englishmen. The fellow was bickering with the silver-haired receptionist over his bill.

The second man looked like a mangy lion. He had pushed past the receptionist, who was too busy arguing with the tall man to notice, and snatched a key and an envelope from one of the pigeon-holes. He came back and hurried across to the bar.

Ah, the bar! the CRS man thought. That's where they all go. Drinking at the bar. Writing their stories at the bar. They should try a few years in the CRS. Try breaking up a few riots. He did not think this with bitterness, he was a sanguine man; and anyway, it probably meant an easy evening for him.

An American television film unit had just arrived outside, with two trucks mounted with cameras, sound-booms and folding canvas chairs with the team's names on the back. They came in noisily, tearing off dark glasses and shouting for their keys. 'We got sixty feet of battle film that would make old Zanuck sweat!' one of them yelled. 'And those goddam CRS grabbed the lot!'

He came striding past the desk, throwing a scowl at the CRS man who ignored him. The tall Major Thompson figure had finished his dispute with the receptionist, and the CRS man watched him walk across the foyer to join his red-headed colleague in the bar.

CHAPTER 5

In the bar Mallory opened the envelope which was addressed to 'Monsieur Ingleby, Chambre 274', and read, in a sloping feminine hand in French: '*Mon cher, I have not seen much of you in the last few days and I have many things to tell you. Please, before you go back to England, I must see you and talk to you. Be in your room at the hotel tonight. I will come before the curfew. Please be there. Many kisses! A-M!*'

He finished reading it just as Winston St. Leger came up. 'Well done, you old decoy-duck!' he croaked, holding up the key to Neil's room.

St. Leger eyed it dubiously, 'I suppose these cloak-and-dagger tactics are necessary,' he muttered, 'but I can hardly say it's a métier I enjoy. Do you think it will work?'

Mallory shrugged: 'It may make 'em think he's still in the hotel — or at least that he's due back and not at the airport. It's a chance, anyway. Drink?'

'Thank you. Pink gin.'

'Poor old Ingleby,' Mallory went on, 'he'll just have to miss his oats this time.' He passed the letter to St. Leger, who glanced at it with a hint of distaste. 'A little birdie he had up in his room the other night,' Mallory explained, 'the one somebody said was old Broussard's stepdaughter.'

St. Leger nodded and passed the letter back. 'Whoever started that rumour is a malicious fool. I admit that Ingleby's made a pretty big ass of himself out here, but that story's going too far!'

Close by, a despondent BBC man was prowling about with a tape-recorder, fretting over his transmission to London. Mallory heard him say, 'I wanted to get gunfire fading into the sound of grasshoppers for Radio Newsreel. Well, I got plenty of gunfire all right, but the damned grasshoppers wouldn't make a bleep.'

Mallory laughed: 'And old Ingleby's sitting out there worrying about the best scoop of the year.'

'I hope he gets away,' St. Leger said gravely, sipping his gin. 'You think he's in real danger?'

Mallory shrugged: 'Could be.'

'How was he when you left him?'

'Pissed. Kept on babbling about girls. I don't think his nerves are too good.'

CHAPTER 6

Neil watched the rim of fire die out in the green sky, as the sun went down behind the mountains and a swift submarine darkness fell that made the mountains look very close and the airfield no wider than a boulevard. The sabotaged Caravelle still glowed on the tarmac, a frail black wreck like burnt paper in a grate.

He stayed at the bar till it grew dark. He drank only coffee, feeling cold and shivering, although outside the desert wind boomed against the walls and the air in the main hall became stale, stifling, full of the wailing of terrified children.

A CRS officer had told him that it was now hoped that special crews would be arriving from Paris to fly the planes out. But he did not know when. Perhaps tomorrow. Perhaps later.

Since the destruction of the Caravelle, Neil had made three telephone calls. The first had been to the British Consulate, where he had spoken to a fruity-voiced young man called Wynne-Catlin who had listened to his troubles and said, 'Oh, sounds a bit tricky to me — better stay at the airport and get on the first plane out.' Neil had said, 'Thanks!' between gritted teeth, and the fruity voice had added, 'Right, I'll look into it. All the best!'

The next call had been to Pol. There had been the three familiar pips, then the woman's voice reciting the number back to him. When he had asked for Pol he had been put through to a M. Julien, who told him that Pol had been moved to another department. After a lot of explanations he had been at last transferred, and the resonant voice, slightly subdued now, came on the line: '*Comment ça va, Monsieur Ingleby?*'

Neil had described his plight, and the answer had had a lyrical sadness to it: 'Ah, there are good days, my dear Ingleby, and there are bad days. This is a bad day. But you ought to get on a plane tomorrow. There's nothing more I can do.'

They had said goodbye, and Pol had promised to look him up at his newspaper offices if he came to London. It was the last he ever heard of Pol. It had not been one of the most satisfactory relationships, Neil reflected.

His final call had been to Mallory, put through to the upstairs bar of the hotel. His voice had come over in a piercing electronic hiss, largely unintelligible, wishing him 'Good luck, old boy, have lots o' drinks on me! Send my love to the airhostesses!' Then he added, 'We fixed about you in the hotel. You stick there. Should be all right.'

Neil hung up and walked back to his stool at the bar, feeling alone and vulnerable, dreading the approach of night when the CRS would be growing tired and might even be withdrawn. Then the commandos would come in, pretending to be refugees, and prowl round among the crowds until they found him, and empty a couple of machine-pistol clips into him while he slept. Or maybe they would do it more silently — with a knife, perhaps. And pin a notice on him: '*JE SUIS UNE BARBOUZE*'.

Darkness fell, and the lozenge lamps along the ceiling came on with a sombre orange glow; while outside, down the highway into the city, special arc-lights had been set up to illuminate the column of cars that now stretched for more than a mile, under a heavy CRS guard.

In the main hall they tried to sleep, nerves inflamed by the hot howling wind and the claustrophobic longing for escape.

Neil had bought a série noire edition of Simenon at the bookstall and started to read, sitting propped against the wall; but the print crawled in front of his eyes like slabs of insects. He felt tired, sick, trembling after six cups of sour black coffee. Later he sought relief in the toilet which was splashed and choked, without water or towels or paper.

He slept at last, hunched up with his face against the skirting, dreaming that he was in the Dorchester Hotel with Colonel Le Hir and the two German legionnaires who were somehow improperly dressed, and there was a row with the management; and then Caroline had appeared in her wedding dress, but her face somehow indistinct, and Neil had made some appeal to Le Hir who had taken him outside and called a taxi.

He woke staring at the distant ceiling, listening to the wind and whimpering of children, then remembered with a pang of relief that Caroline was not yet married, and that perhaps he had a chance after all — if he could only get out of here, on to one of those planes, across to Paris and back to London.

It was nearly midnight. Duxelles had told him that if he were still in the country after midnight he would be arrested. But he felt too tired to care anymore, his mind lulled into a torpor which was the final antidote to his state of tension.

Most of the people in the hall were asleep, but their breathing was loud and fast and uneasy; and he noticed what he had feared all along — that there were now far less CRS about. Instead, numbers of young men were wandering up and down buying sandwiches and coffee at the brasserie. He closed his eyes again; but no one came near him.

It was after midnight now. He decided he might try to ask the CRS to arrest him; but when he stood up and saw the length of the floor packed with sleeping figures, he felt dangerously conspicuous. They can still get me here, he thought, and he burrowed down again into the wedge of bodies, lying still, heart beating, feeling as he had done as a child when he came out of the freezing night into a large room with people crowded round a fire in one corner. He remembered the terrible urge to get into that crowd, away from the cold darkness; and he crept deeper among the warm breathing bodies.

Then he began to nurse a new fear: that someone would try to talk to him and find out that he was English. Earlier, when he had been drinking with Mallory, it had not seemed to matter. But now, in this sleeping sepulchre, he felt his only salvation was to remain anonymous, buried among the crowds. He lay with his eyes closed, waiting for morning.

He slept badly, waking every few hours, sweating yet cold, his mouth full of fur and his head slamming with a slow deliberate pain.

It was some time in the small hours. He had been dreaming again, fighting to get through the crowds to the smoking Caravelle, weighed down with cardboard boxes and marble clocks, feeling a nudge in his buttocks, somebody shaking him by the arm. He saw two boots with black gaiters in front of his face. A CRS man was standing above him, gun over his shoulder.

'Papiers!'

Neil sat up and looked round. About a dozen CRS were moving between the rows of refugees, examining papers. He dragged out his passport with the deportation order inside. The CRS man frowned at the document for several seconds, then looked at him: 'You know you were supposed to be out of the country two hours ago?'

Neil tried to concentrate, to make sense of what was becoming a confused nightmare muddled up with his arrival with Le Hir at the Dorchester. He said, 'Yes, yes, I know I'm supposed to be out of here. I want to get out of here. I can't. They blew up the plane.'

'You're an English journalist?' said the CRS man, still frowning.

'Yes. I'm in danger. They're going to kill me. Can you arrest me?'

The man shook his head and handed the passport back: 'You have to stay here. There may be a plane tomorrow. And you'd better be on it!'

Neil lay back and watched the lamps burning above him like red-hot pendulums. The CRS man had moved on to wake someone else. Neil had a fierce thirst; he saw that the bar and brasserie were closed. A couple of men in berets were lounging against the wall near the glass partition of the Garderie d'Enfants. There were now only about a dozen CRS in the hall. He crouched down and closed his eyes again, but he could not sleep.

There was a man's head lying a few inches from his own. It was bald and creased like putty, the mouth half-open, making no sound. It was like the face of a dead man. He turned the other way and saw a tiny child staring down at him with big round eyes, its lips quivering on the point of tears. It was so young that he could not tell whether it was a boy or a girl. It had thick curls, like a print of David Copperfield as a child, and wore a miniature white duffel coat with pegs the size of pretzels.

He looked away and went on trying to sleep. His back ached, and he lay stretching his legs to work out the cramp in his thighs and calves, but each time he moved he only awakened some fresh, overstrained muscle, and the ache began all over again.

Something brushed lightly against his face. It was the hem of the child's duffel coat. He said in a whisper, not unkindly, '*Vas-y! Où est ta maman?*'

The child goggled at him for a long time, repeating in a murmur, '*Maman!*' Then slowly, unsteadily, it tottered away among the sleeping bundles, calling '*Maman!*' — over and over again without anybody taking any notice.

Neil began to crawl away from the putty-faced man, and his fingers touched the edge of a trampled magazine. He opened it up and lay with the pages folded across his face, and at last fell asleep.

He woke suddenly, dazzled. He was looking into the glare of morning sunlight. Somebody had lifted the magazine from his face. He twisted his head round and blinked painfully.

Standing above him, with a heavy black handbag slung over her shoulder, was Anne-Marie.

CHAPTER 7

Anne-Marie said quietly, 'Get up, Monsieur Ingleby. We're leaving.'

He lay for a moment staring at her, not quite certain where he was. He had a sore throat and his eyes stung and his hair was itching, rubbed against the grain of his scalp like cat's fur stroked the wrong way. He sat up, trying to collect his faculties, feeling very unwell.

She repeated, with a curious wooden expression, 'Come on, we're leaving.'

He began to think more clearly. His watch was still stopped. He looked at the clock above the departure desks and saw that it was just after seven o'clock. There was a sluggish movement in the hall: people arranging their luggage and queueing up for the toilets and for coffee. The airhostess and the CRS men, in smart dark-blue, were still on duty, and the wind still roared outside.

He stood up, rubbing his eyes, and looked at her. Her face was cold and empty, like a grainy black-and-white photograph. 'What are you doing here?' he said dully, still half-asleep.

'We're leaving,' she said again. 'You can't stay here anymore.'

He opened his eyes wide and shook his head. He wondered if he were still dreaming: 'But what are you doing here? How did you know where I was?'

'I went to the hotel to find you. You didn't get my letter?'

He frowned: 'I'm sorry — I'm not really awake yet.' He pressed his hand to his forehead: 'I don't quite understand what's going on.'

'You're coming with me, Monsieur Ingleby.' Her eyes had a blank icy look; and for a full ten seconds they stood facing each other without moving or speaking.

'I can't go with you,' he said at last, 'I'm booked on the first flight today. I've got a deportation order.'

'There will be no flights today,' she said, hitching the bag higher on to her shoulder, 'the CRS captain has just told me.'

He swallowed dryly, tasting the bitter aniseed on his breath, wishing he had a toothbrush and razor. The stubble on his chin felt like an extra skin. He said, 'I must go and wash, I can't talk to you like this.'

She called after him, 'Hurry! We haven't much time.'

There was a queue outside the toilets, and it took him several minutes before he found a vacant cubicle. The lavatory seat had been torn off, and he sat for what seemed a long time on the cold china rim, his head in his hands, trying to arrange his thoughts into some order.

He remembered what Mallory had said about her. Even if she were not Broussard's stepdaughter, all logic warned him against her. But logic was no longer with him. Again he felt that perverse compulsion to stay close to those who threatened him — to explain to them what had happened, to seek protection by telling only the truth. There was no protection awaiting him from the CRS or from Pol or the man called Wynne-Cadin. But there was just a chance that Anne-Marie might be able to help him.

He stood over the washbasin and splashed tepid water on to his face and into his eyes, flattening down his hair with wet hands.

She was waiting for him outside. He looked at her more carefully now. She was wearing a tight sea-green dress. Her hair was scraped back and her face had a stiff drawn look with scoops of shadow under the eyes as though she had not slept.

She looked at him with a vacant stare. 'I've got my car outside,' she said, starting to walk across the hall towards the entrance.

'Wait a minute! Anne-Marie!'

She paused, her shoulders hunched slightly forward: 'Yes?'

'Where are we going?' He stood beside her, wanting to lean on her, to seek her support while the crowded hall seemed to be revolving round him.

'I know a way out of the country,' she said, 'I'm going to take you.'

She turned and strode on, and he followed her, past the brasserie where they were selling paper mugs of steaming coffee and salami sandwiches. He said, 'I must have something to eat.'

She turned again, her eyes flashing darkly: 'I told you, we don't have much time.' She glanced round the brasserie, at a group of CRS by the door, and added, 'Come on, please! I don't want to be seen around here.'

He remembered the deportation order just in time, changing it to his breast pocket before they reached the CRS at the entrance. 'What are the chances of a plane today?' he asked, as the guard flipped through his passport.

The man shrugged: 'I don't know anything. The crews are still on strike.' He looked again at Neil's passport:; 'You're a journalist? You want to leave today?'

'Yes.' Beside him he saw Anne-Marie watching them both with eyes narrowing into fierce slits.

The CRS man went on, 'You'll have to take your chance here. It depends on when they get the special crews from France.'

'What are the roads like? Are the frontiers open yet?'

'I wouldn't try going by road,' he said grimly, 'there are a lot of Arab Front terrorists about. All the roads in the Bled are dangerous — especially after what happened yesterday with Ali La Joconde and his friends. *Beaucoup d'effervescence!*' He turned to Anne-Marie: 'Are you both together?'

She nodded and flicked a dog-eared identity card at him. Neil tried to catch a glimpse of the surname on it — whether it began with a 'B' — but she was too quick. The CRS man saluted and she walked past him through the entrance. Neil caught her up, and on an impulse of affection tried to take her hand. She snatched it away as though he had touched her with a flame. Her fingers, with their pearl-white nails, felt small and cold.

She ignored him completely as they walked down the concrete steps into the sunlight where the dust swept stinging into their faces. They walked with their heads down, shielding their eyes, and Neil called to her above the wind, 'You heard what the CRS man said — that it's dangerous to try and drive out?'

'The CRS know nothing!' she cried. 'I know what I'm talking about.'

They had to walk nearly a quarter of a mile, past the lanes of dust-brown cars, full of the frightened faces of people who were preparing to camp out here for perhaps days.

Because of the wind they hardly spoke to each other. Neil wished again that he could have a shave and some breakfast — at least one coffee and a glass of Fernet Branca. The wind battered him, making his face raw and dry. Anne-Marie walked in front of him, her head and shoulders bent forward, the bag swinging against her hip. It gave her a heavy, slouching appearance; and he thought of her running down the sands, strong and brown, smiling with white teeth, hair swirling. She was not the same girl any more.

The car — the Simca convertible in which they had gone down to the Casino de la Plage — was parked off the road on the edge of a maize field sprinkled with poppies. It was empty, with the black hood closed. She unlocked the door on the driving side and let him in beside her. Her movements were deliberate and unhurried.

He sat back in the bucket-seat and she switched on the ignition. Above the grunt of the engine he said, 'Anne-Marie, I want to get one thing clear — about what happened yesterday with General Guérin.'

She said nothing, swinging the wheel over, and they screeched round in a tight circle into the empty lane leading back towards the city.

'Do you think I betrayed General Guérin?' he said, raising his voice against the whine of the car.

'No, I don't think you betrayed anybody.' Her voice was quite calm: 'General Guérin and Colonel Le Hir were arrested — that's all.'

'I was with them. It was because I was in the car that the CRS knew it was Guérin.'

'I know.' Her profile was rigid, her sun-filled eyes on the road.

'Do the others think I betrayed Guérin?' Neil shouted, as the car began to lurch from side to side, buffeted by the wind. She did not answer. The road raced towards them, curving into a roundabout, and she braked violently, dust rising like steam, the car howling into the turn, out on to a wide road between the tobacco fields.

Neil clutched at his knees, peering through the brown-caked windshield, his heart thumping hard. He turned to her again: 'Anne-Marie, listen!' Her face remained immobile, watching the road. 'I must talk to you before we go any further. Does the Secret Army think I betrayed Guérin?'

She made a sudden movement with her hand. The windshield-washers spurted, dribbled down, the glass and the wipers swept the dust aside in a clean arc. The road ahead was empty, the sky blue with brown drifts of dust swooping and spiralling in the wind like ghosts.

'Anne-Marie, listen! Slow down, will you! I have to talk to you! What have you come here for? How did you find me?'

'I went to the hotel last night. I told you, I left a letter asking you to meet me. You weren't there.'

'How did you know I was at the airport?'

She turned with a quick look of triumph in her eyes: 'Where else would you be? You were trying to get away.'

'I was frightened,' he said, in a hoarse voice that was lost in the scream of the slip stream. The car slowed and turned on to a track like the one up to the farm yesterday. Neil felt a nasty sinking in his stomach: 'Where are we going? This isn't the way along the coast. We're supposed to be making for the frontier!'

She made no reply, steering the car up the bumpy track towards a line of trees, with the mountains beyond.

'Anne-Marie, this isn't the right way!'

'We can't take the main roads. There are too many patrols out — we wouldn't get through. I'm taking you a special way I know.'

He knotted his fingers together, watching the track bump towards them, trying to remember how far it was to the frontier. They were coming into a village, chalk-white with bulging walls, patched up with newspaper and straw and tin cans under roofs of sagging corrugated iron. Two French soldiers sat in a jeep on the roadside. She accelerated, her hand down on the horn; and as they flashed past them, Neil had a glimpse of one of the soldiers shouting and waving towards the village.

They passed a mosque with a mud wall crumbled like biscuit. A bald dog limped across the road in front of them, cowering against the broken pavement as they roared past.

There was only the one street. Halfway down they passed a café with a single table outside the door and a row of scrawny, dry-brown Moslems squatting barefoot in the dust, doing nothing.

As the Simca drove by, one of them leapt up and drew a finger across his throat, teeth bared. Anne-Marie saw him and shrugged. Neil remembered that she had made just the same gesture on that first morning when he had asked her what happened to the barbouzes.

'Those are Moslems!' he blurted out, stupidly.

'It's only a small village,' she said, 'afterwards, behind the trees, we get on to the road to the frontier.'

They were almost out of the village now, and the road narrowed between stone walls, winding into the trees ahead. Two Moslems in jellabahs sat on the wall staring at them.

'How far is it to the frontier?' said Neil.

'Two hundred and eighty kilometres.'

He looked at the petrol gauge. It was showing a quarter empty. He said nervously, 'Are we going to have any difficulty getting petrol outside the city?'

Without turning her head she replied, 'We don't need any petrol.'

He stared at her: 'But we've got a hundred and eighty kilometres to go!'

She said nothing. They were driving under the trees now: tall eucalyptuses with silver-green leaves bending, falling gracefully like a girl's hair, tossed and parted by the wind, the branches flattened back against the slender trunks. The soil here was deep red, and behind the trees Neil caught a glimpse of bony white-haired goats.

He said, 'Were not going to the frontier, are we? We were never going there?'

She swung the wheel and braked, with the leafy branches slithering over the canvas roof. The car stopped. Calmly she switched off the ignition and sat back, smoothing her green skirt over her knees. In the silence after the engine noise they listened to the trees sighing, throwing flashing streaks of sunlight into the dirt.

Neil waited, staring at Anne-Marie, feeling a sudden unreasonable panic: 'Why have we stopped?'

She turned to him. Her face was a handsome mask; he hardly recognized her. 'Monsieur Ingleby, you are a traitor.'

He heard a buzzing in his head. Leaves swept across the windshield, and he thought he saw something move under the trees ahead. The hairs on his neck felt like wet dog's fur. 'What do you mean?' he said.

'You know what I mean.' She leant down and lifted the handbag. He grabbed at it, She flinched away, and he felt her fingernails sting against his cheek. He lunged at her, and something hit him over the eye. '*Sale lâche! Sale traître!*' she screamed

He put his hand to his head, sitting back, feeling dizzy. Then he realized that she had suddenly become very still. He looked at her, and saw her staring ahead out of the window. Her face was as white as the edges of her eyes.

There were men coming out of the trees towards them, from all sides, closing round. She slammed up the handle of her door, locking it. Instinctively he took hold of the handle on his side.

'Lock, it!' she shrieked. 'Lock it!' She switched on the ignition, her foot stamping on the throttle, and the car lurched forward, bumping into one of the men who let out a yelp and jumped aside, shaking his fists.

The wheels skidded out into the road, leaping over the broken ground, under the waving trees, round a corner.

A roll of barbed wire stood across the track a few feet ahead. She could not stop in time; the wire scraped over the bonnet, up against the windshield. The engine stalled. She switched on again. The car was still in gear and it bucked forward further into the wire, puncturing both front tyres.

Neil seized her arm: 'Stop, for God's sake!' He turned and saw them coming round the bend, running. They were laughing and waving sticks and scythes that flashed in the sun. Neil had snatched out his passport and international Press card. He pushed down the handle on his side and started to open the door. She threw herself across his lap, screaming, 'No, no!'

It was too late. One of them had pulled the door open, and he felt himself being dragged out, shouting, '*Anglais! Suis anglais!*'

One of the men was wearing an open khaki tunic with no buttons and dungarees tied up with string. He had bare feet, scaly with dust, and the vest under his tunic was blotched with oil stains. He was grinning, pressing a revolver into Neil's stomach. Neil looked into a broad brown face with hair chopped so short that he could see the man's scalp. He shouted again '*Suis anglais!*' — waving his passport.

The man went on grinning. Neil had a glimpse of nickel teeth and black eyes glittering; and he heard Anne-Marie scream.

They were dragging her out, head first, down into the dust, wrenching the handbag from her, laughing. The green skirt was pulled up over her thighs and he saw her face, brown with dust, giving him one desperate half-mad look as he tried to duck down and run towards her.

Something hit him from behind and his arm went numb. A thin man in a woollen cap had grabbed her legs and was dragging her under the trees. One of her shoes came off and lay on its side in the road.

Neil had dropped his passport, noticing dimly that his arm was wet, the sleeve dripping into the dust. He stood shouting in English and French, 'I'm English! I'm a journalist! English journalist!'

They laughed, not understanding. One of them was emptying Anne-Marie's handbag on to the road. A purse and mirror fell out, a comb and handkerchief. The man held the bag up and shook it, and a pistol, lodged in a pocket of the bag, dropped with a thud. The barrel was wrapped in a thick bandage.

They all began shouting together in Arabic. Neil was rushed towards the side of the road. He saw Anne-Marie's legs kicking out across the sun-scorched grass. She writhed round, her face dappled with moving shadows from the trees, and he saw her eyes turn to him again, the whites long and shining, her mouth opening in a scream.

The air exploded round him, and he watched the bullets smacking against her tight green dress. And her face crumpled and fell away under the waving branches of the eucalyptus tree.

He tried to run to her again but they were all round him, lifting sticks and knives, one of them moving forward with a burp-gun, across where Anne-Marie's legs lay motionless under the leafy branches.

Then the sky grew dark.

CHAPTER 8

The man came through the swing-doors out of the rain down Fleet Street, into the bar of El Vino. They were there at the back of the room, round a table near the glass partition that closes off the rear saloon where guests are allowed to bring women in to drink.

He was a tall man with carefully combed grey hair and a worried face. 'I'm sorry I'm late,' he said, 'there's a jam right across Aldwych.'

'What will you have?' asked one of them, a florid man with a bowtie.

'Hock and seltzer, please.' He hung up his coat and began dusting the rain from his hair. Opposite him a small dewy man sat sucking the tip of his thumb: 'Nothing new, I suppose?'

'Nothing.'

The florid man returned with the glass of hock. 'The nationals have been on all morning,' he said, sitting down, 'I told them to wait for a statement from you or the editor.'

The tall man nodded: 'That's right. I'm seeing David at three. We'll be putting one out after we've heard officially from the Foreign Office.' He took a deep breath: 'I still don't understand it! We know from Tom Mallory that he was out at the airport with a pass on to the first plane — and that left the next afternoon. Why on earth wasn't he on it?'

The dewy man said, 'We must bear in mind that there was a lot of confusion. The French admit that it looked pretty doubtful right up to the last moment, what with all the crews on strike. It's possible he just didn't think any planes would take off that day.'

'But what was he doing riding off into the country with that girl?' cried the tall man. 'Did he know who she was?'

'Obviously he didn't,' said the dewy man. 'Perhaps she was offering to drive him out of the country?'

The florid man leant forward and said, 'What I don't understand is why he was out there in the first place. I thought he'd gone to Greece to write a book?'

'He did,' said the tall man, 'but he met some Frenchman in Athens who got him over there in a boat. He was one of the first people in — we can't hold that against him.'

'Who are you sending now?' said the dewy man.

'Saunders, from the Paris office. He's a pretty tough reporter — he should be able to get to the bottom of it all. The trouble with these sophisticated university graduates is they get too involved.' He sat staring at the rows of wine-casks behind the bar. 'It's all quite frightful!' he added suddenly. 'And the only copy I got from him was that eye-witness piece about the Casino. I wanted him to do some intelligent digging into the political background.'

'He seems to have done enough of that,' said the dewy man, 'too much, in fact!'

'As far as I can see,' said the tall man, 'he spent most of his time running around with the stepdaughter of one of the terrorist leaders and getting himself tied up in every kind of dirty deal in the country. That's all right if you're writing a book about it perhaps, but my job is to get out a newspaper!'

They all looked up as a black-haired man in a raincoat approached and said with a grave smile, 'Ah, Foster, there you are.'

The tall man nodded to an empty chair: 'Well, have you heard anything your end?'

'Yes.' He took off his raincoat and sat down, taking his time: 'A.P. have just put over some pictures of the bodies. At least, what was found. They're not very nice.'

The tall man, Foster, put his hand to his eyes. 'Oh, God!' he murmured.

'The French think they may have been shot first,' the black-haired man added. 'They found quite a lot of clothing and part of a British passport. I don't think there can be any more doubt about identity. There were French troops on the other side of the village. They saw the car go through and apparently tried to warn them.' He looked round the table: 'The other thing is that a French engineer from the Sahara was shot dead in the hotel the night before in the room directly above Ingleby's. I don't know if there's any connection there.'

Foster stood up and began putting on his coat: 'I'll have to get in touch with the editor right away.' He paused just as he was leaving: 'Ingleby was a good lobby correspondent — he should have stuck to it!' He shook his head wearily: 'What did the damned fool think he was trying to do out there?'

'Perhaps,' said the dewy man, 'he was trying to help?'

A NOTE TO THE READER

Dear Reader,

If you have enjoyed the novel enough to leave a review on **Amazon** and **Goodreads**, then we would be truly grateful.

SAPERE
BOOKS

Printed in Great Britain
by Amazon